Dear Reader

When my publishers a   next romance in 1899   immediately thought,   intended to write a furt   *Schuyler* *Chronicles* about the adv   es of a poor relation of the family, and what could be better than making him the hero of my new novel? So Allen Marriott, who concealed his charismatic power behind his reputation as *The Quiet Man*, was born. I was able to show him in the company of Gerard and Torry Schuyler in their late thirties, now part of the set around the Prince of Wales, as well as at the other end of society where he is the friend of Mr Nance, a clockmaker and shopkeeper off Piccadilly.

The 1890s were a time of great change and of great hopes for the future. My heroine, Trish Courtney, like many women then, was interested in the possibility of female emancipation. It was exciting for me to discover how many of the issues which moved the nation then were similar to our concerns today. I feel sure that you will find as much enjoyment in reading about Allen and his dear Trish as I did when creating them.

Paula Marshall

Paula Marshall, married with three children, has had a varied life. She began her career in a large library and ended it as a senior academic in charge of history in a polytechnic. She has travelled widely, has been a swimming coach, and has appeared on *University Challenge* and *Mastermind*. She has always wanted to write, and likes her novels to be full of adventure and humour.

Recent titles by the same author:

MISS JESMOND'S HEIR
THE WOLFE'S MATE
THE DEVIL AND DRUSILLA

THE QUIET MAN

Paula Marshall

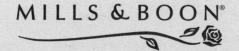

MILLS & BOON®

First published in Great Britain 1999
Harlequin Mills & Boon Limited,
Eton House, 18-24 Paradise Road, Richmond, Surrey TW9 1SR

© Paula Marshall 1999

ISBN 0 263 81895 0

Set in Times Roman 10½ on 11½ pt.
04-9912-84460

Printed and bound in Spain
by Litografia Rosés S.A., Barcelona

The Schuyler Family

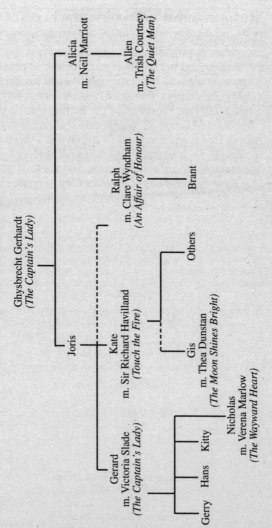

ACKNOWLEDGMENT

The author would like to thank the following for their assistance in providing her with information to make the background to this novel as authentic as possible. Any mistakes are her responsibility and not theirs.
Mr Christopher Tarratt of George Tarratt Ltd;
Lord Midleton, President of the British Horological Institute; Major A. G. McDonald, Librarian to the British Horological Institute's Library at Upton, near Southwell; Dr Jonathan Betts, Curator of Horology of the National Maritime Museum; and the staff of the Reference Library, Leicester City Libraries.

Prologue

New York, 1890

'This way, Mr Marriott. Mr Gerard will see you now.'

Allen Marriott, who had been kicking his heels in Mr Gerard Schuyler's outer office for the last half-hour, rose, frowning, from his uncomfortable seat. He was a tall, slim young man, about twenty years old, with fashionably cut darkish hair, hazel eyes, and a pale, slightly worried face. He was dressed in impeccable taste. He looked, apart from the worried face, exactly like the sort of gentleman who could call cousin that intrepid international financier Mr Gerard Schuyler, being the son of Mr Gerard's father's sister, Alicia.

The office he was shown into was tastefully, but not over-expensively furnished. The most magnificent thing in it—apart from Mr Gerard Schuyler—was the oak desk at which he sat.

He was busy writing when Allen was announced, and continued to do so for some minutes. He did not offer Allen a seat, either when his flunky showed him in or when he had finished writing. Instead he looked up at his cousin, and said curtly, 'You know why I have sent for you?'

Overwhelmed by meeting for the first time the man of whose exploits he had often heard, Allen simply nodded an answer.

Gerard flung his pen down and leaned back in his splendid chair. 'Come, come, Mr Marriott, that will not do. We must start as we mean to go on. Yes or no, please.'

'Yes.' Allen knew that he was being sullen, but he could not stop himself. The errand on which he was engaged was so supremely distasteful to him—but so necessary—that he could barely speak.

'In that case, I would ask you to detail the circumstances to me.'

'Why?' Allen blurted the question at Gerard before he could stop himself. 'You know perfectly well why I am here.'

'Is it your habit to answer a question with another? If it is, it's a bad one. Yes, I know why you are here. Do you? Tell me—or you may consider this interview closed. The door is over there.'

Allen gritted his teeth, and said, as civilly as he could, 'I am here because when my father, Cornelius Marriott, died my mother and I discovered that he was bankrupt, and that we should have to leave our home immediately. Which we did. We are now lodged in a poor hotel in Queens, which we can only afford because my mother, illegally, smuggled two pieces of her jewellery out of the house when we left it.'

He did not need to tell Gerard that they had been living on Fifth Avenue in one of New York's most palatial mansions—now up for sale.

'Fortunately I had just finished my education at Yale, having gone there two years early, but I have no immediate means of earning a living sufficient to keep my mother and me in even moderate comfort. Consequently she wrote to your and my grandfather, Ghysbrecht Schuyler, the Captain, for financial assistance to tide us over.'

He stopped and looked out of the window before resuming.

'The Captain has a reputation for being a hard man, and he lived up to it. He wrote to my mother saying that she had made her own bed and must lie on it. Her dowry when she married my father had been a magnificent one, and on top of that her husband had inherited three million dollars when his own father died. That he had chosen to squander his fortune on failed financial dealings, drink, gambling and other women was no fault of his father-in-law's, and consequently he saw no reason to assist us.'

He stopped again.

Gerard said, his voice pleasant, 'Go on—and remember that I am a hard man, too.'

'My mother then wrote to you to ask for help, reminding you of old family ties, and you wrote back saying that if we needed any assistance I was to present myself at your office today and you would see what you could do for us.'

'Admirably lucid. Couldn't have put it better myself. What would *you* do in my position?'

Allen stared at him. He felt sick and ill. A fortnight ago his whole world had crumbled about him. He had come down from Yale where, despite his youth, he had had a distinguished academic career as a scientist and mathematician determined to investigate the meaning and workings of time. The Cornelius Marriott who had settled in America in the early eighteenth century had been a bankrupt clockmaker who had set up in business in Boston, made himself a small fortune and enhanced it by marrying into the then rich De Lancey family.

Every subsequent Marriott—until his wastrel father, Cornelius—had enhanced it further; clockmaking had been left long behind. Allen had found the first Cornelius's notebooks, and had become an amateur clockmaker and repairer in his spare time. Once his university career was over he had promised himself that he would set up his own laboratory and carry out the experiments he had been dreaming of ever since he was a boy.

That dream was dead and he was reduced to begging for help from the hard man before him.

He was aware that Gerard was waiting for an answer to his question. He decided to be honest—and damn the consequences.

'I don't know. I can't imagine myself in your position.'

Well, that should have dished any chances of help from Gerard, and no mistake.

Gerard sat up and made a note on a piece of paper.

'I like that. An honest answer. Let me tell you what I propose to do—and then you must decide for yourself whether you will agree to it. It's this. I am prepared to settle an annuity on your mother which will keep her in comfort. Unlike my grandfather I am not prepared to see a Schuyler starve. There is a condition: that you will take up the position of junior clerk in my office here in New York. That will enable *you* not to starve. Your mother's annuity is conditional on that and on your continued employment.'

'But…' began Allen. 'I have been expensively educated at Yale…' He stopped at the expression on Gerard's face.

'For what practical end?' said his cousin dryly.

How could he answer that?

He remained mute for a moment. Gerard added, 'Do I take that to be a refusal?'

'N…no,' said Allen, almost stuttering at the prospect of starvation rising before his face again. After all, what had his education fitted him for in the real world in which most people lived?

'No, I accept. Of course I accept. I would be a fool not to.'

'Agreed. There is, however, another condition. I know that your name is Allen Schuyler Marriott. You will drop the Schuyler and you will not reveal that you are related to me—or any of the Schuyler family. That is all.'

'Yes, I understand. I shall be only too happy to obey you.'

If there was a double meaning in his answer Gerard chose to ignore it. He handed a piece of paper to Allen, who took it nervelessly. At least his mother's troubles were over—his were just beginning.

'You will arrive for duty tomorrow morning at seven of the clock and give your name to the receptionist at the desk in the front hall of this building. She will tell you to whom to report, and you will hand him this paper. I know that he has a vacancy in the counting house downstairs. You have done some maths at Yale, I understand, which should mean that the post should not present you with any difficulties. Do your duties well and diligently and you will have the prospect of advancement.

'I bid you good day.'

It was the signal for him to leave. He began to utter a belated thank-you, but Gerard said, white teeth flashing, 'Thank me if you survive. I am taking a chance in thinking that you will—for, after all, your pedigree is suspect. I don't believe in visiting the sins of the fathers on the sons, but a wise man is always cautious. I was harsh with you at the beginning of this interview in order to discover whether you could survive in a world where you will be an unconsidered subordinate who will have to do as he is told—and quickly.'

'Oh, yes, sir,' said Allen submissively. 'I quite understand.'

'Good—you know the way out, I believe.'

Outside, in the corridor, Allen leaned his head against the wall, trying to collect himself enough to face a future far different from the one he had always dreamed of. Somehow he would succeed—and some day he would repay Gerard Schuyler for today's humiliating interview, come what may.

Chapter One

London, Spring, 1899

The London train had been making peculiar noises, but then trains often did. Allen Marriott, who had been holidaying in Stratford-upon-Avon, but had decided to return to London a few days early, was far too busy worrying about his future to worry about a train's funny noises.

Five years ago he had been rewarded for his dedication and his diligence by being transferred to Schuyler Incorporated's London office as a junior clerk. Once settled in London he had succeeded again, to the degree that he had been made the chief clerk's second-in-command. After one piece of work which had necessitated him co-operating with the prestigious Rothschild's firm, Rothschild's had offered him a post at a greatly increased salary which would enable him to support his mother.

Inasmuch as he could ever be happy—for he had become a lonely soul—he had been happy in his London work, and the temptation to rid himself of his last Schuyler ties was great. In the beginning he had dreamed of revenge, of making Gerard Schuyler pay for having sentenced him to a life of servitude, but that dream now seemed childish, the delusions of a spoilt boy.

Once such a splendid offer to leave Schuyler's would have had him out of the front door in no time, but that desire was nearly as long gone as the fortune which his father had squandered. To his surprise he felt a strange compunction about leaving. He had kept his promise to Gerard and no one knew that he and the head of the company were cousins. He had asked Rothschild's for time to consider their offer, but that time was now running out. He needed to make a decision soon...

The train was halfway between Banbury and Oxford, and he was almost asleep after the effort of trying to make up his mind what to do, when the whole world turned upside down in a great burst of grinding sound. Dazed with shock, assailed by ever-increasing noise, scarcely believing what was happening to him, Allen was hurled from side to side of the small compartment.

Finally, the noise and movement subsided, and he landed on the floor across his own valise with a thump which nearly drove the breath from his body, so that for a moment he lay there winded, unable to move. His head had ended up among the dust under the opposite seat. Dust, indeed, had settled everywhere.

At first he was too dazed to understand what must have happened, until, in the silence which seemed to be even more menacing than the hideous noise which had preceded it, common sense told him that the train must have crashed. His right hand was grasping someone's foot—presumably that of the elderly gentleman who had been sitting opposite to him.

Nauseated, and a victim of shock, Allen at last summoned up sufficient resolution to sit up, to look around him and try to find out how serious the accident was. He soon discovered that it must be very serious indeed, for the coach was lying on its side.

On his right the compartment's door and windows were consequently at an odd angle, giving him only a view of blue sky and clouds. On his left there was no view at all. The old gentleman was lying with his back to the door. He was unconscious, but was still breathing. Allen crawled towards him, took his pulse and discovered it to be strong. He decided that he could be safely left where he was for the time being.

Because of the coach's untoward position, standing up proved difficult, but he managed to struggle to the window and look out of it. The view was limited, but he could see enough to confirm that the train had met its accident on a high embankment above open country. There was nothing for it but to open the door and risk jumping down.

It took yet another struggle to force the door open, and a great deal of blind faith that he would not permanently injure himself before he jumped out and down on to the track. He landed heavily, but fortunately suffered no injury beyond a few more knocks and bruising—unlike the train, which he discovered had been completely wrecked.

He was standing alone on the embankment down which the locomotive had plunged, taking its coaches with it, to lie like a wounded snake, leaving only the last one, in which he had been travelling, with some connection to the railway lines. Smoke and steam were rising from the locomotive, but the eeriest thing about the whole dreadful business was the dead silence which had fallen on the scene. Allen began to wonder whether the blind chance of his being in the last coach had left him and the old gentleman the only passengers alive.

Looking around, he saw that a road ran alongside the field below the embankment. Cows stolidly chewed the grass beyond. Overhead, birds turned and wheeled merrily, ignoring what had happened beneath them. Gradually, noise and life returned to the wrecked train.

A man in one of the coaches halfway down the embankment had his head out of the door and was calling to him for help in opening it. The acute angle at which the coach lay was making this difficult. Allen slithered down the slope to help him, then found that once the door was open the man was so weak that he had to pull him out and lie him down on the narrow patch of grass which bordered the track.

Shock still had the man in its grip. He remained passive for some moments, breathing hard, blood trickling gently down from a cut on his temple. Allen pulled his handkerchief from his pocket and tried to stanch it before the man sat up and gasped at Allen, 'I am a doctor. Are you hurt?'

Allen gave him the handkerchief to hold to his head. He shook his own head, saying, 'Miraculously, no. But I think that the other passenger in my compartment may be. I'll try to haul him out if I can get in again.'

The doctor, not forgetting his manners even though the heavens had fallen, introduced himself. 'My name is French. When I feel a little better I'll go back in and try to recover my bag. There are sure to be survivors whom I can help, although I fear that many may be trapped.'

'Indeed,' said Allen. 'It occurs to me that it could be useful to discover if the guard is still living—he might be able to tell us what to do. I doubt whether he will know anything, but we ought at least to try to find him. Do you feel fit enough for me to leave you?'

French assured him that he was. Allen ran back to the guard's van, where he found the guard lying half-in and half-out of it, unconscious. His leg was doubled up beneath him, obviously broken. Allen debated whether or not to move him, but decided that it might be unwise. Instead he took off his jacket, rolled it up and put it under the guard's head before leaving him to return to his compartment to see whether it would be possible to help the old gentleman to safety.

By now a few men and one woman had struggled out of the wreck, either to stand, dazed, or to sit or lie, shocked, on the grass. These, Allen guessed, were the relatively un-injured ones; the heavily injured were lying trapped uncon-scious, or semi-conscious, in the wreckage. He tried not to think of the dead who were there too. Others would have to worry about them: his concern was with the living.

Getting back into the compartment was no easier than climbing out of it had been. After falling over the valise containing his overnight gear he threw it out of the open door, before a low moan told him that his travelling com-panion was conscious, but had not moved. He was still huddled against the far door. When Allen bent down to speak to him, he croaked in a puzzled voice, 'What on earth has happened?'

'The train has been derailed,' Allen told him.

He had originally concluded that the old gentleman was more shocked than injured, but when he turned his head to speak again Allen could see that the whole left side of his face was heavily bruised and bleeding. Like the doctor he had a wound on his temple, and it was also possible that he had other, unseen injuries.

'If I were to help you,' Allen said gently, 'do you think that we could get you out of the carriage and into the open? I'm very much afraid that the train is lying at such an angle that it isn't safe to remain in it.'

'I think so,' came the muttered answer.

With a great deal of difficulty, and an occasional cry of pain from the old gentleman before he lapsed into uncon-sciousness again, Allen succeeded in getting him out and on to the grass. The doctor, who had recovered his bag from the train, came over to where he lay and shook his head at Allen after he had examined him.

'I think his collarbone is broken,' he whispered. 'All I can do is try to make him comfortable.'

'The guard is unconscious,' Allen told him, 'and quite badly injured, so there's no help for us there. We are on our own, I fear, until someone further along the line realises that the train is hopelessly late. Until then it's up to us.'

In later years, looking back at his memories of it, and what came after, Allen would realise that the accident to the train had been responsible for changing his whole life. At the time, though, he was only aware of a desperate desire to rescue as many as possible. He and the doctor were not to be alone for long. Others had struggled out of the train, eventually to join them in their life-saving efforts.

It was Allen who organised the survivors into teams, to ensure that the efforts of the rescuers were co-ordinated, not haphazard. During his difficult apprenticeship he had learned that he had inherited much of the Schuyler powers of management and control, although he had found few opportunities to use them. Now he found himself directing operations as though he had done so all his life.

It was Allen, too, who took the most risks, clambering onto the locomotive and half into the cab to discover the train driver's dead body. He shuddered afterwards at the thought of what he had done, although at the time it seemed normal and right. The fireman had been thrown clear, and later on he was found lying by the track, badly injured and unconscious. His injuries, indeed, were severe, and he had no memories of the crash or what had preceded it.

A little later on, ignoring the exhaustion which threatened to overwhelm him, Allen climbed into one of the first-class coaches at the front of the train. He had heard a woman's voice calling for help from it: a voice which was perfectly controlled, not desperate.

Once inside, Allen found himself looking down at just
about the prettiest young woman he had ever seen. She was
seated with her back against the far door, cradling an unconscious girl in her arms.

Her great violet eyes looked up at him out of an ashen
face distinguished by its classic features. Her long and
lustrous black hair had come down and her expensive travelling costume had a great tear in its right sleeve. Like him,
she had somehow survived the crash without suffering any
major injury.

'Please,' she said to him, as calmly and politely as
though she were addressing him in a society drawing room,
'can you get Hetty out soon? She's badly injured and I'm
afraid that she might die. There's a poor woman opposite
who I think was killed when the accident happened. Some
luggage from the overhead rack fell on her head. But those
still living, like Hetty, must come before the dead, mustn't
they?'

Her composure was remarkable, Allen thought, for someone in her very early twenties. The only evidence of shock
was her trembling mouth, which betrayed the strength of
the resolute will which was keeping her steady.

'I'll do what I can,' he told her, 'but it may take a little
time.'

He called up to those who stood by the door and who
were ready to assist him to haul out anyone who wasn't
trapped. 'There are two in here we can do something for.
I'll try to get them up to you as soon as possible.'

First he examined the woman lying on the floor, to discover that the girl had told him no less than the truth: he
could do nothing for her. It was time to look after the living. He immediately found that the girl was prepared to
help him as much as she could.

Between them they managed to lift the unconscious
Hetty up to where the rescue team was waiting. After that

it was the girl's turn, and finally Allen himself clambered out.

She was waiting for him, refusing to sit on the grass, or to allow a sturdy woman, a qualified nurse who had been rescued earlier, to examine her until she had thanked him. The doctor was looking after Hetty.

'It was very brave of you,' she told him solemnly. 'I cannot thank you enough for what you did for Hetty, my maid, and me.'

'It was my duty,' he said, bowing. Now that she was in the open he could see at once that she bore all the signs of great wealth and great position. Her clothing, her carriage, everything about her bore the stamp of her class. What was unique to her was her courage.

'It was more than that, I think,' she said spiritedly. 'You put yourself at risk for me—and for many others, I am told.'

Allen was about to disclaim any credit again when there came a grinding noise from behind him. The train, that mechanical snake, moved and writhed as though it were truly alive, falling even further down the embankment after such a fashion that the last coaches crushed still more those which had originally been ahead of them—among them that from which he had lifted Hetty and her mistress. Dust arose from it in a great cloud.

'You see,' she said to him, almost reproachfully, 'you *did* put yourself in great danger. Suppose that that had occurred after you had climbed in to our compartment—what would have happened to you then?'

'Fortunately for the three of us,' he replied, 'it didn't.'

'It doesn't lessen your courage,' she told him earnestly. 'I can never forget that I owe you my life, nor will Hetty when I tell her.'

'Hear, hear,' said another of the passengers whom Allen had pulled from the wreckage, and who had later joined one of the teams of rescuers he had organised. 'There are many of us who owe our lives to him and to the doctor. A Yankee, aren't you, sir, by your voice?'

He was about to say more when far below them, on the road beyond the embankment, two men on bicycles appeared. They were wearing the navy blue uniform of railway workers.

Dr French said, cheerful for the first time, 'Ah, the sheriff's posse has arrived—from the next station up the line, one supposes. The signalman, once he realised that the train had never reached him, must have notified them. I expect that the police and the fire brigade will be here next. And ambulances, of course, from Oxford or Banbury. Our work is almost over.'

Allen nodded. He was holding exhaustion at bay by an act of will, but he knew that there was one thing which he needed to do, and that quickly. He had no intention of staying once professional help had arrived. Nor was he prepared to reveal his name. From what he had overheard while moving among the rescued he was going to be celebrated as the hero of the train crash, and would probably end up on the front page of various newspapers.

Were that to happen it would almost inevitably result in his relationship with the Schuylers being discovered, and he not only intended to keep his promise to Gerard, he had no wish for publicity for himself. It was true what the doctor had said: their work was almost over. Before the professionals arrived he would slip away as quickly and as secretly as he could, which ought not to be too difficult in the confusion which would follow. He could then strike out across country until he came to a village from which he could arrange his journey back to London.

He had already hidden his valise beneath a bush on the embankment, from where he could quickly recover it before he disappeared. His one regret was to leave behind the gallant young woman whom he had rescued without learning who she was. She would remain forever a ship which had passed him in the night, never to be seen again, but there was no help for it.

After all, he had spent his adult life sacrificing himself for his mother; this was only one more in a long line, and certainly not the greatest. Or so he told himself when he slithered down the embankment again, picked up his valise and began his journey back to London.

Nevertheless, among his many memories of the accident, both good and bad, the one which was perhaps the most poignant of all was his first sight of the beautiful violet eyes which had gazed up at him so bravely.

Chapter Two

'Oh, my dear,' exclaimed Torry, now Lady Schuyler, for her husband, Gerard, had been knighted for his services to Anglo-American co-operation soon after he had become a British citizen, 'what a terrible thing to have happened. To be caught in a serious train accident. Thank God that you are safe, but poor Hetty! The only consolation is that the doctors say that she will soon recover and be able to live a normal life again.'

Patricia 'Trish' Courtney, Allen's 'girl with the violet eyes'—the name by which she still lived on in his memory—had just arrived at the Schuylers' Park Lane mansion. She had been detained overnight in hospital at Oxford until they were satisfied that she was fit to travel home.

For the last four years she had been the Schuylers' ward. Her widowed mother, whose husband had been a great friend of Gerard's, had asked him to be her guardian shortly before she had died of a mysterious wasting sickness. Trish's father had left her money tied up in a trust, only to be inherited when she reached the age of twenty-five. Gerard was its Chief Trustee. Consequently, for him to look after Trish had seemed to be both right and proper. This was a particularly sensible arrangement since Trish's only other near relative was an elderly great-aunt who had been relieved to have the girl taken off her hands.

Torry had been living in an agony of anxiety ever since the news had broken that the train on which Trish had been travelling had been involved in a serious accident which had resulted in many deaths.

Trish had telephoned them late the previous night to assure them that she was unharmed but that poor Hetty had not been so lucky.

'Oh, I have so much to tell you,' she had said at last, 'but it will be better told face to face.'

She had arrived home to be greeted with as much love and affection as Torry would have given to her own daughter. They were now in the drawing room, drinking tea and waiting for Gerard to come home.

'I do hope that you weren't too distressed by such a dreadful experience,' Torry was saying anxiously.

'I have no right to be distressed,' Trish told her, 'for I have survived unharmed where many didn't. And the reason for that was a young man to whom I shall always feel the deepest gratitude. In order to save us he risked his life by climbing into the coach where Hetty and I were trapped. We are not the only ones who owe their life to him. I thanked him at the time, of course, but it grieves me that I do not know his name and that I can't write to him to tell him that Hetty is not too badly injured.'

'Was that the young man whom the newspapers are calling the "mystery hero of the Oxfordshire train wreck," who disappeared shortly before the fire brigade and the police arrived?'

'Yes, dear Torry. He truly did save us, because almost immediately after he lifted us out the coach we had been trapped in was crushed when the train moved again. Most of those who were unfortunate enough to be killed were in it.'

'You have no notion of who he might have been?'

'No, and nor had anyone else when the police questioned us about him. It seems that he was travelling alone. He had a slight American accent—something like yours—as though he had lost it a little by living in England for some time, and was obviously a gentleman by his clothes and manners. I told the police that, and the other passengers agreed with me.'

She sighed, and leaned back against the sofa cushions. Her extreme pallor and the shadows beneath her lovely eyes were the only signs of her recent ordeal.

'He was a handsome young man?' ventured Torry shrewdly.

'Yes, though of course he was very much knocked about—not only because of the accident, but because of his clambering in and out of the train to rescue people. The other passengers told me that before he saved me and Hetty he had even climbed into the locomotive to see if he could do anything for the driver, but the poor man had been killed instantly.'

Torry did not say aloud that the young man, whoever he was, seemed to have made more impression on Trish than the many young men who had besieged her since she had arrived in London and become a prominent member of high society. She had refused all offers of marriage from them, saying more than once, 'Oh, it's only my money they're after, not me.'

A judgement with which both Sir Gerard and Lady Schuyler had ruefully agreed. One of their worries had been that the beautiful heiress in their charge might become the victim of one of the unscrupulous fortune-hunters who were society's plague, but there seemed to be no danger of that happening.

It had taken an unknown man whom she most likely

might never meet again to arouse her interest in the opposite sex!

Torry's questioning of Trish was ended by Gerard's arrival. Like his wife, he was relieved to learn that she had taken no real harm from her unwanted adventure.

'And you met the mystery man—as the newspapers call him?' he asked her.

'Oh, yes, he saved me, as I have been telling Torry.'

'From what I hear he deserves all the praise heaped upon him,' said Gerard, after listening carefully to Trish's tale. 'Highly resourceful also, I gather, from what you say. I could do with him now that my secretary has chosen to leave me.'

'Hall? Hall is going?' queried Torry. 'That must be a blow after you have had him so long.'

'Indeed, I shall scarcely be as lucky again. I am allowing him to retire without notice since he has inherited a small estate. All in all it has been a most vexatious day. I spent the afternoon with a pompous flunky of a senior civil servant who is exercised over this business of when the next century begins. Everyone is assuming that the date will be the first of January, 1900, but he has been taking quite seriously the proposal that it will really begin on the first of January, 1901!

'He wanted to know what the business world's opinion of the matter was. I scarcely knew how to answer him. What I really wanted to say was that the only persons who can be troubled about such a thing are those who have nothing better to think about! That fellow Austin, in the *Illustrated London News* last December, had the right of it when he said that they were having a severe fit of arithmetic—'

Torry broke into Gerard's typically headlong oration, much as Trish had heard her do before, by saying in a teasing voice, 'Really, Gerard, you will have a fit yourself if you don't calm down. Do drink your tea. The last thing poor Trish wants at the moment is any more excitement.'

'Sorry, my dears,' said Gerard with a grin. 'But when I think of the number of our rulers concerning themselves with such nonsense I can't help thinking that it explains why they are making such a mess of things in South Africa. They have their priorities jumbled.'

'Well, Trish and I are with you there. And your main priority is replacing Hall immediately, not with lamenting the shortcomings of the government—I have heard quite enough about that from you lately.'

'True. I have asked Cope, my chief clerk in the City house, to send me his best man to act as a stopgap until I have time to waste on finding a permanent secretary. Being an MP as well as a businessman leaves me with little of it to spare.'

It was Trish's turn to tease him. 'But you wouldn't have it otherwise, would you, Gerard? I can't imagine that doing nothing but sit around being a fine gentleman would ever please you. Both Torry and I would think that you were sickening for something if you weren't always on the go.'

Laughing, Gerard rolled his eyes heavenwards. 'Was ever a man so plagued by his women? Do neither of you have any respect for me? I pity your poor husband when you come to marry, Trish, you have had enough lessons from Torry on how to put a man in his place to keep him in order.'

'And so many lessons on how to make his life comfortable while I do.'

'And that is true also. No pleasure without pain, eh, Torry?'

Trish, watching them, wondered whether she would be lucky enough to have such a happy marriage as Gerard and Torry's was, where love and mutual respect ran hand in hand—something rare in the society in which they lived.

For a fleeting moment she thought of the young man who had lifted her to safety and wondered whether he might, if she ever met him again, give her the loving kindness which that stern buccaneer, Gerard, had brought to his marriage with Torry.

Not that she *was* likely to meet him again.

'Allen! When your trunk arrived back two days ago I had not thought to see you back as early as this. And until your telephone call late last night I was a trifle worried about your non-appearance yesterday. I was afraid that you might have taken harm in that dreadful accident to the Birmingham-London train which has been filling the papers for the last two days.'

'Oh,' said Allen carelessly, 'I came home on another line.' He acknowledged to himself that this was not a total lie, for he had, indeed, done just that after he had left the scene of the accident and spent the night in a little inn in the country.

'You look very tired, though,' said Mr Nance. 'Do sit down. Shall I make you a cup of tea—or would you like something stronger?'

'That would be kind,' Allen returned. 'Tea and brandy, perhaps.'

He sank into an armchair by the small fire burning in the grate of Mr Nance's living room at the back of his shop which was situated in a street off Piccadilly.

Mr Nance was a clockmaker and repairer of Huguenot origin. His family name had been Nantes, but when his remote ancestor had arrived in London in the late seventeenth century, after escaping from the persecution to which the Huguenots, being Protestant, had been subjected in France, the locals had mispronounced and misspelled it Nance. The family had not corrected them: Nance they had been rechristened and Nance they had remained.

He was an old man who had lost his wife and young child in one of the fevers which were endemic in London's summer and had never remarried. Five years ago Allen, who had just arrived in London and had still been living in temporary quarters in a small and dingy hotel, had walked into his shop. A clock in the window had caught his attention. It had reminded him of one which was a family heirloom and had reputedly been made by Cornelius Marriott, the original emigrant from England.

They could not have been more unalike, the tall and sturdy young man—Allen had filled out and matured since that dreadful interview with Gerard—and the small, slight old man with his white hair and gold-rimmed spectacles.

His shop was not a large one, but it was full of clocks and of sound: tickings, tockings and chiming bells.

'Good morning, sir, what may I do for you?' Mr Nance had asked.

'I should like to take a look at the small carriage clock in your window, if I may. I am interested in its origin.'

'Certainly, sir, it is a rare piece. One moment and I will get it for you.'

Rare it was, and the young man and the old one inspected it reverently, the old man gaining a growing respect for the young man's knowledge of his craft.

'Have you any notion who made it?' Allen asked.

'I believe it to be from the workshop of a man called Marriott, who shortly afterwards went bankrupt and emigrated in the mid-eighteenth century to settle in Boston and start a business there. Not much of his survives here.'

'But a lot does in the States,' smiled Allen, 'where I have seen one very like it. He was by way of being my great-great-something or other.'

'Was he indeed?' Mr Nance's respect grew. 'And you are in the business, too?'

'No, no,' said Allen. 'I am merely an amateur. I am a

clerk with a City business house, but I am interested in horology. I have been less than a month in London and already I have encountered a souvenir of my ancestor. If you will suggest a price I shall consider buying it.'

'In a moment,' said Mr Nance. 'I was about to shut the shop in order to have my afternoon cup of tea. Would a visiting American care to share it with me? I rarely meet a young man who is so knowledgeable.'

'With pleasure,' said Allen, who had been feeling lonely since he had left the boat at Liverpool. He found himself in a small cosy room, full of clocks and bric-à-brac and books, being waited on by the kind of bustling servant he had thought only lived in Dickens's novels.

The tea and scones were excellent. He and Mr Nance conversed eagerly on clocks and time and the fables relating to the ends of centuries. Allen revealed that he was looking for rooms and Mr Nance immediately offered him most of his first floor—'until you find something better.'

Allen bought the clock, accepted the offer—and was never to find anything better. Mr Nance gained a son to replace the one he had lost, and Allen, at last, found a father and a home, since they lived, ate and talked together. The loneliness which had dogged his life since he had become a clerk at Schuyler's disappeared.

Mr Nance was a member of the Literary and Philosophical Society and introduced Allen to it, where he soon proved himself to be a valued member. More than that, Allen became his assistant in his spare time, and Mr Nance, who was the last of his line, had dreams that his semi-adopted son might carry on the work of the shop which Philippe Nantes had founded long ago.

'And your holiday is over already?' enquired Mr Nance now.

'I was lonely, and I had seen all that I wished to. It's

back to work on Monday for me,' said Allen, stretching a little. 'Back to the grindstone.'

'You know what I have offered you,' his friend said. 'Whenever you wish you could take over the shop. I am growing old. My offer was not made lightly.'

'I know,' said Allen. 'Your kindness overwhelms me.'

He paused before saying, 'While I was away I decided that I would give Schuyler's another six months and if I were no happier at the end of it, then I would reconsider your offer.'

He had no idea why he was hesitating. He loved the work of the shop, but always at the back of his mind, like the earlier Marriotts, he thought that somewhere, somehow, there might be something more for him than that. What, he did not know. It was not that he did not wish to become a shopkeeper, but if he did it would take away his last hopes of accomplishing something in the world—the hopes which his father's folly had destroyed. Perhaps the offer from Rothschild's might do that—if he accepted it.

Allen was still thinking about these two contrary offers when he returned to work on Monday morning, when he was told that Mr Cope had left word that he was to report to his office immediately on arriving.

He found his superior at his desk, surrounded by files and writing busily. He did not look up until Allen coughed and stared at the ceiling.

'Oh, there you are, Marriott. I trust that you had a restful vacation. I assume that you were not involved in that dreadful railway accident the other day.'

'Very restful,' Allen answered, dodging the last sentence neatly.

He need not have troubled himself for his superior roared on without listening to him. 'Good. Excellent. You will be ready, then, for what I have in mind for you.

'It is this. Sir Gerard Schuyler's secretary has resigned

and he wishes me to send him my best and most reliable man as a temporary replacement. You, Marriott, are undoubtedly my best and most reliable man, so I am sending you to him. I shall be sorry to lose you but you deserve the chance of better things. Work as well as I know that you can and I would not be surprised to learn that your appointment will be more than temporary.

'You will, of course, be required to live at Park Lane, and be one of the staff there. You are of gentlemanly appearance and behaviour. I have no fear that you will not fit in.

'Well?'

Allen stared at him. Work for Gerard, his cousin? Did he wish to? He could almost have laughed aloud.

'I have a question for you, sir,' he came out with at last. Mr Cope was tapping his chin with his pencil, wondering why Marriott was not immediately leaping forward to accept this splendid offer.

'Yes, well, what is it?'

'Have you informed Sir Gerard of whom you propose to send to him?'

'What an extraordinary question, Marriott! I cannot see its relevance to what I have just told you. But, no, he left the matter with me. He is, as you know, a very busy man. He said that he trusted my judgement.' He paused, meaningfully. 'Implicitly.'

For the first time since he had arrived from the States Allen favoured him with a broad grin, although for the life of him Mr Cope could see no humour in the situation.

'In that case,' said Allen, forgetting his role as humble and subservient Marriott for a moment, 'I accept.'

And if he sends me back, he told himself, wanting no part of me, then I shall leave Schuyler's and either go to Rothschild's or take up Mr Nance's offer. What a turn-up for the book this is, though, when suddenly everyone wants unknown and hitherto disregarded Mr Allen Marriott!

'Good. You would have been a fool to have refused such a splendid opportunity, but I suppose you know that. You are to report to Sir Gerard at his Park Lane home tomorrow morning at nine o'clock. Clear your desk before you leave this evening, and collect from me your letter of recommendation to him.

'Good luck, Marriott, don't let me down. Make the most of this splendid opportunity; you may not get another.'

He held out his hand to Allen, who was still smiling, baffling Mr Cope even further.

Allen was wondering what his cousin Gerard's reaction would be when he presented himself in the morning as Cope's 'best and most reliable man'!

'Gerard can't come with us this morning after all,' Torry told Trish. They were seated in the carriage, about to leave for a reception and luncheon given by the Committee for the Welfare of Poor Women, of which Torry was a valued member. A number of men prominent in public life had been invited in order to persuade them to make a donation to the cause.

'Not having Hall to remind him, he had forgotten that he was due to accompany us and had arranged with his City office to interview his new secretary after breakfast. He has promised faithfully to arrive in time for lunch and use his influence to persuade some of the more tight-fisted to "cough up," as he puts it. I sometimes wonder whether I shall ever civilise Gerard completely, but I have to admit that I like him halfway there, so to speak. Most civilised men often seem to be effete!'

Gerard, seated in his office, was congratulating himself that he had managed to avoid the boring part of the morning. One of the drawbacks of being an MP was having to appear cheerful and interested at a variety of functions which he would not willingly have chosen to attend.

He had genuinely forgotten this one, and had debated telephoning his City headquarters and ordering them to delay sending their man for a day, but it was being without a secretary which had caused this mix-up and the sooner one was in post the better.

Downstairs in the entrance hall, a room far larger than the entire ground floor of Mr Nance's home, Allen stood waiting for the butler to return. There was a long, gilt-framed mirror on one wall and he could see himself in it. He was wearing his best black jacket and black and white pinstriped trousers. His linen was spotless, as were his stiff and glossy collar and cuffs. His black silk stock was modest, as befitted his station. He was carrying a small leather briefcase in one hand and his top hat and gloves in the other.

The man who wore them was quite unlike the one whom Gerard had interviewed nine years ago. Time, hardship and the experience of fending for himself had changed him completely. He was no longer thin and pallid, but had the strong, muscular body and bronzed face which was not only typical of the Schuylers, but of his own ancestors. He held himself well, and his confidence was not the empty pride of an untried young man, but that of someone who had learned to respect others as well as himself.

He even found himself wondering whether Gerard would recognise him. He had seen his cousin several times, both in New York and again in London when he had walked through the office, Cope and his previous secretary in tow, but he could not recall Gerard having glanced even once in his direction. It was quite possible that he was not aware that he had been transferred to London, since he had been such a junior employee at the time.

London had changed him, and Mr Nance, who had given

him a pride in himself and his abilities by valuing him as
a man and a friend. If Gerard did not want him for a secretary then he was beginning to think that he might owe
the old man a duty for what he had done for him.

The butler had reappeared. 'Sir Gerard will see you in
his study, sir. Come this way, please.'

He was led up the great main stairway at the top of which
Sir Gerard and Lady Schuyler entertained their distinguished guests. Like the hall, it was lined with good oil
paintings. Either the Schuylers had excellent taste or their
advisers did.

Finally they arrived before a massive door which the
butler threw open, saying loudly, 'Mr Marriott, Sir Gerard.'

His cousin was sitting at a desk of similar massive pro-
portions to the door. The room was more of an office than
a study, although one wall was lined with books and over
the large hearth there was an oil painting by Sargent of a
beautiful woman seated in a rose garden. Lady Schuyler,
presumably.

Unlike himself, Gerard had not changed very much. He
was even larger and more dominant-looking; self-assurance
oozed from his every pore.

Well, what of that? He had self-assurance now, and the
knowledge that he did not really need this post which Mr
Cope had thought such a boon for him, whereas when he
had last met Gerard he had been desperate. Now, if he went
to Rothschild's or took over Mr Nance's shop, he could
well afford to support his mother himself.

He walked forward to stand immediately before the desk.
Gerard looked keenly at him. Allen thought that he had not
recognised him when he walked into the study, but the
amber eyes which surveyed him were all-seeing—and they
saw that it was his cousin standing before him, exchanging
stare for stare.

'Well, well, well,' drawled Gerard, his voice sardonic.

'If it isn't Cousin Allen. You are Cope's most reliable and trusted man, are you? I didn't even know that you were in London, let alone that you were reliable and trusted.'

Allen inclined his head, his own eyes steady on Gerard. 'I have been here for five years. I arrived as a junior clerk. I am now Mr Cope's second-in-command.'

He said nothing more: merely waited.

It was almost a clash of wills as to which would speak first. Allen was determined not to give way. He had inclined his head a little when he spoke, but now raised it to stare challengingly at his cousin.

'You allowed yourself to be put forward for this position?'

'Is that a question?' Allen asked politely. The words were insolent but his manner was not. Gerard recognised himself a little in the young man before him.

'You may take it as one.'

'Then the answer is yes.'

Gerard wanted to whistle. He said instead, 'That must mean that you have no objection to working for me.'

'Indeed not. The objection might lie in your not wanting me to.'

Gerard rose and walked round the desk. 'You have changed, I see.'

'I regret that I cannot say the same for you, sir. But, changed or not, I am willing to be your secretary and to serve you as diligently and humbly as I have served Mr Cope. More I cannot say.'

Gerard said gently, for he thought that in some way his once unconsidered cousin had become formidable, 'You understand that you will have to live in. It might be fairer to you for your Schuyler connection to be revealed.'

His cousin's reaction surprised him.

Allen threw his head back and said haughtily, 'No, on no account. You made it plain nine years ago that I was to claim no relationship with you, and by doing that you conferred on me an unexpected favour. You made me my own man. I am now Allen Marriott, with no Schuyler in my name, and I have not the slightest wish to be connected with you and your family in any way other than that of the work for which I am to be paid.'

'Suppose I made that a condition of your employment?'

'Then I should offer you my resignation from Schuyler's on the spot. If you wish to hire me you will offer me the same terms as anyone else who was sent to you. No less and no more.'

Gerard thought that it might have been his own young self speaking. 'Very well, you shall have your wish. I think that we might deal well together.'

'So long as we both understand, sir, that our relationship is only one of business. I want no favours, nor do I want to be judged more harshly than you would judge an Allen Marriott whom you had never met before.'

'Very well. I find it odd that the man I interview should be the one laying down conditions, but for once I shall be happy to accept yours. When can you start?'

Allen lifted his briefcase. 'Immediately, but I shall require a little time to move my possessions from my present rooms to Park Lane.'

'You have not asked me what your hours and duties will be.'

'From all I have heard, and what I have been told of Mr Hall's, they will be fair. Neither onerous nor over-generous.'

Gerard began to laugh. Yes, it was like interviewing himself. He tossed a piece of paper over to Allen. 'Your conditions are listed there. If they are not to your taste, you may change your mind. I shall quite understand.'

Allen picked up the paper, looked at it and said, 'You will allow?' before reading it.

His terms of service were indeed fair, and, together with his salary, would enable him to retain his rooms with Mr Nance and also give him a little time to continue his clock-making activities. He had to give Gerard a quarter's notice, but he thought that if, after a suitable length of time had passed, he wished to leave, his cousin would not stand in his way.

It was done. Gerard said easily, 'I now have to attend some flummery of my wife's at the Savoy Hotel. While I am out you might like to begin the task of moving in. Tomorrow morning will be soon enough for us to start to work together.'

Allen inclined his head; it was his *congé*. The die was cast. He would be working with Gerard, living in his home—and whether he was glad or sorry, he did not know.

Chapter Three

Torry had told Trish that they were dining alone that night. She accordingly dressed quite simply. She disliked the elaborate clothing which most society women wore, preferring a classic elegance of line to frills and flounces. Similarly her lustrous dark hair was devoid of the elaborate curls which fashion favoured. Nor did she wear what were known as rats, small pads arranged under the hair to give the impression of having a greater wealth of it than nature had given her.

She rarely needed to resort to paint and powder to enhance what was a perfect complexion without them. Her violet eyes were already famous, and, like many late nineteenth-century beauties before her, her photograph had appeared in the *Illustrated London News* above a caption reading simply, 'An English Violet'—in imitation of the description of Lilly Langtry, once the Prince of Wales's mistress, as 'The Jersey Lily.'

Trish disliked her fame and tried to ignore it. What she could not ignore was people standing on chairs at balls to look at her, and the myriad of young men who pursued her for her money as well as her looks.

Tonight she had chosen to wear a pale amethyst gown

with a high neck and a simple lace collar. Her only jewellery was tortoiseshell combs decorated with some small
diamond studs, and she carried nothing but a small fan. She
liked these informal evenings—they reminded her of home
and the simple life which she had lived before her mother
fell ill.

She had just reached the black and white stone-flagged
entrance hall when one of the doors into it—the one directly opposite to her—opened and a young man wearing
a dark suit came through it.

They stared at one another. Allen immediately recognised 'the girl with violet eyes' and Trish recognised her
rescuer. It would have been difficult to tell which was the
more astonished.

'You!' they both exclaimed together—and then fell silent.

Trish, surprisingly, was the first to recover. She thought
that her saviour looked even more handsome in his dark
suit than he had done when he had lifted her out of the
coach—and she'd thought that he had been remarkable
then.

'Oh,' she breathed, dropping her fan and clasping her
hands to her breast. 'How wonderful to meet you again!
Why did you disappear? How surprised and pleased Gerard
and Torry will be when I tell them I have found you.'

'No!' The word almost exploded from Allen. 'Please, I
beg of you, say nothing of the accident to them—or of my
part in it.'

Trish was so overcome that she could only stutter at him.
'But why? What you did was heroic. Oh, I am not speaking
of what the papers said, but of what I saw you do. How
can you not want people to know?'

Allen did something entirely spontaneous. He would
wonder afterwards what anyone who had come upon them
then would have made of it. He dropped on to one knee,

took her small hands in his and looked up into her glorious eyes before he said urgently, 'I know how you must feel, but you must do me this one great favour in return for the one I did for you. It is vital to me that no one knows of what I did. For reasons I cannot explain to you I wish to remain anonymous.

'Will you do as I wish, my violet-eyed beauty?'

The last words flew out of him. In response Trish, also scarcely knowing what she was doing, lifted one of his hands to her lips and kissed its palm. A great shudder went through him, but he did not withdraw it when he stood up.

She said slowly, 'It beggars belief that you require this of me, but since I owe my rescue to you—and Hetty's life—then I will keep silent, even though my dearest wish is for the world to know you for what you are.'

For a long second they remained standing thus, face to face. Then time's clock ticked again. Allen surrendered the hand he still held and she handed him his back.

He bowed, and said stiffly and impersonally, after a fashion quite different from the one he had previously used to her, 'I must inform you that I am Allen Marriott, Sir Gerard's new secretary, and you are?'

'I am Patricia Courtney, always known as Trish, and I must ask you whether, when we meet before dinner, you wish us to appear to be strangers.'

Clever girl, thought Allen, but said aloud, 'I think that would be best, don't you, Miss Courtney?'

'If that is what you want, yes.'

'And I also think that you should enter the drawing room before me. It would not do for us to arrive together.'

He also thought that it would give them both time to recover from the shock of their unexpected meeting. No, it was more than shock; something had passed between them which was deeper than that: a powerful and mutual attraction which seemed age-old, not new. It was as though they had known one another long ago in some distant past. He watched her walk to the drawing room door and pass through it with a sense of loss which, although he could not know it, Trish shared.

She had recovered her usual calm composure, and consequently she did not betray her surprise on finding that Gerard and Torry were not alone. Lord Moidore, Gerard's original patron in London society, and now his best friend, was seated before the fire, a glass of sherry in his hand. He and Gerard put their glasses down and rose to greet her. Tom Moidore, a widower who had recently lost a wife to whom he had always been faithful—unlike many—was finding it hard to adjust to life without her. He was a large man in his early fifties.

'You know Tom, of course,' Gerard said to her, 'although he has not been seen much in society lately. He was at the luncheon today and, finding that he was at a bit of a loose end, I invited him to dinner. I assured him that it would be a quiet family one, the only other guest being my new secretary, who should be here any minute.'

He pulled out his gold hunter and inspected it. 'One more minute, in fact, and he will be after the hour I told him to be here. Not a good way to start one's new post, eh, Tom?'

Trish flushed. The only reason the new secretary looked like being late was because of their chance encounter in the entrance hall. She was debating whether to say something to mollify Gerard when the door opened and Allen entered.

Gerard looked at the hunter which he was still holding and said, grinning a little, 'Punctual to the moment, Marriott. As you see this is the family dinner I spoke of earlier. May I introduce Mr Allen Marriott to my wife, Lady Schuyler, and to Miss Patricia Courtney, our ward? The other gentleman present is not a gentleman at all, nor a member of the family, although our long friendship quali-

fies him to call himself one. He is, in fact, a nobleman.
Lord Moidore, may I present my new secretary to you?'

Allen bowed. Lord Moidore, responding, said lazily,
'How do, Marriott?' and to Gerard, 'Hall has finally gone,
I see. Now he *was* a member of the family. How many
years had he been with you, Schuyler?'

'Fifteen,' returned Gerard. 'But all things change in the
end.' He was looking at Allen as he spoke, so that Allen
wondered if there were a double meaning in them for him.

'Do let us sit down,' said Torry briskly. 'This is not a
formal gathering and we may as well be comfortable. Is
this your first post as a secretary, Mr Marriott?'

'Yes, Lady Schuyler. I have been working as a clerk in
Schuyler's London house for the past five years. Sir Gerard
will have to be my tutor, I fear.'

'Well, then, I pity you,' returned Torry frankly. 'He is
not the most patient of men.'

Allen could not resist saying, in as neutral a voice as
possible, 'I have been told that, Lady Schuyler, but I trust
that I shall prove an apt and willing pupil.'

Trish was not the only person in the room to think that
there was something slightly satirical in Allen's tone. What
impressed her about him was the calm with which he was
behaving, as though it were quite usual for him to find
himself hobnobbing with a leading member of Her Maj-
esty's Government and one of America's robber barons
turned English gentleman and MP.

Torry said, 'I can tell by your voice, Mr Marriott, that
you are either an American or have spent some time in the
States. From what part do you hail?'

'The East Coast,' Allen answered, choosing the largest
piece of territory he could think of in the hope that Torry
would not pursue the conversation by asking which part of
it, compelling him either to lie or be unconvincingly evasive.

Fortunately for him the butler cut all conversation short by entering and announcing that dinner was served. Lord Moidore took Trish in and Allen made up the rear. Lord Moidore made a small joke about his presence spoiling the perfect symmetry of the meal by creating an odd person at table.

Allen found himself seated alone, facing him and Trish. It was Lord Moidore who started the conversation by saying to Trish, 'Do I understand, Miss Courtney, that you were involved in that dreadful train accident outside Oxford?'

Trish flushed again. 'Yes. I was on my way home from a visit to my great-aunt, who lives just outside Leamington in Warwickshire. I suffered very little, fortunately, but my poor maid Hetty was quite badly injured. She is still in hospital, but the doctors say that her chance of a complete recovery is good.'

With Allen seated across from her Trish had not mentioned that she had been rescued by the 'mystery hero.' Lord Moidore, however, knowing nothing of why she was being reticent, said cheerfully, 'I understand from Gerard that you and your maid were among those whom the "mystery hero" plucked from the crash.'

Trish, without looking at Allen, said, 'That is true, and I shall always be grateful to him, and many others must be too.'

'How strange that he should disappear afterwards. What sort of person was he?'

'Young,' said Trish, still studiously avoiding Allen's eye.

'Quite the gentleman, I believe you said,' remarked Torry, who was wondering why Trish was being unforthcoming—particularly when she had been so lyrical about the young man when she had told her of the accident.

'The *Morning Post*'s man reported that one of those

whom he rescued said that he spoke with an odd accent. Did you think it was, Trish?'

'Not particularly.' Trish's voice was non-committal. Who would have thought that Lord Moidore would be interested enough in the accident that he was determined to pump her about it?

'The reason I ask,' he said, 'is that there will be an enquiry set up, and it would be extremely useful to have the young man's evidence. I understand that he was the first out of the train and the first to examine the locomotive. I was hoping that you might have remembered something about him which would help us to trace him.'

'Only that he was very brave and took a large number of risks. If he left the scene in order that he might not be questioned I think that we ought to respect his wishes, don't you, Lord Moidore?'

He smiled. 'Yes, I suppose so, my dear. Seeing that you owe him a debt of gratitude, I quite understand why you should feel as you do. The press are to print an appeal to him to come forward, but if he remains determined to avoid publicity that may not answer either.'

Fortunately for both Allen and Trish that disposed of the matter, for Torry, aware that Trish had disliked speaking of the accident and putting her reticence down to her over-vivid memories of it, steered the conversation into other channels.

'Gerard,' she told the company, her voice amused, 'has been complaining about the current obsession with the question of whether the new century begins on January first, 1900, or on January first, 1901. He considers it frivolous since, whatever the mathematicians might say, no ordinary person—the fabled man on the Clapham omnibus, for instance—will consider that it starts in other than 1900. I wonder what your opinion is, Tom?'

Allen had drunk his soup while adopting the junior

clerk's habit of not looking at anyone in particular when he was not part of the discussion. He was inwardly amused to note that his cousins were on Christian name terms with the nobility, and at the same time relieved that Lady Schuyler had turned the conversation away from the accident. He had tried to look as innocent as a man could while Lord Moidore had questioned Trish and was sorry that his plea to her for silence had put her in such an awkward position.

He was so busily determined not to be noticed that he almost missed the fact that Lord Moidore had included him in the vigorous dinner table discussion about the date. Gerard was dismissing it as mathematicians' nonsense, while Lord Moidore, partly to roast him, was taking the opposite point of view.

'After all,' he said, 'these days accuracy in such matters is more important than it was in the past, when times and dates were delightfully vague. But science has taught us the necessity for precision if we are to make the most of the brave new world which the next century will surely bring. Marriott, here, is at the sharp end of your business, Gerard, I wonder what his views are on the matter?'

Allen's surprise at being named was such that he almost dropped his soup spoon. He had hoped for anonymity at the dinner table at least, but apparently he was not to be allowed it.

The footman removing his soup plate gave him an instant's grace in which to collect himself.

'Why, m'lord,' he replied, aware that Gerard's considering eye was on him, 'I am a little of your opinion. I have a friend who takes these matters seriously and is investigating the possibility of inventing a machine which would not only tell the time but would measure the days, weeks and months of each year after such a fashion, and with such accuracy, that merely to look at it would tell us precisely which week and month we were in and when the century changed. For ordinary, unscientific purposes, though, I agree with Sir Gerard, and the man from Clapham.'

Tom Moidore gave a loud laugh. 'Oh, splendid! You should be in Parliament, young man. With one short paragraph you have managed to please all parties here present. You have also intrigued me, and, I believe, Sir Gerard, too. Is your friend's proposition serious—or is it mere speculation?'

'Both,' said Allen, permitting himself a small smile. 'I understand from him that earlier this century an Englishman called Babbage was experimenting with a similar machine which would add, subtract, multiply and divide mechanically, thus saving me and my fellow clerks a great deal of hard work—as well as saving time.'

Allen had a sudden vision of Mr Nance sitting opposite to him over their humble supper in front of the big black range in his small kitchen, which was quite unlike the splendid room in which he was eating the rarest of delicacies, his questioner a peer of the realm. Mr Nance would most likely be talking animatedly about all the experiments he might be able to undertake if only he were younger or richer. For Allen's part he would be silently regretting that he would not be able to use the fortune which he had hoped to inherit at twenty-one—and which had been lost with his father's—to help finance such projects.

'You are speaking of a machine like Babbage's, but operated by electricity,' said Gerard shrewdly. 'Has your friend considered that?'

Allen was aware that both men were watching him curiously. 'Yes, even though it sounds as impossible as the time machine of which Mr Wells wrote recently. The problem is that the capital necessary to carry out even a small project of that nature is far beyond his touch.'

'Hmm,' said Tom Moidore. 'Something for you to think about, Gerard.'

Gerard shook his head. 'Not yet,' he said. 'I don't think the time is ripe. In the future, perhaps.'

'Oh,' said Torry, smiling, 'in the magic new century— if it turns about to be magic, that is. You mentioned Mr Wells, Mr Marriott. He quite frightened me by prophesying that strange creatures will be coming from Mars to murder us all—not a very happy prospect for the future, you will agree.'

Tom Moidore nodded. 'That was in *The War of the Worlds*, was it not? That man has the most gruesome imagination. He's something of a social reformer too, I understand.'

Allen forbore to mention that he had met H.G. Wells shortly after he had arrived from the USA, when Wells had been living in London and had discussed social reform and other matters with him at the Literary and Philosophical Society to which Mr Nance had introduced him. He had no wish to draw any attention to his life outside the Schuyler orbit.

Trish said eagerly, 'I have read *The Time Machine*. I liked the bit when the traveller went back into the past, but, like Torry, I was frightened by his description of our future. One can only hope that the next century will not become a scene of desolation.' She gave a little shiver when she had finished speaking.

Tom Moidore comforted her jovially. 'Oh, you need have no fear of that, my dear. The Peace Conference at the Hague—which I shall shortly be visiting—will, I hope, pass a resolution prohibiting the production of all new firearms and explosives. We are growing far too sensible to engage in war, particularly in one which might involve mass destruction.'

Allen forgot his self-denying resolution to be as nondescript as possible. Had Mr Nance said anything similar he would have responded immediately, as he did now, to a statement which he felt the speaker did not wholly mean but was meant rather as an encouragement to a fearful young woman. Trish deserved better than that.

'Do I take it, m'lord,' he asked, 'that your last remark means that the present critical situation between Britain and South Africa will *not* be resolved by war—as it was on the last occasion when the two countries were at odds?'

He saw Gerard raise his eyebrows, Torry smile, and Trish look sideways at him, her face glowing with approval. It was the first time since dinner had begun that their eyes had met. The table between them disappeared and for a second they were in a world of their own before they returned to the Schuylers' dining room.

Neither Gerard nor Torry sensed anything amiss, but Tom Moidore, that shrewd man of affairs, despite sitting opposite to Trish and Allen, felt rather than saw the silent message which passed between them. How in the world had Master Secretary, who had arrived in the house only a few hours ago, managed to make such an impression on a young woman who was notoriously cold to most of the men she had met in society?

She was famous as the epitome—in the nicest possible way—of the so-called New Woman, who regarded herself as equal to men and therefore considered herself entitled to have opinions on subjects which had been traditionally reserved as the preserve of men.

Fortunately for Gerard and Torry she had drawn the line at joining what was known as 'the shrieking sisterhood'— the suffragettes—women who campaigned noisily and vigorously for the vote.

What was more, if he had read matters aright, she and Master Secretary had not even had the opportunity to speak to one another before the meal began—Gerard had introduced him to Trish in the drawing room in a way which had made it plain that it was their first meeting.

His answer to Allen, though, was pleasant in the extreme. 'Oh, one does hope that reason will prevail—indeed, I am sure that it will. Neither we nor the Boers can possibly gain anything by going to war over matters which common sense says can be settled peacefully.'

Mr Nance had once said that the reason one could not predict the future was because so many odd and quite unpredictable things might occur to change it. Allen risked being considered insolent by remarking quietly, 'In my opinion m'lord, which I well know is a humble one, it is those events which have no reason behind them which often precipitate nations into war.'

He gained unexpected support from Torry Schuyler. She leaned forward, saying eagerly, 'What a very perceptive remark, Mr Marriott. You mean, I suppose, like the firing on Fort Sumter which sparked off the American Civil War?'

Allen bowed his head in her direction to show his agreement without speaking further. Trish did it for him. 'If that is true then we must hope that nothing untoward occurs in the future.'

'Which is like hoping that it might not rain tomorrow,' said Torry dryly. 'I am always in hopes that electricity—about which everyone is enthusiastic—might be used to make the weather more amenable—and more predictable.'

'Like arranging for it to be fine every day and only to rain at night,' put in Trish. A remark which gained appreciative laughter from the whole table and led discussion into calmer waters.

Gerard had decided that since the party was small the ladies and the gentlemen would retire to the drawing room together once dinner was over, instead of the ladies leaving the men to their port and cigars. 'Most civilised,' Tom Moidore commented once Gerard had raised the matter.

Allen said nothing. He had remained silent after his re-

mark about South Africa and—last again—he walked to
the drawing room to sit quiet, and outwardly deferential,
on a chair near the sofa on which Torry and Trish sat, away
from the armchairs of Gerard and Tom Moidore. He was
suddenly tired to the bone. It had been a long and difficult
day, and having to behave himself at a semi-formal dinner
when he had understood that it would be a family one had
'put the tin lid on it'—a favourite saying of Mr Nance's.

His exhaustion was not only of the body, even though
he knew that he had not fully recovered from his exertions
of two days ago. It was partly, also, of the mind, caused to
some extent by his wishing that he was back in Mr Nance's
kitchen, able to speak his mind freely—something to which
he had become accustomed during the last five years. He
had retained his rooms there, as a bolt-hole to which he
could retire if the strain of being Gerard's unacknowledged
cousin became too much for him.

'You didn't want this post, did you, Allen? Why did you
accept it?' Mr Nance had asked shrewdly, and Allen had
answered him in kind.

'Would you understand me if I told you it was a challenge?'

'I think I might—although I don't understand why it
should be a challenge.'

He couldn't tell the old man the truth. That he wanted
to prove something to Gerard: God knows what; he scarcely
knew himself! He was busy asking himself what folly had
led him to this magnificent, but comfortable room, which
yet offered him no comfort, when Gerard remarked suddenly, 'You look tired, Marriott. Not surprising—you've
had a long and hard day. I give you leave to retire.'

He rose, bowed to the company, and made his adieux
short, but gracious.

Torry said, after the door had closed on him and conversation had continued desultorily for some minutes, 'I,

too, am feeling weary, Gerard. If you and Tom will excuse me, I would like to retire also.'

'And I,' said Trish, rising. She alone knew that Allen's pallor was the result of the accident and had been happy to see him let off the leash, as it were. She also knew that to leave Tom Moidore and Gerard alone would give them the opportunity to speak freely of matters which they might not want to discuss before the women.

Indeed, the moment that she and Torry had left, Tom Moidore leaned forward to say confidentially. 'I hope that you won't take this amiss, Gerard, but there's something dam'd odd about your secretary.'

'Oh?' said Gerard, pouring his friend another glass of brandy. 'In what way?'

He knew very well what was odd about young Marriott, but he was not about to tell Tom what it was. He had given his word to his cousin that he would not reveal his identity to anyone and he meant to keep it. What did intrigue him was what Tom thought that he had discovered.

'Difficult to say,' Tom answered, swirling his brandy round and round in its balloon glass and taking a sniff at it. 'His manner, so outwardly deferential, for one thing, but I sense that there's a totally different attitude beneath it— almost as though he despises us.'

'That's a remarkable judgement to make,' returned Gerard coolly, 'on a few moments' idle conversation.'

'Not idle on his part. He's a clever young devil is Master Secretary, beneath all that humility, if I don't mistake. What's his background, do you know?'

What answer could Gerard make but an evasive one— which didn't sound evasive?

'Only that Cope sent him to me as his best and most reliable man—and you know what I think of Cope's judgement.'

'Quite, that it's spot-on, but there's another thing. Have he and Trish met before?'

Gerard looked up sharply, his languor gone.

'No, certainly not. What makes you ask that?'

'You've always trusted my—what do you call it?—second sight. Only that twice something passed between them, with no words spoken—the sort of communication which usually only occurs between men and women after a long and intimate friendship or affair.'

Gerard said, not angrily but searchingly, 'I have the best of reasons for knowing that they have never met. Marriott has been a clerk in my London office for the last five years, living God knows where, but somewhere humble, no doubt; his pay wouldn't run to more. For the last few years, since Trish came to live with us, she has barely been out of Torry's sight—until she visited this old aunt in Warwickshire three weeks ago. She'd hardly meet Marriott there; the aunt's a recluse, which is why she came to us. How, therefore, could she and Marriott have had a long relationship—or a short one for that matter?'

'Nevertheless,' Tom said slowly, 'and again at the risk of offending you, I'd swear that they've met before tonight. I'd wager good money on it. But from what you've just said it's an impossibility—so I'd lose my good money, wouldn't I?'

That ended the matter, but Gerard privately decided to keep a firm eye in future on Master Secretary, as Tom Moidore had dubbed him. At least Tom hadn't guessed at the relationship between them.

After the dinner party with Lord Moidore Trish was determined to talk to Allen Marriott again; he was such an interesting person, quite unlike all the young men she had previously met in London society. His question to Lord Moidore about the possibility of war in South Africa had been very acute, and his remarks about the ending of the century had been both interesting and informative.

She was not being quite honest with herself: her real reason for wanting to meet him again was that he attracted her strongly—and strangely. She found herself fantasising about him. Where had he come from? Why, every time that she looked at him, did the oddest sensation shoot through her? A kind of thrill which involved her whole body. She could hardly wait to see him again, if only to discover whether the thrill would occur again.

Unfortunately, on the following evening Gerard had given a grand dinner party to a collection of French diplomats—a dinner party to which his secretary was not invited, which was another opportunity to meet him lost. The morning after that Gerard had gone to chair a committee at Westminster before attending a Commons debate in the afternoon. Torry had invited her to go shopping at Harrods, but she had pleaded a headache, thinking that this would be a splendid opportunity to contrive a meeting with Allen.

She dressed herself quite plainly in a neat blue morning gown, ran up to Gerard's office, knocked on the door before entering and pretended to be surprised to find that Gerard was not there.

'No,' Allen told her, looking up from his desk by the window, 'Sir Gerard has gone to the House.'

For one moment when he had lifted his head, his eyes blind before he acknowledged her presence, something about him had reminded her of Gerard. She dismissed the fleeting sensation as having occurred because he was in Gerard's study, surrounded by his possessions.

'Oh, I'm sorry to have interrupted you at your work…'

Allen drank in her whole charming appearance, trying not to drown himself in her violet eyes. 'No need to be sorry. To be truthful I have been at my desk for several hours and I need a break.'

'Is your work very hard?' asked Trish, desperate to keep him talking to her so that she had no reason to leave.

'Not really. The problem is that my way of keeping files in order is quite different from my predecessor's, which means that I am having to rearrange his work at the same time that I am pursuing my own.'

The smile he gave her when he finished speaking set Trish's legs trembling. That strange thrill was running through her again. And it only came when she was with him.

She pulled out her little fob watch. 'Aunt Torry and I usually drink coffee at this hour. Suppose I ordered it to be served in the library next door. We could drink it together and then neither of us need be lonely.'

Allen hesitated. Had she no notion of the temptation which she presented to him? In his lowly position he had no right to socialise with her. She, he had discovered, was a rich heiress, and what was he but a poor man who needed to earn his own living? But the look which she gave him was such a pleading one that he almost surrendered to her immediately—and then decided not to.

It hurt him to say it, but it was necessary. 'My dear Miss Courtney,' he told her gently, 'I don't think that either Sir Gerard or Lady Schuyler would approve of you hobnobbing with his secretary. I'm sure that you never drank coffee on your own with Mr Hall.'

'Indeed not,' she said vigorously. 'He was not at all the kind of person with whom I could either hob or nob. Neither had he saved me from a train wreck. He was also old enough to be my father and consequently presented no temptation to me at all.'

'But I do, Miss Courtney. Is not that true?'

How handsome he looked whilst he was denying himself to her.

'I do wish that you would not call me Miss Courtney,'

she told him crossly. 'My name is Trish. I would like you
to use it when you speak to me.'

'Now you know I ought not do any such thing.'

'No, I don't. Everyone else calls me Trish; why shouldn't
you? I was given the nickname as a child. At least I wasn't
called Pat or Patty; that would have been the very end.
Don't you find it strange that all the people in the best
society have such weird nicknames? I find it most childish
to hear some huge guards officer addressed as Binkie by
another giant who's always known as Tuffy.'

'Agreed,' he said, his small smile appearing again like
the sun coming from behind a cloud.

Trish gave a little crow of delight, naughtily taking his
agreement to be that to her first statement, not her second.
'There! I knew you'd give way. Trish it shall be.'

Allen gave way. 'In private only. In public—Miss Courtney.'

'If that is what you want. Now I shall ring for coffee to
be served next door. No one will think anything of that.
Gerard and Torry often take coffee in the library. You and
Gerard would have had coffee there today if he weren't at
the House.'

She pulled the bell and when the footman arrived ordered
coffee for two. When he had gone she flung open the door
which led to the library and motioned Allen through. There
was a table in a tall window at which she often sat with
her guardians. It looked out on to Hyde Park where, later
in the day, the cream of society would appear walking, or
on horseback, or in their carriages.

And Allen would still be working. He was watching her
mobile face with its changing expressions and thought that
he had never seen anything so charmingly artless. Not that
she was a fool. Everything she said betrayed a lively mind,
and if she had not been formally educated she had obviously educated herself.

'I like the library,' she told him. 'The books and the pictures, and the feeling that all the great minds of the past still live in them.'

'True,' he said, 'but before we discuss them, I have to offer you my thanks for not betraying the ''mystery man'' to Lord Moidore. You must have been sorely tempted to reveal that he was sitting at table with him.'

'Indeed I was. I find it strangely satisfying, however, to know something which he doesn't. He is kind to women, but he thinks that we are fools and talks down to us. He's good, though, really good—not like that ghastly Mr Asquith whom Aunt Torry warned me never to be alone with because he wasn't safe around young girls. I suppose I shouldn't say that to you, but it's the oddest thing, I feel that I have known you all my life and can say anything to you.'

What a fool he will think me, thought Trish despairingly, babbling away like that. But it's the truth. I feel comfortable with him. I suppose that because he's quiet and self-contained I believe that I can confide in him and he won't betray me.

What was nice was that when she had finished chattering a companionable silence fell before he said, 'I know what you mean, Trish. Remember, though, that many men of affairs, and men of no affairs at all in society, talk down to all those whom they consider their inferiors. Not only women but servants, tradesmen and even professional people are addressed in exactly the same fashion in which Lord Moidore talked to you at dinner the other night.'

The coffee arrived, served by a footman who promptly returned to the servants' hall and told the staff, 'That new secretary's a fast worker and no mistake. He's already chewing the rag with Miss Courtney as though he's known her all his life. When the cat's away, the mice will play. I wonder what Sir Gerard would have to say about that!'

'Enough, man,' the butler commanded magisterially whilst trying to decide how best to drop a word in Sir Gerard's ear. He disliked men who were neither servants nor masters trying to get above themselves. Drinking coffee with the Schuylers' well-protected ward, was he? What next!

He would have had a further fit if he could have heard Allen and Trish discussing quietly and sensibly the vexed question of female suffrage. Trish's original nervous chattering, provoked by the excitement of being alone with Allen, had at last subsided.

Shortly afterwards Allen pulled out his watch and said, 'Pleasant though this is, I must go back to work.'

Trish answered him eagerly. 'Sir Gerard and Lady Schuyler are lunching with the Prince of Wales tomorrow, before the Prince and Sir Gerard attend a meeting of architects interested in designing suitable homes for the poor. I see no reason why I shouldn't ask the butler to serve coffee in here again at ten-thirty tomorrow morning, do you?'

'Every reason in the world,' replied Allen, rising to leave, and offering her one of his slow smiles which clutched at her heart strings, 'but that does not prevent me from saying that I shall find it necessary to retire to the library tomorrow morning at about that hour, when I shall be as surprised to find you there as you were to discover that Sir Gerard was not in his office this morning!'

'Fairly caught out,' riposted Trish with a gamine's grin. 'I can see that I shall need to take care to be absolutely truthful when next we meet. I've grown too used to being with young men whose one weapon against me is flattery.'

'Oh, I can do that, too,' Allen told her, before he closed the door behind him, 'but I rather thought that you would prefer me to be honest.'

'Indeed I do,' Trish murmured softly to herself. 'And I

can't wait for tomorrow morning when we shall meet again.'

This first rendezvous set the pattern of their days. Whenever possible—that was when they were left alone in the house—Allen and Trish met for a few snatched minutes over coffee. Otherwise they were constrained by being in the company of Gerard and Torry, separately or together. On evenings when the Schuylers dined alone, Allen dined with them, sitting silent at the table unless spoken to, and equally silent in the drawing room after it.

'I had always thought my fellow Yankees a talkative race,' Torry remarked to Gerard at breakfast after Allen's first week in Park Lane, 'but Mr Marriott seems determined to prove me wrong. Mr Hall, who was scarcely a sociable soul, had more to say for himself than your new man.'

'Better that than an idle flow of vacuous chatter,' was Gerard's only reply. He was somewhat surprised by his cousin's determination to remain aloof from them, but respected it. 'I can only suppose that he is something of a recluse. He never addresses me on other than matters of business. His efficiency, however, is undoubted, and that is what I want most in a secretary, not an unending stream of witty conversation.'

Trish, listening to them, thought of the man whom she was coming to know, who talked interestingly to her on a wide variety of subjects. He had a quiet humour, making small jokes which she did not always pick up until he had left her. He never took any advantage of their secret meetings, remaining always a perfect gentleman, something which was beginning to annoy Trish a little.

Did he really feel for her what she was beginning to feel for him? He showed little sign of it. His self-control was so absolute that she had no notion of what he might be thinking except when he gave her that heartbreaking smile. They were both, she thought crossly, behaving so properly that they might as well be a pair of bishops at a convocation!

She would have been heartened to learn what it was costing Allen not to give way to his very real attraction to her, not to lean forward and take her hand in his, and… At that point in his post-meeting musings he usually gave up and concentrated sternly on his work for Gerard—which was the equivalent of throwing a bucket of cold water over himself.

On his first full day off Allen visited Mr Nance. He found him in his workshop, examining the innards of a striking clock which he had spread across the bench. He looked up at Allen, showing little of the pleasure which he felt on seeing him again.

'You come at an apposite moment,' he remarked somewhat ruefully. 'My eyes are betraying me these days.' He handed Allen the loupe he was holding. 'Perhaps you can help me.'

It was a gesture of confidence which set Allen smiling. He sat down, asked his master what the problem was and set about solving it.

'I see that living among the mighty has not yet destroyed your skill.' Mr Nance's voice was dry. 'You look tired. Are they overworking you and not feeding you properly?'

'Neither,' said Allen, pausing from his labours for a moment. 'Sir Gerard is a reasonable taskmaster and the food is superb. On the other hand…'

He paused tantalisingly, picked up a tiny screwdriver and concentrated on his work before finishing his sentence. 'On the other hand, I prefer your kitchen and your company to the fleshpots.'

Without thinking he added, 'I have grown unused to high living, I fear.'

'Which means that you were once used to it—something

which I had guessed from little things you have said and done.'

Allen shrugged his shoulders. 'Oh, one gives one's self away without meaning to. Here, I believe that I may have repaired your broken piece.'

Mr Nance took it from him. 'You will be my master soon, Allen, and my heir. I would like you to be my heir in every way. You have a gift, a creative gift, which is better than the other gift you have, which is a barren one used to make other men rich.'

They had had this argument before, and again Allen said nothing in reply.

'Does this mean,' Mr Nance went on, 'that you are wedded to this man for whom you are now working? That you see no future here? That you will leave me to make my clock of the century on my own?'

'You are a blackmailing old gentleman, are you not?' said Allen, laughing. 'You and Sir Gerard Schuyler are not as unalike as you might think. I spoke to him of our ideas for a year-long and dated clock shortly after I arrived in Park Lane, and he was full of electricity and the wonders which it might perform.'

'If he was, he is a shrewd man. Old age prevents me from considering its advantages. You, on the other hand…'

'I on the other hand,' said Allen, 'am hungry. I skipped breakfast in order to come to you as soon as possible in the hope that you would serve me one of your fry-ups. I've missed them.'

He could not have said anything more calculated to please the old man. He beamed at his protégé. 'I shall only do that if you will tell me if you have met any charming young ladies in your new home. It is not good for you to live like a monk.'

Allen's answer was careless. 'Thus far, I have only met Sir Gerard's wife, who is charming but not young, and their ward, Miss Courtney, who answers to both your descriptions. Both of them are equally beyond my touch, and, since the servants despise me for not being one of them, my future dealings with any young ladies, charming or otherwise, look likely to be bleak.'

'Your trouble,' said Mr Nance, who had now taken over the task of repairing the clock, 'is that you are too particular, too finicky. But it is a good failing. You are not likely to end up hitched to someone inappropriate because you could not keep your hands off her.'

This was one of the many pieces of down-to-earth wisdom with which he favoured Allen, whom he saw as a son to be advised. Allen had a sudden vision of himself *not* keeping his hands off Trish. He banished the vision of a Trish who was slowly being stripped of her clothes in order to reveal the glories of her beautiful body.

He thought of fry-ups instead, and plaintively reminded Mr Nance that he owed him one for telling him about the women he had been meeting in Park Lane. After that setting the table, making tea and slicing bread for a late breakfast sufficed to keep at bay lecherous thoughts about someone whom he was foolish enough to hanker after—seeing that he had become that most dubious creature of all: someone who was neither servant nor master.

Chapter Four

Trish was walking along Piccadilly, mooning about life. More accurately, she told herself, she was mooning about Allen Marriott, whom she had not met much lately—other than in brief encounters on stairs or in corridors. This was the busiest part of Gerard's year, which would climax in mid-July with a grand dinner which the Prince of Wales had promised to attend—the Prince being one of his friends and admirers.

The Prince liked Yankees, some unkind commentators said, because unlike him they could get things done. His mother's tenacious hold on life meant that he would be an old and tired man before he succeeded to the throne—if he did not die before her, that was.

Allen being very busy and constantly in attendance on Gerard, their little meetings in the library had come to an end. Time was slipping by, and, although she was encouraged by her guardians to meet as many young men in society as possible, she knew that neither of them would encourage her to pursue her friendship with Gerard's penniless secretary. The thing was, though, the more time she spent with Allen the more boring she found all the young gentlemen of her acquaintance.

She was on her own in the West End, for Torry being from America, where young ladies were allowed much greater freedom than the over-chaperoned English girls, allowed her to visit it without a maid in attendance. She dawdled along, looking in shop windows and wondering why she felt so lonely these days, when before she had met Allen these little expeditions had been life-giving because she could please herself.

The pavement was crowded, and weaving her way through the pedestrians before crossing a street jammed with horse-drawn carriage of all kinds she thought that she saw Allen walking briskly along on the other side of the road. It was almost as though thinking about him had conjured him up!

She knew that it was his day off, and also knew that it was his custom to leave the Park Lane house before he had eaten breakfast. It was, therefore, not unlikely that he might have travelled to the West End. Reaching the opposite pavement at last, she set off in the same direction to try to catch his apparent double up, in order to discover whether it *was* Allen she had seen. This little adventure seemed to give her whole morning a point and purpose.

Unfortunately, just when she nearing him, she was prevented from any further progress by a procession of men who were carrying large boxes from a pantechnicon into a newly opened shop. By the time that the last man had gone by her she could no longer see her quarry.

Of all the rotten luck! Trish could only console herself by assuming that it had not been Allen she had seen. On the other hand the man had disappeared so quickly that it was possible that he might have turned into the alley full of shops which were just beyond the line of removal men. It wouldn't hurt to go down it herself—who knows what she might find?

Alas, there was no sign of him. The alley was empty of

life except for a Persian cat which sat sunning itself in the doorway of a small shop whose one window was full of clocks and watches. Perhaps it was the cat which led her there, but for whatever reason—or no reason—Trish walked over to inspect the window and the small and large treasures displayed therein. For treasures they were, she soon discovered. One watch in particular lured her by reason of its beauty.

It was a lady's watch on a chain, meant to be worn around the neck to make inspecting it easy. It was gold, decorated with tiny enamelled flowers. Beside it was a matching gilt box in which to keep it safe when not in use. Trish could not resist the delicate thing.

The cat had risen and padded over towards her, arching its back in order to rub itself gently against the full skirts of her elegant walking dress. She bent down to stroke it before pushing open the door into the shop.

She found herself in a small room full of clocks of all kinds. Grandfather clocks, grandmother clocks, bracket clocks, travelling clocks, mantelpiece clocks, banjo clocks, all of them chiming the hour of eleven, some early and some late. Behind the counter stood a little old man, white-haired and wearing an embroidered skull cap.

'Good morning, madam. How may I assist you?'

'Good morning,' Trish responded. 'I wonder if I might have a look at the small watch on a chain in the window.'

'Of course, madam. One moment and I will fetch it out for you. It is a charming piece, is it not?'

'Very. It caught my eye immediately.'

'Which shows your good taste,' the shopkeeper told her, laying the watch, the chain and the box reverently on the blue velvet mat which lay on the counter.

He was about to lift the watch up to show her its beautifully enamelled back when the door behind him opened and a man came through it.

It was Allen.

It was also an Allen whom she had never seen before.

He had discarded his sober black jacket, his stiff glossy collar and formal cravat. Instead his shirt was open at the neck and its sleeves were rolled up to show a pair of muscular forearms. He was also wearing a coarse linen apron and holding something in his hands.

Surprised, they stared at one another.

Trish broke the silence first. 'It *was* you I saw. I thought it was.'

'Did you now?' he said, with his small smile. 'And when was that?'

She might have known that he would never allow anything to shake his calm control.

'Just now. In Piccadilly, walking ahead of me. I knew it was you, and then I lost you. I decided to investigate the next side road—and here you are.'

Allen shook his head. They had both forgotten that interested spectator Mr Nance, who was turning his head from one to another as though he were watching a game of singles at a tennis club.

'You knew me in a crowded street?'

'Of course. I would know you anywhere.'

For the first time since she had met him Allen laughed. He was not mocking her; the laugh was rueful.

'What a girl you are, Trish.'

The laugh, though, had broken the spell which had held them alone in their enchanted world.

Allen turned to Mr Nance. 'You will think me mannerless, sir. Allow me to introduce the young lady to you. Miss Trish Courtney meet Mr Louis Nance, who is by way of being my friend, teacher and benefactor. Miss Courtney is the ward of my new employer, sir.'

'Enchanted,' murmured Mr Nance, taking in the whole charming picture which Trish presented in her mauve and white walking dress, her pretty white straw hat with its circlet of pansies, her white gloves and white kid shoes. This, then, was the young lady whom Allen had so briefly mentioned and who, judging by the way they had just rallied one another had become a challenge to his monkish life. He had to commend his protégé's taste.

Instead he complimented Trish's, leaving his previous thought unspoken. 'Miss Courtney had the good sense to wish to examine this handsome little piece, which you may remember I acquired at a recent sale.'

He saw that Trish was looking curiously at them both, and decided that an explanation was in order. 'Mr Marriott has lodged with me ever since he arrived in London and, like you, almost by accident found his way to the shop. He lived here until he was employed by your guardian and visits me once a week. He has become my friend.'

'Ah,' murmured Trish. 'You are, then, the friend who is trying to build a remarkable clock which will tell the day, the month and the year. He spoke of it when Lord Moidore came to dinner on his first day with us.'

Mr Nance looked at Allen, who said, 'We were discussing time and the next century, were we not, Miss Courtney?'

'Trish,' she said evenly. 'This is not our coffee meeting, but I am still your friend and I must be Trish to you—and to you, sir, for if you are Allen's friend then you are my friend, also,' she added, smiling in Mr Nance's direction.

He was as captivated by her as Allen was. 'Then if you are my friend,' he told her, 'you might perhaps care to join us for a cup of tea. We usually indulge in one at this time of day.'

'Nothing would please me more.' She watched Allen lay down on the counter the clock which he had been holding before he opened the door to admit the cat, which went straight to Trish to rub himself against her skirts. After that he turned the placard in the shop door's window from 'Open' to 'Closed'.

Mr Nance said, 'You see how welcome you are, Trish. Cyrus seldom makes a fuss of strangers.'

'Well, he made a fuss of me outside,' said Trish forthrightly, bending down to stroke him. 'Cyrus, you say?' And then, 'Oh, of course, after Cyrus the Persian! What a clever name.'

'You may well say that,' said Mr Nance, opening the door to the back room for her. 'Allen named him.'

The back room was a workshop where repairs were carried out. Bits and pieces of clocks stood on a bench. Some odd-looking machinery was on another table. Shelves, crammed with a wide variety of books, covered one wall. At the far end of the room was another door which led to a living room of a kind which Trish had never seen before.

On the wall opposite to her was a large black kitchen range in which a fire blazed. On either side of it were two comfortable armchairs. A dining table stood before a window which looked out on to a yard. A settle and a writing desk took up the whole of the right-hand wall. To the left of the door by which Trish had entered was a large Welsh dresser on whose shelves an array of crockery was arranged. The floor was covered with blue and gold linoleum. Another open door led to a scullery with a red quarry-tiled floor.

Allen had gone to its small sink and was filling a sooty copper kettle with water. He carried it through to the range and placed it on the fire. Mr Nance motioned Trish to one of the armchairs and then sat down in the other himself. Allen had returned to the kitchen from where, after a few moments he came back, carrying a brightly patterned tin tray on which stood a tea-caddy, a sugar bowl, a milk jug and a large brown teapot.

After he had laid them out on the table he collected from

the dresser three cups and saucers, four plates, and three apostle teaspoons from one of the dresser's drawers. From a cupboard in the dresser he fetched a tin biscuit barrel, with the words 'Peak Frean's' on the side, took some biscuits out of it and carefully arranged them on one of the plates.

He caught Trish's eye when he moved over to the fire to check whether the kettle was boiling, and said, with his small smile, 'You see, Trish, that Mr Nance has thoroughly domesticated me. When I arrived in his shop I could scarcely boil water. Now I can cook a dinner and, if the occasion demands it, bake bread. Mr Nance doesn't like the shop kind. His first present to me was a copy of Mrs Beeton's immortal recipe book.'

Trish said suddenly, the words wrenched from her, 'Oh, Allen, you both make me feel quite useless. Gerard told Torry that you were the best secretary he had ever had; from what I have seen here you can help Mr Nance to repair clocks and watches, and now you tell me that you can cook. The only thing which I can do is look decorative.'

'But you do that very well,' Mr Nance told her, echoing Allen's thoughts.

'But it isn't enough,' exclaimed Trish mutinously. 'Nothing I can do is enough. I can ride a little, draw a little, paint a little, embroider a little, crochet a little, play the piano a little, sing a little, dance a little. What a useless catalogue that is, to be sure. Now, if I had been a boy, I might have been taught something practical. But I'm not, so I wasn't.' And she shook her head at them both.

'But I'm very happy that you aren't a boy, Trish,' said Allen, looking tenderly across at her before pouring boiling water on to the tea leaves in the big brown earthenware pot.

'Now you're patronising me, both of you.' Trish was

looking mournful, so mournful that Allen wanted to go to her, put his arms around her and comfort her.

'Do you know what?' she said. 'I once thought I would like to go to Oxford, to Somerville. Then Mother fell ill, and that was the end of that.'

'Who nursed your mother?' Allen asked her.

'Mostly me, because she couldn't bear the notion of a trained nurse in the house. She said that it made her feel an invalid. It was only in the last few months when she became so ill that we had to have a nurse to look after her.'

'But you did do something useful if you nursed your mother.'

'I suppose. Only by the time I came to live with Uncle Gerard and Aunt Torry, as I used to call them, then it was too late for me to go to Oxford—and I wasn't really prepared for it, either. I wasn't sent to one of those schools which educate girls for university. First of all Father didn't approve of them, and then Mother fell ill. It may be selfish of me, but if I'd been a boy none of that would have happened.'

Allen brought a little table over to where she sat and placed her tea, the small jug of milk, the sugar bowl and a plate for her biscuits on it.

'Lady Schuyler told me once that you were sympathetic towards those who call themselves New Women and demand the same rights and education as men. Hearing your story makes me understand why you feel like that.'

'Indeed,' echoed Mr Nance, who liked to think of himself as a Fabian socialist, like Bernard Shaw, the playwright, and Mr and Mrs Sidney Webb, wealthy people who sympathised with the lot of the underdogs, be they working class or women, and believed in helping them by slow change, not revolution.

Trish drank her tea and ate her biscuits. Mr Nance, who had a gift for drawing people out, and who counted music

among his many enthusiasms, talked to her of it, and was
happy to discover that her taste was good—at least accord-
ing to his lights.

'You said that you played the piano. What are your favourite pieces?'

'Nothing too difficult. I accompany Torry when she
sings. But my favourite composer is Mozart, who is not
fashionable these days.'

'You mustn't underrate yourself, for there is something
which you can do and I can't,' said Allen, who had been
sitting quietly beside her, watching the play of emotion on
her mobile face. 'Play the piano, that is. I love to listen to
music, though. Mr Nance and I always go to Sir Henry
Wood's Promenade Concerts.'

The oddest thing was that she would think afterwards,
when she was once again cocooned in the splendours of
Park Lane, that she had rarely enjoyed herself so much as
she was now doing, talking to Allen and Mr Nance in Mr
Nance's humble kitchen—for that was what it really was.
She had never, ever before expressed herself freely and
frankly about her lost education and her resentment that
everything which she did was amateur in the extreme because she had never been taught to do anything properly.

'A young lady is not expected to try too hard,' her
mother had once told her reprovingly. 'Gentlemen don't
like it.'

Most of the gentlemen whom she had met certainly lived
up to her mother's description of them. Except, oddly
enough, Gerard, that supremely masculine man. He was
proud of his clever wife, who organised committees and
wrote articles expressing advanced views which found their
way into the daily newspapers, including, once, that august
organ of opinion, *The Times*. He had never stood in her
way—rather he encouraged her—but then, he was an
American.

Remarkably Allen suddenly started talking exactly like his employer. 'I see no reason why a woman—and by that I include those who are described as "ladies"—should not have the right to express themselves exactly as men do, and if that means that they must be educated as men are, then educated they must be.'

Trish sent a grateful smile his way. 'You aren't just saying that to please me, are you, Allen? Men often give girls false answers in order to please or flatter them, but they don't believe a word of it.'

'Oh, I've no desire to please or flatter you, Trish. As a fledgling New Woman, you shouldn't want me to, and I will respect your wishes, always.'

His eyes were dancing, and again Trish suddenly saw in his gently mocking expression something which reminded her of Gerard. It was gone in a moment, even before she flung at him, her face comical, 'Wretch! You're a wretch, Allen Marriott.'

Her face alive with amusement, she appealed to Mr Nance. 'He's a wretch isn't he, Mr Nance? Tell him he's a wretch. He's always teasing me, but he keeps his face so straight I don't often know that he's doing it. I only understand what he's said afterwards, when he's incommunicado with Gerard and I can't go in to read him the Riot Act.'

'Well, you may read it here, Trish—or would you like me to do it for you?'

'Not so much do it for me, but start me on my way.'

Mr Nance obliged her. 'You're a wretch, Allen Marriott, to provoke a poor young girl who hasn't provoked you.'

Allen bent his head in mock surrender. 'OK, OK, I give in.'

'Now what in the world does "OK" mean, Allen Marriott?' Trish teased him in her turn.

'OK is an American expression which means certainly,

or I agree with you, or that's all right. I'm surprised that you haven't heard it before.'

'Yankee slang—not used in our circles,' retorted Trish grandly. She was enjoying herself enormously baiting Allen, trying to get him to relax his guard even more than he had already done. Oh, he rose to that, didn't he? Like a fish snatching at a particularly gaudy fly.

His smile had grown broader than ever when he tossed the conversational ball back at her with, 'When *are* you going to read me the Riot Act? That's one of your British expressions, I take it. I'm not quite sure what it means.'

'And that, Allen Marriott, is the biggest whopper I've ever heard. I've never before met a man who was so sure about everything—unless it was Gerard!'

Mr Nance was also enjoying himself. He had never before seen his lodger and friend express himself so freely and easily. This charming young woman obviously possessed the power to pry him out of the protective shell into which he often retreated.

'Then you must have met some odd men,' Allen riposted. 'Mr Nance will tell you what a shy creature I am.'

'Then it must be me who has this odd effect on you.' Trish flung this out at him without thinking: but it was true, no doubt about it. Gerard had frequently complained to Torry of his new secretary's taciturnity, and she knew from something her maid had once told her that the servants also thought him stiff and uncommunicative. Nothing stiff about him now, though. They might have been verbally sparring together all their lives.

She flushed, knowing that she had just given herself away. Whatever would Allen say next? Mr Nance saved her by looking at the big clock on the wall, which resembled the large clocks in railway stations, before saying regretfully, 'Back to work, both of us. Perhaps, Trish, you might like to stay here until twelve o'clock, when I am sure that Allen would be delighted to escort you to the nearest ABC for a light lunch. Unless, of course, you have arranged to return home for it.'

Trish said rapidly, before Allen could object or demur, 'What a delightful notion! I have never visited an ABC, and Allen will be able to stop me from doing all the wrong things there and making a spectacle of myself.'

Allen could not resist leaning forward to say, 'Oh, Trish, wherever you go you are always a spectacle: the most charming spectacle in the whole world.'

'I'm not sure whether I should take that as a compliment or not,' said Trish doubtfully. 'I fear that it may be one of your remarks which takes on quite a different meaning when thought about later.'

This set Mr Nance laughing, 'Come now, children,' he told them, pretending to be stern. 'Enough is enough. Time to cease squabbling. Trish, my dear, you will find a large number of books and magazines on my shelves which will help you to pass the time.'

He hesitated, then said, his old voice kind, 'My dear girl, I have really enjoyed your visit. I hope that you will not hesitate to come again—you will always be welcome.'

'And I have enjoyed being here. Next time I come you must tell me something about clockmaking. Oh!' she exclaimed. 'I have enjoyed myself so much that I have forgotten about the little watch. Before I leave you must tell me how much it costs. If for nothing else I would like to buy it as a souvenir of a happy morning.'

What Trish had just said came from the heart. She was not unhappy with Gerard and Torry at Park Lane, but there was a formality about life there which she often found constricting. Here, in this small room, quite different from everything she knew, she was more at ease than she had ever been in her whole previous life. It was not only being able to talk and joke with Allen without fear of being interrupted, but her pleasure had also been enhanced by Mr Nance's gentle charm.

Allen's pleasure had been enhanced by her lack of patronage in her dealings with his friend and patron. She was gold all through: a thought he took with him to his work on the bench, which seemed more fulfilling than ever because he knew that she was sitting in the kitchen, waiting for him to finish.

'Trish must be the charming young lady whom you dismissed so lightly in our recent conversation,' remarked Mr Nance, a trifle provocatively, when Allen returned after buying Trish poached egg on toast and a cream bun at the ABC before putting her in a cab for Park Lane. 'I commend you on your taste. She is not only charming but clever and kind. She will always be welcome here—and you must know what I mean by that.'

Allen knew.

He knew that the old man had clearly seen the growing attraction between him and Trish.

He said, however, and it pained him to admit it, 'You must understand, sir, that she is a great heiress. I'm not sure whether I am doing either of us a kindness by encouraging her to come here. She is much above my touch.'

'Nonsense,' said Mr Nance robustly. 'You are a gentleman and she is a lady. I might prefer to say that you are a man and she is a woman, but it would not exactly describe your relationship in 1899. Since I believe, however, that we are shortly to be living in a century where our present social system will soon be outdated, such considerations should not weigh with you.'

'Nevertheless,' said Allen, 'they do. Perhaps, sir, the best thing would be that neither Trish nor I ought to place too much stress on our current feelings. We may find that what we share is a fleeting thing, soon to pass, and worrying about our unequal stations in life will disappear with it.'

He did not really believe in what he was saying. His delight in being with Trish was so strong that he could not think it was a purely temporary sensation. He had never experienced anything like it before, and, rightly or wrongly, he thought that Trish's response to him was the same as his for her.

'You know,' he said later, putting down his dessert spoon at the end of their evening meal, 'I have need of your advice. I have been rearranging my predecessor's files, and I have discovered some oddities which I can't explain to you—only someone well versed in book-keeping and in numbers would understand them. In fact, very few of them would detect anything wrong. You'll have to take my word for it.'

'Oh, I know my talents lie elsewhere,' said Mr Nance. 'But I believe you. Before you go on, may I ask you one thing? Does your employer know of your mathematical genius—for it almost amounts to that—and, as you well know, others more knowledgeable than I hold that opinion, too.'

'No,' said Allen, curtly for him when speaking to Mr Nance, who raised his eyebrows.

'May I ask why?' he said. 'It could be of use to you for him to know, even more than to him.'

'I have no wish for him to know anything about me other than that I perform my secretarial duties quietly and competently. For example, I have taken great care to tell him nothing about you, and I shall need to ask Trish for your— and the shop's—existence to remain a secret between the two of us. The trouble is that I am unearthing something whose explanation might raise questions which no one would want to be asked, or would wish to give an answer to if they were.'

'It involves dishonesty?'

'I believe it does.'

'Possibly your employer's?'

'Possibly, and therein lies the rub. What sort of hornets' nest might I bring about my ears if I raise the matter with him? Especially since, clever though he is, I might have difficulty in making him understand something so nebulous.'

He could not tell Mr Nance of the odd relationship which existed between him and Gerard, where there was, in essence, no mutual trust.

'You suspect your predecessor?'

'I'm not sure who the devil I suspect. What I *do* suspect is that I might have to do even more research into Schuyler's financial past—and monitor its present.'

'In that case,' said Mr Nance, 'my advice is that you do nothing until you are absolutely certain of your facts.'

Allen lay back in his chair and gave a short laugh. 'Exactly what I expected, nay, hoped you would say. If I am right there are only two possibilities I can see: one of them is that Schuyler Incorporated is being robbed, and the other is that Schuyler Incorporated is doing the robbing. Not a pretty thought either way.'

'No, indeed. Let us talk about more pleasant things. Your paper to the British Horological Institute for instance. How is it going?'

Allen grimaced. 'Slowly, since I am mostly working at night. Basically it's finished. What I'm doing now is sharpening and polishing it at the same time. Two contrary things at once, you might argue.'

'I can see that working for Sir Gerard Schuyler isn't addling your brain. Do you have much to do with his duties as an MP?'

'Oh, yes. It's interesting, but time-consuming. Now that my probationary period is over I frequently have to go to the Commons with him. The best part of that is when the weather is fine and we take tea on the terrace, surrounded by the rulers of the British Empire.'

He pulled out his watch. 'It grows late. I'll help you to wash up before I resume my fancy dress and return to Park Lane. Next week we can take in a Music Hall: I could do with an earthy bit of fun for a change.'

'Perhaps Trish would like to come with us?' Mr Nance's smile was sly.

'Now there's a thought,' smiled Allen, rising from his chair and beginning to pile the used crockery on to a tray. 'The poor girl will never have had such a treat before, I'll be bound. Roll on next week!'

A sentiment which Mr Nance heartily applauded.

Chapter Five

'That's a pretty bauble you're wearing, Trish,' remarked Torry Schuyler. 'I haven't seen it before.'

She was admiring Trish's new watch pendant on its gold chain.

'No?' said Trish, determinedly following the late Duke of Wellington's maxim, Never explain. 'It *is* pretty, isn't it?'

Allen had asked her not to tell anyone about Mr Nance and his shop full of treasures, so she was 'keeping mum'— a phrase borrowed from her maid. If Allen had had nothing to do with the shop she would have told Torry about it, but since he did it was better to keep quiet. She was shortly to appreciate how necessary it was to be conspiratorial.

After Torry and Trish had left the room Gerard was enjoying his breakfast when the butler, who had the housekeeper and many of the staff's full support, approached him, saying, 'Ahem, sir. There is a matter which I do not like to raise with you, but which I feel that I should.'

This arcane statement set Gerard snorting inelegantly. 'Don't waste time, man. Spit it out.'

'It's about Mr Marriott, sir. On the days when you and Lady Schuyler are absent he leaves the office to take coffee with Miss Courtney in the library. I wondered if you had given him permission. I thought that I ought to take the liberty of asking.'

Gerard grunted, 'Yes, it is a dam'd liberty, but you were right to ask me.'

The butler thought to embroider. 'Seeing that Miss Courtney is an heiress…'

Gerard glared at him. 'That's all. You may go.' Belatedly. 'And thank you.'

Best to say nothing to Torry yet, but to consult Timson, his know-all valet, a most useful hidden aide.

A Commons committee of which Gerard was chairman was meeting later that morning. He walked upstairs to his suite of rooms and bellowed for Timson to 'finish him off'—his inelegant phrase for 'see that I look like a proper English gentleman.'

Timson duly arrived. 'You called, sir?'

'You might say so.'

Gerard let a few moments go by before remarking casually, as though it were an afterthought, 'By the by, Timson, what does the servants' hall know about my secretary and Miss Courtney?'

Timson, who was used to this intimate, but blunt sort of questioning, said, 'Only that they seem rather sweet, shall we say, on one another.'

'To the degree of taking coffee together in my absence?'

Timson was one of those who rather liked Allen Marriott—he was a considerate sort of man, unlike Mr Hall, who had been a bit of an uppity swine—but he could not resist saying, 'When the cat's away, the mouse will play, sir—as you surely know.'

'Yes, I do know that, Timson, thank you. A pity no one informed me earlier of these meetings.'

But Tom Moidore had warned him, hadn't he?

Timson gone, Gerard decided that he would say nothing

to Torry or Trish but that he would warn Marriott off in as harsh a way as possible. He had not appointed him in order that he might go fortune-hunting after young heiresses— and if he didn't like it he could lump it.

Becoming an English gentleman had done nothing to make Gerard's thoughts any more gentlemanly than they had been when he had first set foot in England after leaving the States. His public image, however, was quite different. He was propriety personified.

Allen was seated at his desk, poring over some accounts, when Gerard came in. He was a little surprised to see him. Gerard had already given him his orders for the day before he went in to breakfast.

He rose to his feet, his head bent a little. He rarely looked Gerard directly in the eye for fear his expression gave something away. Gerard said, harshly for him, 'No need to look dam'd humble, Marriott, when you are busy deceiving me behind my back.'

Allen raised his head as this was thrown at him. He squared his shoulders and said, 'Sir?' He managed to make the simple one-syllable word a statement of acute puzzlement.

This had the effect of infuriating Gerard even further. 'Oh, damme, Marriott, did you expect to go on sweet-talking Miss Courtney over coffee in the library during my absence for ever?'

Allen, now looking squarely at Gerard, said quietly, 'I had not known, sir, that you expected me to inform you of the details of my mid-morning break, or I would, of course, have done so. I would be grateful if you would instruct me on what other aspects of my spare time of which you would wish to know.'

He had the intense satisfaction of seeing Gerard turn puce with rage.

'Don't be so dam'd insolent, Marriott. You know perfectly well of what I am speaking. I have no intention of allowing you to exploit your post as my secretary in order to engage in fortune-hunting one of England's richest heiresses, to whom I owe a duty of care.'

Allen's rage, had Gerard but known it, equalled his employer's. Nevertheless, his face stony, he answered Gerard in the even tones which Trish would have recognised as those he used to unsettle whoever he was speaking to at the time.

'I am at a loss, sir, to understand how an infrequent cup of coffee, taken over—' he looked at his watch '—about fifteen minutes, on average, could be construed as fortune-hunting.'

'An activity,' snarled Gerard, who had not yet understood how much he was underrating the man before him, 'which, I have reason to believe, has already caused unpleasant gossip in the servants' hall.'

'Oh?' Allen raised his eyebrows as high as they would go. 'I hadn't heard that, sir. I rarely spend my limited spare time listening to the gossip of the servants' hall, unpleasant or otherwise, so you must forgive me for being unaware of it.'

His expression remained unchanging, one of polite interest. He had, and both men knew it, succeeded in rebuking Gerard.

Gerard pulled himself together. He must not allow the young devil standing before him to bait him further. Coldly, his own face iron, he said, 'Well, now I *will* give you an order. This activity must cease. You may make what excuse you like to Miss Courtney, but as long as you remain in my employ you will have as little as possible to do with her in the future. That is an order.'

'Understood, sir. May I resume work now?'

His total unflappability almost commanded Gerard's admiration.

'What the devil else would I expect you to do?'

Allen inclined his head. 'I am not quite sure, sir, which is why I asked you.' He knew that he was treading the tightrope of Gerard's anger, but if Gerard sacked him on the spot he would, with a few words, solve most of Allen's problems. For now that thought did not trouble him.

On the other hand he was enjoying more than he had expected the challenge which living and working with his cousin entailed. His own strength of will was being daily honed, and the knowledge that he could win a battle of words with Gerard was an exhilarating feeling.

He would leave when he chose, and that was that.

Trish sat in the library, waiting for Allen to emerge from the office. He was often delayed when he was in the middle of doing some important task for Gerard. Consequently she wasn't worried about his late appearance and sat there dreaming happily of her next visit to Mr Nance's shop and what she and Allen might do when they were together there.

It came as something of a shock when she looked at her watch to discover that he was over fifteen minutes late. Perhaps he had forgotten the time! She knocked on the office door before opening it to discover that he was sitting there, his head bent over his desk writing rapidly. He looked up when she moved into the room, but did not speak.

Her heart beating rapidly, Trish said, 'Are you too busy to drink coffee with me this morning, Allen?'

She looked so stricken that he rose and walked round the desk to take her hand. 'No, Trish, I am never too busy to make time for you.'

'But you didn't come today,' she faltered.

'That is because this morning, my darling, Sir Gerard

ordered me not to join you for coffee again when he and Lady Schuyler are absent.'

Trish sprang away from him. 'Why in the world should he do that?'

Allen gave a short laugh. 'It appears that the servants don't like it.'

'Why ever not? What is it to do with them? He cannot mean it.'

'I'm afraid that he does. He thinks that I am after your fortune.'

'How preposterous! Of course you aren't. And even if you were, what about all the other young men I meet to whom he makes no objection? Aren't they all after my fortune, too? I shall make it my business to go to see him this evening and remind him of that sad fact. He cannot treat us like this.'

'Oh, but he can, and if you do go to see him he is almost sure to dismiss me on the spot, and I am not ready to leave yet. Later, perhaps.'

'Oh, how unfair! Whatever shall we do?'

'We can do nothing here but obey him, and while it is brave of you to refuse to believe that I am a fortune-hunter, consider carefully whether you ought to agree to what I shall now propose. May I suggest that there is no reason in the world why we should not continue to meet at Mr Nance's, and elsewhere. We have both come of age, even if you are still his ward.'

'I don't need time to consider,' returned Trish indignantly, 'for that would mean that I doubted you. Which I don't. Of course I shall meet you at Mr Nance's shop—or anywhere else for that matter. I enjoyed myself there very much yesterday—he is such a dear old man—and now Gerard is trying to spoil it for us.'

'Not if you don't let him,' Allen told her, delighted by her immediate and determined response to his suggestion.

It was taking him all his will-power not to put his arms around her and comfort her, but after what Gerard had said he did not wish to go against his cousin's wishes in his cousin's home. What he and Trish might do outside Park Lane was no concern of Gerard's.

Instead he said gently, 'I ought to leave you now. There has been enough idle and spiteful gossip about us without our providing our critics with more. From now on we must ignore each other.'

'But how shall we know when and where we are to meet one another?' asked Trish dolefully.

'Simple,' said Allen. 'We will make arrangements for the next week when we visit Mr Nance on my day off—making sure that we leave Park Lane separately, of course.'

'Of course,' said Trish happily. She would have been happier still if they were not going to have to meet behind Gerard's back, but he had left them no alternative. He ought to have known that neither she nor Allen would ever bend easily to another's will.

'Time for me to leave you,' said Allen, reluctance written all over him. 'Drink your coffee on your own and allow the servants to snigger over my unused cup and saucer.'

'Why do they dislike you, Allen? You are always courteous and considerate when you speak to them.'

'Oh, it's nothing personal, I'm sure. It's just that I am neither fish, flesh, fowl nor good red herring, and being neither servant nor master leaves me out in the cold, since neither side wishes to acknowledge me. It's not like this in the States, you know.'

'Yes, I do know,' Trish told him. 'Gerard has commented on it critically once or twice, which is why I am surprised that he has treated you so cruelly.'

Allen could not tell her the whole truth, only part of it. 'That is because he feels that he is protecting you from a base fortune-hunter.'

'He might change his mind if he knew that both Hetty and I owe our lives to you. I've a good mind to tell him…' Trish began.

Allen put a gentle hand over her mouth. 'No, no, my darling. I doubt whether it would help matters, and that is my secret, not to be told.'

'Very well,' grumbled Trish. 'All the same, he ought to know how brave and true you are.'

'I doubt whether that would change his mind, and since what he thinks of me doesn't trouble me, then don't let it trouble you.'

All very well for Allen to be airy, Trish told herself later, seated lonely in the drawing room, I'm the one who is having young men paraded before me like male mannequins so that I may choose one of them for a husband. Which she knew, if she were honest, was exaggerating somewhat, since Gerard and Torry had never put any real pressure on her to accept any of them.

That last sentence wasn't strictly true, either. This very evening Lady Norman and her son Harry were among the Schuylers' guests for dinner. Harry was by way of being the very rich heir of an elderly and now paralysed baronet who had married a young woman late in life to get an heir. Lady Norman had brought her son south from the Western Highlands to find a suitable heiress to be his bride. Trish fitted the bill because she was not only rich, but beautiful. Harry had been stubbornly refusing to marry, but once having met Trish she was sure that Harry would find her beautiful violet eyes irresistible.

Both she and the Schuylers had been clever enough not to push them at one another. They had simply arranged for them to meet at suitable intervals and hoped that nature and propinquity would do their work. To Trish's relief, Harry had been friendly, but never lover-like, and now she was going to have to spend the evening with him after being deprived of Allen's company. It really was too bad, but there was nothing she could do about it.

She passed Allen on the stairs on the way down to dinner. He gave her a bow so slight that it was barely an acknowledgement, and she averted her eyes from him as though he were beneath her notice. The butler, standing at the bottom of the stairs, grinned. There was no doubt that his few words to Sir Gerard had destroyed the young man's hopes.

He should stick to young women of his own station— whoever they might be—not go lusting after his betters.

He opened the door for Trish, whom he silently complimented on having come to her senses, and hoped that she would find the handsome young fellow who had just preceded her more to her taste.

Alas, handsome Harry might be, and charming, too, but he was not Allen. Oh, he was agreeable, talked to her on matters which interested her, asked her how she was enjoying the season, and all in all was just the pretty, rather vacuous, young man she might have married if she had not met Allen in the accident to the Birmingham to London train.

Trish, trying to eat food which lay like ash upon her palate, remembered overhearing something which a society beauty had said to a friend. 'My trouble is that I married a man who was the season's catch and after the honeymoon I found that I had no feeling for him at all—nor he for me—and now we are stuck with one another.'

It hadn't meant much to her at the time, but now it meant everything. Did Harry have any feeling for her, or was he simply netting his heiress in obedience to his dominant mother's wishes?

After dinner was over, and the men had returned from their port and cigars, Torry had the windows to the terrace thrown open for the evening was warm. Harry, all outward gallantry, bent over Trish and asked her if she would take a turn outside with him.

For a moment Trish was on the verge of refusing, but thought better of it. What harm could it do?

'Certainly,' she said, rising and smiling at him. 'I could do with a breath of fresh air.'

'And I,' said Harry, who didn't smoke very much, and didn't drink either, and found the obligatory staying behind to do both when the women had gone a frightful bore.

He offered her his arm and they strolled on to the terrace. In the distance, despite the lateness of the hour, London was humming with lights and life. Cabs and carriages went their way, and even the pavement was crowded with pass-ers-by.

Where was Allen? What was he doing? Where would he eat? Would he visit Mr Nance? If so, why was she not with him? Why had she fallen desperately in love with a dark quiet man, with an interesting as well as a handsome face, and not with blond and beautiful Harry, who was talking to her so kindly and considerately?

She must listen to what he was saying. It would never do to ask him to repeat what he had just said. Apparently he was only asking her to sit down with him in the warm evening. The moon was rising above the trees in Hyde Park, where earlier she and Torry had taken the carriage and had met other men who were interested in a wealthy heiress.

'I have a question to ask of you,' he said abruptly. 'Do you hate this horrid business as much as I do?'

'Horrid business?' asked Trish, startled. 'What horrid business?'

'This marriage market,' he told her, serious for once, his usual carefree air quite gone. 'All these meetings arranged for us to get to know one another because our fortunes match. Forgive me for being frank, but I believe that you feel the same about it as I do—distaste.'

Trish stared at him. 'You mean that you are not dying of love for me?' she asked him mockingly.

'Exactly. Oh, I like you, I like talking to you, and if we had met in the normal way liking might have become something more, but as it is…' He shrugged. 'It's all so cold-blooded. If I have offended you, please tell me and I will apologise.'

'No, you haven't offended me. I merely wondered whether you were genuinely interested in me, and if you were how to let you down without hurting you—as it is—'

'Good,' he said eagerly. 'And I was afraid of hurting you. You see, I have fallen in love with someone entirely unsuitable—back in Sutherland that is. Oh, she's a lady, but she's poor, and Mama is quite adamant that I am to marry wealth. My whole family is determined that I shall marry wealth, but what I really want is Lizzie. All I can do is refuse everyone paraded before me until Mama realises that I meant it when I said that I would never give her up.'

Trish began to laugh, and if there was something hysterical in her laughter it was quite understandable.

'Paraded before you! And all the time I thought that you were being paraded before me!'

Harry's face lost something of its desperate look. He grinned. 'You, too? Have you a poverty-stricken lover?'

Time to be honest. 'Yes.'

'And for the moment it's hopeless?'

'Very.'

'Then we can help one another.'

Trish looked puzzled.

'Don't you see,' he explained eagerly, 'that if we pretend to be interested in one another then the parading and the pressure will stop? If we're clever enough we can hold them off for the season and then have a grand falling-out!

I'm sure that we can be friends if we're determined not to be lovers.'

This all seemed rather like a society play written by the unfortunate Mr Oscar Wilde, who had been exiled from England for some misbehaviour which Trish had not been allowed to understand.

'Decadent,' Torry had said evasively. 'He was very decadent. Probably something in the air at the end of the century. We had the French Revolution at the end of the last one, now we've got decadence. Mr Wilde, Mr Aubrey Beardsley and *The Yellow Book*.'

This had all seemed rather vague to Trish, who thought that Robespierre and Oscar Wilde were not a bit alike, but it was obviously one of those matters about which young ladies were not expected to ask questions. Blaming the end of the century for everything seemed to be a popular pastime these days.

'We can blame the end of the century for our falling-out,' she remarked, inspired, and then had to tell a puzzled Harry what she meant. She left Mr Oscar Wilde out, though, just talked vaguely about decadence.

'Splendid,' he said. 'Now let's go in looking very happy, and give the company quite the wrong idea of what we've been doing.'

Yes, it was all very much like one of the convoluted society novels Mr Henry James wrote, which were so vague that at the end you were never quite sure what had happened except that everyone had been very clever and rather wicked on the way there. Next time she read one she would ask Allen to explain it, seeing that, like Mr James, he came from America, too.

Harry seemed quite resourceful, despite his slangy manner and his rather obvious good looks, which, a friend had once told her, were a bad thing in men. He certainly wasn't conceited. But what made Trish really uneasy was that she was now engaged in two conspiracies at once!

'You got on well with Harry, did you?' remarked kind Torry when all the guests had gone.

'Very. He's very pleasant to talk to.'

Now this wasn't a lie, but it did serve to deceive Torry, who, to give her her due, knew nothing of Gerard's warning off of Allen, nor of Trish's involvement with him. However, she was pleased to see that Trish and Harry were apparently interested in one another, and before preparing for bed she said to Gerard, 'I do believe that the child really likes Harry Norman. Marriage to him would settle all her problems.'

'And ours,' said Gerard dryly, but, remembering his conversation with Allen that morning, added, 'Do you really think that she's interested in him?'

'Well, she seemed happier with him than with any other young man to whom she's been introduced.'

Happier than with Allen Marriott? Gerard would have liked to ask her, but didn't. Although he told himself that he had done the right thing in reprimanding his cousin, something about the whole episode disturbed him to the degree that he had not told Torry about it. He was not certain that she would have approved of what he had done, even though he was sure that it was in Trish's best interests.

Trish, meanwhile, was busy hoping that Allen wouldn't mistake her and Harry's play-acting at being lovers for the real thing before she had had time to tell him about it. On the very first day after the dinner party Harry came to call and asked if he might drive her to Hyde Park—he had two new horses to show her.

'It's the most splendid wheeze,' he told her excitedly, once they were alone together. 'It will be quite a declaration of intent for us to be seen together this afternoon. My mother was on her highest ropes when I told her that it was my intention to take you there—if you agreed, of course. I've always refused to oblige her with all the other girls she's trotted out for me to inspect. I feel a bit of a cad for deceiving her, but she's been so persistent I've no alternative.'

'My sentiments exactly,' murmured Trish. 'I shall have to deceive Gerard and Torry if I am to see my young man, and my only excuse is that they've driven me to it.'

'Sad, isn't it?' said Harry, melancholy written all over his usually jolly young face. 'And they are driving us to it with the best of intentions, I'm sure.'

'The road to hell is paved with good intentions, they say.'

'Exactly,' Harry agreed. 'I say, these chestnuts of mine are rather splendid, aren't they? Got them for a bit of a song from a young fellow who had gone bankrupt. Too much betting on the wrong sort of gee-gees, I fear.'

The more she was with Harry the more Trish liked him—and the less she thought that she could ever have married him, since he was the exact opposite of Allen. Something which she told him when they next met at Mr Nance's.

In order to spend the day with him Trish had found it necessary to embark on yet another conspiracy. Her particular friend in London was Miss Lucy Chalfont, whose family lived in a fine house just off the far end of Piccadilly Circus—a most fortunate thing seeing that Mr Nance's shop was quite near. She frequently spent the day with her, and on her last visit, immediately after Gerard had forbidden Allen to have anything to do with her, she had asked Lucy if she would do her a great favour.

Lucy, a rather jolly girl who was a female version of Harry Norman, had fairly squealed with delight when Trish had said hesitantly, 'You see, I've made a great friend of a really worthy young man of whom my guardian doesn't approve because he's poor. I should like to spend the day with him occasionally and I wondered if I could say that I was visiting you when I was really with him.'

'Oh, Trish, don't say you're kicking over the traces at last! I thought that you never would. Of course I'll cover for you. I did the same thing for Phyllis Tracy, when Brentford was courting her and her parents didn't approve of him. Then he came into all that money unexpectedly and they changed their minds. They're married now and are quite the lovebirds. Who is he? Is he handsome?'

'Handsome and brave. Forgive me if I can't tell you who he is, but I do assure you that you would like him enormously if you ever met him. But he must remain my secret for his sake.'

Lucy had nearly exploded with delight. 'How exciting. Why does nothing like this ever happen to me?' she'd wailed.

Yes, she would make a perfect partner for Harry Norman if he weren't already head over heels in love with some young lady in Sutherland.

'Oh, thank you, Lucy. If you ever do need this sort of help be sure to ask me. I shall owe you such a debt of gratitude.'

'Only think,' she told Allen now, a trifle despairingly. 'I'm involved in *three* conspiracies at once.'

'Three?' queried Allen, raising his eyebrows at her. 'Which is the third?'

They were in Mr Nance's workroom. Allen was mending a clock and Trish was perched on a high stool watching him. She was fascinated by his loupe and had even tried to wear it—something which proved more difficult than she had expected.

'Mine with Harry Norman.' And it all came tumbling out. That they had agreed to pretend to be interested in one another because they were both in the same boat.

'Ah,' said Allen, after a moment's pause while he negotiated a particularly tricky bit of repair work. 'That's the blond half-wit whom you've been accompanying to Hyde Park. I was beginning to think that you'd thrown me over. I was quite relieved when you turned up this morning.'

'How did you know that he's a half-wit? I must admit that he is rather.' Then, anxiously, 'You didn't really think I'd thrown you over—without a word.'

'I'm happy to learn that I shall have a word when you do,' said Allen teasingly, putting down the clock's innards. 'As for knowing that he's a half-wit, something in his expression, plus the fact that I heard him talking to you in the entrance hall yesterday, told me. Not one of Scotland's greatest brains, is he?'

'No, but he's nice. Which is more than you are, Allen Marriott, teasing me so relentlessly.'

'Oh, but you like it, don't you?' he said softly. 'Tell me that you like it. More than you like that fellow sweet-talking you.'

Trish was rapidly learning how to respond to Allen's version of flirtation. She tossed her head and said in a melancholy voice, 'Goodness me, Allen Marriott, you do take a lot upon yourself. Suppose I teased you back. What would you say then?'

'That *I* would like it,' he told her promptly, before leaning over to give her a kiss on the cheek. 'And now we must behave ourselves. Mr Nance's customer has gone and he will shortly be coming back. Let him find us behaving ourselves.'

Trish fingered the favoured cheek mournfully. 'Oh, I have no worries on that score since we never do anything else—unfortunately.'

Her reward was a laugh and a blown kiss. Mr Nance's reward was to be handed the mended clock when he bustled into the workroom. Allen's reward was the satisfaction of a job well done—and Trish's rosy face.

'I see you have been working,' was all Mr Nance said, eyeing them knowingly. 'Have you told Trish of our plans for the afternoon?'

'Not yet,' said Allen, pulling off his workman's apron. 'I thought that I would save that for lunch. We are going to eat it here. Mr Nance's daily makes a most superior shepherd's pie, something which I had never heard of until I came to live here.'

'No shepherd's pie in America?' queried Trish. 'I must confess that I've always known it as nursery food.' She, tactfully, did not add that it had never arrived at any grown-up dinner which she had ever attended.

'Mr Nance's shepherd's pie does not remotely resemble nursery food, as you will discover when you eat it. Before that, for *hors d'oeuvres*—or starters, as we say in the States—we shall have a dish of mussels in white wine with new bread and butter. For dessert, we shall eat strawberries and cream as a special treat.'

'I'm feeling hungry already. But who will have cooked this splendid feast?'

'Mr Nance and his daily have prepared everything but the strawberries, which were my responsibility. While he has improved my culinary knowledge I cannot hope to equal him in that department. It's his French ancestry coming out, of course.'

'French ancestry?' Trish looked puzzled, so Allen explained to her the origin of Mr Nance's name.

'How interesting! What a cosmopolitan trio we are,' she added. 'You are an American, I am English and Mr Nance is of French extraction—between us we could organise an international conference like the one which Gerard and Lord Moidore were speaking of the other week.'

'Well, I propose that this cosmopolitan trio adjourns to the kitchen,' Allen said. He had resumed his dark jacket, which Trish deplored a little. She thought that he looked even more handsome in his shirtsleeves. How strange and interesting it was that Harry Norman, who was completely every young girl's *beau ideal* so far as looks went, didn't touch her heart at all, while Allen's serious, closed, if handsome face had it skipping a beat every time that she looked at him.

He gave her his hand to help her down from the stool, and, just as his kiss had sent tremors through her, the touch of it set her shivering. Was touching her doing strange things to him as well?

Not for the first time Trish resented the fact that as a young woman of good family she was not allowed to know anything about the realities of what went on between young men and women in love, or how they behaved after they were married. Light flirtation was permitted, but it was never carried on between equals, because most of the young men were experienced and very few of the young women were other than innocent.

It was something which the so-called New Women were always complaining about, and Trish was beginning to see what they meant. Simply to be with Allen was exciting, particularly when she was with him in Mr Nance's kitchen, where the table was already set for three.

To begin with she was offered a steaming tureen of mussels in white wine from which she ladled her share into a large soup plate. To eat with them was a loaf of bread, ready sliced, lying on a round wooden board with a crock of butter beside it.

After she had enjoyed the mussels Mr Nance placed on the snowy cloth a brown glazed pie dish in which reposed the shepherd's pie, its top a bright gold mixture of butter and cheese, and another dish in which a noble cauliflower lay, dressed in a cream sauce. Next he placed reverently before her a small silver gravy boat.

For his final offering Mr Nance lifted from the hearth a

bottle of red wine which he had placed there earlier to bring it to room temperature.

'In your honour, my dear,' he told her solemnly, pouring it into the glass which stood by her plate. 'Allen and I are always finding little excuses in order to treat ourselves, but we needed no excuse today.'

The strawberries had been dressed with fine sugar and were served with another little silver boat full of cream. A plate of shortbread biscuits was handed around to eat with them.

The food was simple, but, as Allen had promised, delicious. Trish was never to forget this meal with him, away from the grandeur of Park Lane. That Mr Nance acted as a kind chaperon troubled her not at all. She ate and drank heartily, with none of the fine-lady finickyness which both Allen and Mr Nance had secretly feared she might be cursed with. The very simplicity of the meal charmed her.

She was used to footmen and butlers, to a table elaborately laid, with a huge epergne in the middle of it on which every sort of fruit, both in and out of season, was elaborately arranged. Sometimes smilax and ferns were trailed across the tablecloth. Her napkin was always of the heaviest damask, held inside a silver ring with the letter 'S' engraved on it. The plates were of the finest porcelain, the cutlery was silver, and the three or four glasses which stood by her plate were miracles of the glassblower's craft.

In other words, she suddenly realised, the table itself was a work of art, as was the food laid upon it. Even when the Schuylers dined alone the meal was never simple in the way in which Mr Nance's was.

During the meal the three of them laughed and talked together. Trish, fascinated by what she had seen in the workroom, asked questions about clockmaking, which both men eagerly answered. Mr Nance leaned forward at the end of one explanation and said confidentially, 'He's such a modest chap that I'm sure Allen hasn't told you that he's been asked to give a paper to the British Horological Institute on the further possibilities of using electricity as a way of refining the accuracy and running time of clocks. I keep telling him he's wasted as a mere secretary—his mathematical knowledge is extraordinary.'

Allen said, 'Come, come, sir, you exaggerate. Trish must not think that I am a prodigy.'

What Trish *was* thinking was that when Gerard had spoken of the further uses of electricity in time-keeping, Allen had been very non-committal, speaking as though he was referring to someone else, when all the time he must already have been writing his paper.

'If you wanted money to develop your ideas,' she said thoughtfully, 'then perhaps Gerard might be interested in financing you. After all, he has a finger in a large number of pies. Torry told me that he has invested a great deal of money in this new underground line which is due to open next year. I believe she said that it would be an electric one.'

To her surprise Allen's face, hitherto softer and more carefree than she had ever seen it at Park Lane, assumed the frozen look common to it there.

'No,' he said shortly, 'by no means. Besides, my ideas are as yet very speculative—as I believe I told Lord Moidore at dinner.'

Mr Nance said hurriedly, 'So your guardian is one of the rich Americans behind the Central Line which is going to make all our lives easier. The motor car is beginning to drive out the horse-drawn cabs and trams; the new underground will surely finish them off.'

'At least the streets will be cleaner when the horses are gone,' said Allen, smiling at Trish, his good humour restored. She wondered at the note of hostility in his voice

when he had mentioned Gerard: she had understood from
Torry that he and his new secretary worked well together.

The shepherd's pie finished, Mr Nance fetched out the
strawberries, and after they had eaten every one of them
they sat and talked companionably over a pot of coffee.

Finally Allen wiped his mouth on his coarse cotton table
napkin and said to her, 'You have most heroically never
asked what Mr Nance and I propose for you this afternoon,
and your reward is that I shall tantalise you no longer. We
decided that you have probably never visited a Music Hall,
and, since there is a matinée today, we have bought tickets
for you to be entertained by Miss Marie Lloyd. You have
heard of her?'

Yes, Trish had heard of her, but had never thought that
she might be able to see her.

First, though, the pots had to be washed, dried and put
away. Allen had assumed his apron again, and did the
washing up while she and Mr Nance dried them.

And then it was time to visit the Music Hall, something
which Trish had never done before, and indeed had never
thought she would do.

Chapter Six

'We're going to the Canterbury Theatre on the other side of the river,' Allen told Trish while they queued for the horse-drawn bus—another new experience for Trish. 'It's not quite as respectable as the ones in the West End, but it's more like the real thing, and the atmosphere is remarkable. Isn't that so, sir?'

'True,' agreed Mr Nance, who was privately a little worried as to what such a gently bred creature as Miss Patricia Courtney might make of visiting a Music Hall. On the other hand the Prince of Wales frequently visited them; consequently one had to suppose that it was not too *infra dig* for her to be seen there.

Trish was too excited to care whether it was beneath her dignity or not. After all, here they were at the end of an old century, ready to move into a new one when everything would surely change, particularly everything which stood in the way of young women living as free a life as young men. After all, young ladies had become doctors and were going to university on equal terms with men—and it would surely soon be quite the thing for them to travel on a horse-drawn bus to visit a Music Hall with their young man—particularly if an elderly chaperon went with them.

In her excitement Trish had, for the first time, thought
of Allen as her young man, and she was still digesting the
implications of this when the bus arrived. As it was full
downstairs they climbed up the winding staircase to the top,
where Trish had a splendid view of Piccadilly quite unlike
anything she had ever seen before, and an even more splendid view of the River Thames when they crossed it.

Although it was a sunny day the wind was blowing quite
hard, and Allen advised Trish to hold on to her hat. It was
all completely different from her usually stately journeys
across London with Gerard and Torry, or even in the quiet
privacy of the Hansom cab which usually conveyed her
from door to door. Even when she had travelled in that
new-fangled thing—Gerard's motor car—she had never experienced anything like this journey with Allen, who was
surreptitiously holding her hand and occasionally pressing
it gently.

Once he said in his quiet voice, 'I hope that you are
enjoying yourself as much as I am.'

'Oh, yes,' she told him eagerly, her violet eyes shining
so brightly at him that, had they been alone, he would have
taken her in his arms and kissed her. But here, in the public
eye, on top of the bus, he was unable to do anything more
than squeeze her hand again and yearn hopelessly for her.

They left the bus a little way short of the theatre. Allen
had told her that in the early days of the Music Hall the
ground floor had been a cross between a public bar and a
restaurant with a stage at one end. The spectators had been
confined to a gallery above and around it. Over the years
it had been rebuilt to resemble a normal theatre, and Allen
had booked three seats in the pit which had replaced the
bar.

'I thought of hiring a box,' he said, 'but the atmosphere
is much better down here among the crowd.'

Inside, Trish found that the Canterbury was as splendid

as the West End theatres where she had enjoyed seeing Mr Henry Irving, Mr Beerbohm Tree, Miss Ellen Terry and Mrs Patrick Campbell. Everything was covered in gilt, and what wasn't gilded was scarlet. The stage was huge, and the orchestra seated before it was as large and accomplished as any as she had heard before.

The audience was noisier, though, showing not only its appreciation but also its disdain, by booing and hissing when an act failed to live up to its expectations. A pair of cross-talk comedians would come on first, to warm up the audience, Allen whispered to her, in order to make them feel so merry that they wouldn't be over-critical of the acts which followed.

She was sitting between him and Mr Nance, her hand was in Allen's once again, and all through that happy afternoon she joined whole-heartedly in the laughter and cheers with which most of the acts were greeted. After the comedians, dancing girls came on and performed a lively and daring act involving a lot of high-kicking which revealed their frilly pantalettes and their black silk stockings.

Higher and higher and faster and faster they kicked, to the accompaniment of the jolliest music which Trish had ever heard—the audience clapped and shouted in time to each kick and Trish found herself doing the same.

'The dance is called the cancan,' Allen told her. 'It was originally performed at the Folies Bergère, a Paris Music Hall, and it's supposed to be frightfully naughty.'

'Ought I to be watching it?' Trish whispered back.

'Probably not,' Allen returned. 'But it's too late to worry about that now.'

It was too late to be worried about anything. A magician followed the girls, and to make his act even more exciting and mysterious he combined it with having a ventriloquist's dummy which criticised everything he did. Jokes flew thick and fast, particularly when the magician's tricks failed.

Trish found many of the jokes incomprehensible, but since the spectators around them were weeping with laughter there must be some point to them which she was missing.

The jugglers and the acrobats were more straightforward, but after that the audience grew even noisier and began to shout impatiently for Marie Lloyd to appear. Trish had been expecting someone very beautiful, rather like the singers she had seen in the musical comedies which she had visited with Gerard and Torry, but Miss Lloyd was quite plain.

Somehow that didn't matter when she began to sing and joke with the audience, winking at them and occasionally playfully shaking her fist when laughter drowned her next words. Her songs were nearly as mysterious to Trish as the jokes of the magician and the comedians had been. They all seemed to have very odd titles which resulted in gales of laughter when she announced them. One song in particular had the whole place in an uproar. It was called 'She's Never had her Ticket Punched Before,' and when Miss Lloyd sang it she brought the house down—Allen's phrase.

Trish dutifully laughed as Miss Lloyd sang, winked and nodded her way to the end of her act, although at what she would have found it hard to explain. She whispered to Allen when the song about the girl on the bus came to an end, 'Why did everyone find that funny?'

He stopped laughing to gaze at her charmingly puzzled face, and this time he did kiss her, on the cheek, saying, 'One day, some time in the future, when you are ready, I'll explain. But not now.'

'Now that,' hissed Trish loftily, 'is no explanation at all!'

She supposed that, like the fuss surrounding Oscar Wilde, it was something to do with the secret business which passed between men and women. Next time she was with Lucy she would ask her if she knew anything about it. All in all it would be a good thing when the next century arrived, allowing the New Woman to come into her own and not be left in shaming ignorance.

Allen, sensing that she was a little upset, whispered, 'Dear girl, I did not mean to demean you, but it would be wrong of me to enlighten you now.' This didn't help matters, but was some sort of apology, Trish supposed.

She forgot her annoyance when the dancing girls were joined by some dancing men in a grand finale in which Union Jacks were waved and the company sang, 'We don't want to fight, but by jingo if we do, we've got the ships, we've got the men, we've got the money, too.'

Mr Nance, who had overheard the little dialogue between Trish and Allen, shook his head and wondered again whether they ought to have brought Trish into such a den of iniquity as a Music Hall, but when he saw her happy, glowing face after the curtain went down and the lights went up, he lost his reservations.

It was, he concluded, very silly to bring up young ladies in such dreadful ignorance of the real world in which they lived, and it was no wonder that so many marriages among the upper classes were doomed to failure when the women went to them as helpless innocents while the men, on the contrary, were sexually experienced.

He knew that Allen would never take advantage of his pretty girl, and that he would, on the contrary, gently initiate Trish into the realities of love between men and women—or, to put it into blunt terms, the realities of sex and passion.

Outside, anonymous in the happy crowd which streamed out of the theatre, Trish found that she was still holding Allen's hand. 'What now?' he asked her. 'A cup of tea and a bun at an ABC? And then a cab to take you back to Park Lane?'

'Why can't I go home and take tea with you and Mr Nance?' she said, offering Allen the best thanks she could have given him by wishing to return to what, to her, must seem Mr Nance's humble home.

'Because,' he said in his grave, sensible voice, 'it would not be wise for you to be away from Park Lane too long. Another time, perhaps.'

'Oh, please,' Trish said.

'You are asking for another time?'

Trish slipped her hand out of his and turned to face him. 'If Mr Nance will allow and you are willing, that is.'

'Dear girl,' he replied, longing to take her into his arms, 'of course he will allow, and I am always willing, but remember, the choice is always yours, for you are taking the most risks by meeting me clandestinely.'

'No!' Trish returned passionately. 'It is *you* who are most at risk, for I am certain that if Gerard knew that we were meeting like this he would dismiss you immediately—so the choice must be yours. I cannot lightly ruin you by losing you your employment.'

Oblivious of Mr Nance, as well as the surrounding crowd, Allen took both her hands in his to say, 'Oh, you are gallant, my darling heart, but remember that the world in which you live would argue that you are the one most likely to be ruined; let me tell you this now: I will never do anything to betray or hurt you, and I call upon Mr Nance to bear witness to what I have just said and help me to stay on the straight and narrow path of honour where you are concerned.'

Even though he spoke in his usual quiet manner there was such impassioned conviction lying beneath it that both his hearers were moved.

The crowd swirled about them. They were both far from home, Trish particularly so, but home was here, together. Later, back in Park Lane, Trish was to recall that moment and think of what Ruth had said to Naomi in the Bible: 'Whither thou goest, I will go,' and know that those touching words truly described her overwhelming feelings for Allen.

At the time, though, she simply smiled at him and said, 'Since I first met you I have never doubted that you would ever behave other than honourably, Allen.'

'You honour me by saying that,' he told her, and took her hand again to lead her to where the horse bus waited to carry them back across the river to drink tea in a small ABC before he and Mr Nance saw her into a cab. Trish's one regret was that she could not take her programme home, but Allen made her a solemn promise that he would keep it safe for her as a souvenir of the first time that they had gone out together.

He and Mr Nance watched the cab drive off. Mr Nance said, 'I know you well enough, Allen, to be sure that you will keep your promise to Trish. You have found a pearl in a most unlikely place. Rich girls such as she is are usually spoiled creatures not worthy of your attention.'

Allen nodded his agreement. 'She told me not long ago that she had nursed her mother through a long illness, something which, to me, explains why she is quite different from most society girls.'

Later that evening, returning to Park Lane, he arrived in the entrance hall just as Gerard, Torry and Trish were coming out of the dining room. Trish looked particularly enchanting in a young woman's white dress decorated with silk snowdrops.

Gerard said, 'Early back, Marriott?' his tone indifferent.

Allen, trying to avoid Trish's eye, or anyone else's for that matter, said equally indifferently, 'I was a little tired, Sir Gerard, and thought it unwise to be too late turning in.'

'Most commendable.' Gerard's tone was now dry rather than critical, and its hint of unspoken patronage set Trish's teeth on edge. She was in no position to say anything, and she could not even give Allen an encouraging smile. Not that he seemed to mind, and, as ever, there was nothing servile about him. He always stood, his face impassive, quite erect, his head a little on one side as though he were thinking of something far removed from what was being said to him.

Trish could not help contrasting his frozen, sphinx-like expression with the cheerful animation of the man who had sat by her at the Canterbury Theatre, teasing her and enjoying the jokes which she had thought mysterious.

What had that man to do with this one?

Only later, when she was alone in her room, a little puzzled, did Trish ask herself a question: was she wrong to imagine that there was some unspoken hostility between Gerard and his secretary—and, if she was right, why should that be? Since she could come up with no convincing answer to her question she dismissed it from her mind and thought instead of her happy day, and, with the memory of her hand in Allen's, drifted into sleep, a smile on her face.

Summer arrived, and Allen and Trish met most weeks at Mr Nance's shop and with Lucy's help managed not to arouse suspicion. Sometimes they simply spent the day at the shop, with Allen busy at the workbench doing a necessary repair which Mr Nance's failing sight left him unable to complete. Trish was either sitting nearby, busily engaged in minor household chores such as mending Mr Nance's socks, or leaving him in order to perform some other necessary task around the little house. On one wet afternoon she insisted on polishing all the silver ornaments which were part of Mr Nance's stock, as well as his own small pieces of silver which had grown tarnished.

'You will ruin your hands,' he told her once, finding her in the kitchen washing the lace curtains which hung over the small window above the sink.

'I don't like being idle when you are both working,' she

told him simply. 'I am not a fine lady here. I can cover them with cream when I go back to Park Lane.'

Several times Allen and Mr Nance took her shopping in Covent Garden. When their baskets were full of fruit and vegetables, they visited one of the little booths where coffee, tea and small cakes were served, as well as strong drink. After a few weeks had passed Mr Nance trusted Allen enough to allow him to take Trish about London on his own, while he stayed behind to prepare their supper, which Trish enjoyed with them, refusing dinner when she returned to Park Lane on the grounds that she had already eaten.

One evening, after their meal, Allen went upstairs and came down with a largeish box.

'Guess what's in it,' he asked her. He was always teasing her by making her play the little word games which he had enjoyed as a boy. 'They're designed to broaden the mind,' he had told her once.

She had teased him back with, 'Mine isn't broadened enough, then?'

Now, used to such ploys, she pretended to think very hard before saying, 'A grand piano?'

Allen began to laugh. 'Very near. It *is* a musical instrument, but far from a grand one. Since you were almost right, I will tell you. It's a concertina.'

'A concertina!' Trish exclaimed. 'I thought that only Pierrots played them—on the pier at Brighton.'

'I'll have you know I learned to play this at the Glee Club at Yale,' Allen told her. 'I was regarded as a complete master of it. I thought once of a career on the Burlesque Halls in New York—Musical Halls to you. I do a nice line in hillbilly songs and spirituals—the ones the slaves used to sing on the Southern plantations. I changed my mind when I found out what the pay was.'

'Worse than at Schuyler's?'

'Oh, very much worse—and the hours were rotten, too.'

By now he had fetched the instrument from its box and had begun to play and sing in a light baritone the song which Marie Lloyd had sung about the punched ticket.

Trish was entranced. It was a side of him which she had never seen before, and when he had finished she said, 'You played that by ear. That was something I could never do. I need the music before me to play the piano.'

'I can't read music,' Allen told her. 'And the concertina's not a difficult instrument, like the piano.'

He began another song, an American ballad this time by Stephen Foster called, 'Way Down Upon the Swannee River,' which was quite unlike Miss Lloyd's broad humour, being slow and sad. Trish found the words quite moving, and so, too, did Allen, by the way his face changed as he sang it. A shadow passed across his face in the last verse, where the singer remembers his lost home and his lost past.

'All the world is sad and weary,' he sang, 'everywhere I roam.' He even managed to make the concertina sound solemn, something which Trish would not have believed possible.

'I had a piano once,' Mr Nance grieved into the silence which followed, 'but I sold it when my wife died.' He did not tell Trish that he had found the sight of it painful. He'd often wished that he still possessed it after he had discovered that it was one of Trish's accomplishments.

'Enough of melancholy,' said Allen briskly. 'I'll play you a few jolly ones, Trish, to make up for you having to go home early.'

Home is here, she wanted to tell him, and for the first time wondered how their idyll was going to end. She had been busy enjoying herself and had quite forgotten the future. Something in Allen's voice, or even the words of the song, had told her that sooner or later they must come to a decision, that the version of fairyland in which they had been living could not last for ever.

Indeed, they were lucky that it had lasted so long, that someone had not seen them or that her arrangement with Lucy had not been discovered.

As she had seen Allen's face change he had seen hers, and knew the reason why. He put the concertina down and knelt by her chair.

'My darling,' he said, and his voice sounded old and wise, 'let us enjoy what we have and pretend that there is no past and no future. The Romans had a saying, *Carpe Diem*, which means Seize the Day! Let us seize our day. I should not have sung that song. It tells of loss and sorrow.'

Trish nodded her head slowly. 'How strange it is that we often think alike. I have never had that happen to me before, but it happens with you all the time.'

He seized upon her last word. 'Time! Trish, have you ever thought how odd time is? When we are happy, and wish it to last, it flies. An hour becomes a minute. When we are sad, the reverse happens. A minute becomes an hour. When we are waiting for something nice to happen, it seems an eternity, whereas in the dentist's chair things happen far too quickly. So it is with us. Our time together is short—even though it is the best part of a day.'

Trish shivered. 'And it grows shorter each time I visit Mr Nance—and you.'

'True, and Mr Nance's shop is where time is measured, bought and sold!'

'And you repair it.'

'True, also. Trish, before your season grows too busy, would you like me to take you to Greenwich Observatory where the world's time is measured? I have never asked a girl to do such a thing before.'

This was not strictly true. He had tried to speak of these things with the first young woman he had taken out in London, and she had yawned her boredom at him before he could even propose it. 'If you want to take me somewhere,' she had told him, 'take me to the Gaiety Theatre, to see the new musical comedy there.'

It was not that he did not enjoy going to the Gaiety, but he had hoped to meet someone who might share his other enthusiasms, and until he had met Trish he had never found anyone who would—or could.

And all as the result of a railway accident—which reminded him that chance, as well as time, runs our lives.

'Of course, I would, Allen. You know, I never thought about clocks or time before, but what with the end of the century coming, and getting to know you and Mr Nance, watching you repairing things and talking together, I have become quite intrigued. I still think that you ought to tell Gerard about your—' She stopped, because Allen's face had taken on that frozen look again, which turned him immediately into the man whom Park Lane and the world outside Mr Nance's shop knew.

'No,' she said rapidly. 'I shouldn't interfere. Except that I know that he doesn't value you properly, and he ought to.'

'That doesn't matter,' he told her, his face softening again. 'That you value me, and that Mr Nance does, is what matters. Now forgive me if I tell you that I don't care a fig for his opinion of me.'

He meant it, Trish was sure, and once again she wondered what lay between her guardian, whom she respected and liked, and the man whom she respected and loved. She said no more, but concentrated instead on enjoying her brief hours of freedom—not that living at Park Lane could really be described as servitude!

Allen was not finding his duties at Park Lane servitude. Gerard was a considerate master, although Allen preferred not to think of how his cousin would have behaved had he proved to be an incompetent secretary. Tales about Gerard's legendary temper were always circulating excitedly around the London headquarters of Schuyler Incorporated. Thus far, Gerard had always treated him with cold courtesy, often asking him to carry out delicate tasks which he would not have entrusted to Mr Hall.

On this particular morning he had been sent to Rothschild's, where he had received a warm welcome—indeed, he had been told that he would have had an even warmer one had he decided to change his mind and work for them. His mission over, he made his way back to Park Lane. Gerard was attending a meeting of a Parliamentary committee and was staying on at the House to take part in a debate.

He was met in the entrance hall by one of the footmen—the butler, it seemed, had just gone off duty. The footman took his hat and coat from him, and then said in a confidential voice, 'I thought, sir, that you would like to know that Mr Hall, Sir Gerard's former secretary, called some little time ago. He was hoping to see either you or Sir Gerard. The butler received him and saw fit to tell him to wait in the office for you, rather than in the drawing room. I thought you ought to know.'

What Allen did not know was that the dislike which most of the staff had originally felt for the aloof and quiet young man who had succeeded the jovial Mr Hall had disappeared. His courteous and considerate manner had won everyone over but the butler, who had taken him in great dislike.

'He's always so pleasant,' one of the maids had said over afternoon tea. 'Mr Hall was all right, but you never knew when you was going to have to dodge his hands—if you take my meaning. I prefer 'em quiet myself—it's safer.'

General agreement had followed from everyone except the butler, who had snorted, 'Too quiet for my liking. I thought once he was after Miss Courtney, but not any more. I'd take him for a bit of a soft Miss Molly, myself.'

To his surprise he had been met with a chorus of dissent. Wade, the senior footman had said, 'You wouldn't think that he was soft if you'd seen him when the pantry boy fell out of the tree in the back garden. He not only picked him up, but he carried the great lummox into the house as though he'd been a baby—and when he got him there looked after his broken leg until the doctor came. On top of that the lad told me afterwards that the housekeeper wanted Sir Gerard to turn him off for larking about when he was supposed to be at work, but Mr Marriott told him that boys will be boys, and he'd had a nasty lesson, so Sir Gerard changed his mind and let him off with a warning.

'As for being a Miss Molly—no Miss Molly looks at Miss Courtney the way he does when he thinks no one's a-noticing of him.'

The butler had muttered something under his breath, but the staff's defiance of his judgement—which was usually respected—had done nothing to endear Allen to him. 'Thinks he's a gent, I suppose,' he'd muttered. 'Still dangling after her, eh? Let's see what Sir Gerard has to say about that.'

'Nothing,' Wade had said stoutly, 'seeing as how I should deny I ever said any such thing!'

The butler had given up, but remained quietly determined to do young Marriott a mischief the first chance he got.

Allen thanked the footman now, and made his way to the office as quickly as he could without appearing overhasty and causing more gossip. He reached the closed door, hesitated a moment before opening it as quietly as he could before entering.

It was quite plain that Mr Hall had not heard him. Allen had left some files on his desk and Mr Hall was bent over,

busily going through them. He wondered whether the man
had bribed the butler to let him into the office, although he
now had no business there, or whether, given the butler's
antagonism, it had not been necessary.

He silently turned around and noisily opened and closed
the door as though he were only just entering which, by
the time he turned back, enabled Mr Hall to spring away
and sink into a chair by the desk as though he had been
seated there ever since the butler had shown in him.

'Ah,' exclaimed Mr Hall jovially, leaping to his feet and
saying, 'Mr Marriott, I presume?'

Allen inclined his head a little and said in his quietest
voice, 'Indeed, and you, I take it, are Mr Hall, my predecessor. What may I do for you?'

Mr Hall spread expansive hands. 'Nothing, nothing—a
courtesy call, merely. I am, as you may know, now retired.
I inherited a comfortable little estate from a distant cousin
and am become a man of leisure.'

By now Allen had made his way to his desk, where he
stood for a moment before seating himself and waving a
hand at Mr Hall to indicate that he might do the same. It
pleased him to offer himself as almost a parody of the industrious clerk by leaning forward, steepling his hands, and
murmuring, 'Since, however, I am not a man of leisure,
and Sir Gerard has handed me duties which I must accom-
plish before the evening, your social call must, I fear, be a
short one.'

He heaved a heavy sigh, looked down at his files and
prepared to pick one up. His only regret in carrying out
this pantomime was that he did not possess a pair of pince-
nez which he could perch on his nose to inspect the dubious
fellow in front of him.

*Courtesy call, indeed! And looking through my papers.
He must think that I am a pigeon for the plucking!*

What Mr Hall thought was not plain. He rewarded Allen

with a condescending smile, asking him kindly, 'You have no questions, then, which you would care to put to me regarding the records I have kept?'

'None,' returned Allen, re-steepling his hands. 'Your records are as clear as crystal to me—even though the system which you used was quite different from mine. Nothing which you could tell me would surprise me—quite the contrary.'

This superb piece of double-meaning either deceived Mr Hall or he allowed it to pass him by.

'Splendid!' he announced. 'I am delighted that Sir Gerard has been fortunate to find such a suitable replacement for me.'

Allen inclined his head again. 'I thank you, sir, and now, if you have nothing further to say to me, and since Sir Gerard will not be returning before the evening, I suggest that this interview be terminated.'

This, at least, had the effect of distressing Mr Hall. His air of patronage disappeared; he stammered a little, 'I h…had thought…'

'Yes?' Allen inclined his head again. 'That you might take coffee, perhaps, before you left?'

'Oh, quite. Very gracious. You must be wishing for a break yourself. The butler informed me that you have spent the morning at Rothschild's.'

'You mistake. I drank sherry with young Mr Nathan not long ago. No, I shall ring for the butler and ask him to serve you in the library. Now, if you will excuse me, I have work to do, and the library is more comfortable than this office as I am sure you are aware. Good day, sir.'

He picked up his pen, waved at the door, and, as he had promised, rang for the butler.

With suppressed ill-grace concealed behind a weak smile, Mr Hall disappeared through the door to the library with a muttered, 'Good day, Marriott.'

Once he was safely gone Allen leafed rapidly through the files on his desk which Mr Hall had been inspecting. He could not be sure that nothing had been removed, and he had no notion of what Mr Hall had been trying to find.

What he did know was that all his suspicions regarding the man's honesty—or rather his lack of it—now seemed to be grounded on more than mere speculation. The trouble was that he still had nothing tangible to offer Sir Gerard which might convince him that a man who had been described as 'part of the family' had been swindling him in some fashion yet to be discovered.

Trish had spent much of the morning in the nursery with Gerry Junior and Hans, two lively small boys who already bore a strong likeness to their dominant father. Their mother had gone to visit a friend whom she wished to take part in one of her many charitable enterprises set up to assist poor women.

Nurse finally drove her away, politely, of course, saying that Master Gerry and his brother had had enough excitement for one morning. Left at a loose end, she had decided to visit the library to discover whether it had any books on clockmaking and time. It would, she decided, be useful to know a little more about the subjects in which Allen and Mr Nance were interested.

Since Dr Ryan, the librarian, was spending the morning at the British Museum, she had the pleasure of browsing unchecked among the shelves. She soon found an interesting old book about clocks and was carefully turning its yellowed pages when she heard someone come into the room. Looking across from where she was hidden in a narrow bay lit by a window, she saw that it was Mr Hall, Gerard's late secretary.

Like the maid who had disliked his roving hands, Trish had disliked his roving eyes. Jovial he might be, but it was not the kind of joviality of which she approved, so she kept quiet, reading her book and turning its pages silently.

Shortly afterwards someone else entered. By his voice it was the butler, who had evidently brought coffee for Mr Hall. She was about to make it known that she was present when the butler said slightingly, 'He's made you have it on your own, has he? A right stuck-up young gent is Master Marriott. Not one for a kind word to me—as you were.'

Mr Hall gave a sneering laugh. 'Not one for a kind word with anyone, if you ask me. Practically threw me out of the office—you'd never think I'd been Sir Gerard's trusted man for so many years.'

'Sounds just like him, it does. You take both sugar and cream, don't you?'

'Fancy your remembering that!' exclaimed Mr Hall, flattered. 'Yes, both.'

Their demeaning of Allen kept Trish silent. She shrank back into her niche, wishing herself anywhere but where she was. Perhaps the butler would leave soon—she had no wish to overhear any more, and disliked being an eavesdropper, but to reveal herself and thus disclose what she had overheard would not make the butler love Allen the more.

That she was right to keep quiet was quickly proved. In answer to Mr Hall the butler replied, 'Aye, I don't forget my friends. Especially those who have benefited me—if you take my meaning.'

Mr Hall's response was quick. 'Then perhaps you wouldn't mind assisting me again—for a consideration.'

'Anything to oblige, sir,'

'Then you could keep a weather eye on young Marriott and let me know anything which might benefit *me*. I didn't like the tone he took with me. I wouldn't like Sir Gerard to think any of the less of me on account of what he might be saying to him. Besides that, if you know of anything to his detriment you might let me know of that, too.'

'Oh, I know something already. He's after Miss Courtney, the smarmy young devil that he is. Sir Gerard ordered him to have nothing to do with her, but I have my suspicions about them. He's been altogether too quiet and she's a wilful young piece. From something my head footman said it wouldn't surprise me if they were meeting behind Sir Gerard's back.'

'Right, find out what you can and let me know. Here's my address and a little something on account for you.'

'Thank you, sir. I always knows a true gent when I meet one—but what do you expect from a damned Yankee who tries to sound like an Englishman?'

Mr Hall laughed. The butler echoed him and left.

Trish, sitting silent in her corner, seethed inwardly. Eavesdropping might be very much not the done thing, but she had learned something useful from it and therefore could not regret her involuntary fall from perfect social grace. She waited until she heard Mr Hall leave before replacing the book on its shelf and walking over to knock on the door to the office.

Allen looked up at the sound and wondered who next was coming to interrupt him. He called out, 'Enter,' and put his pen down. The sight of Trish coming through the door filled him with joy.

Words flew from him. 'Yes, my dearest, what is it you want?'

My dearest! He had already called her his darling, and now he had called her his dearest. Trish was so pleased that she almost forgot what she had come to tell him. He was waving her to a seat and saying, 'I think that we are safe for the moment. Sir Gerard will not be back until the evening. Mr Hall was in the library, but I suspect that he has gone by now.'

'Yes, he has, and that is why I came to see you immediately he left. I was there, reading that book about clocks of which you spoke, when he came in. By good luck he didn't see me, for I had no wish to speak to him. Shortly afterwards the butler brought him coffee and they had a most disagreeable conversation about you—and later about me.

'They were obviously cronies of a sort, and Mr Hall had been paying him for information when he worked here. They didn't say what about. After being unkind about you Mr Hall offered the butler money for anything which he knew to your detriment, whereupon he told him about us! By what he said the butler even suspects that we might be meeting secretly, and Mr Hall gave him money for that.

'Oh, Allen, we must be careful—I do hope that you don't think that I might be making something out of nothing.'

Allen came round the desk and took her hands in his. 'I don't think anything of the sort, and I agree that we must be careful. But tell me, did he say anything else—anything to do with my work?'

'Yes, and that was odd. Mr Hall thought that you might be saying unkind things about him to Sir Gerard. Why should he think that?'

Allen knew perfectly well why Mr Hall should be worried about what he might say to Sir Gerard, but since he had no evidence to back his suspicions he felt that it would not be fair to tell Trish of them.

'I'm not sure,' he said. 'Perhaps he judges others by himself.'

'I suppose he might. He sounded very vindictive. What I don't understand is how, if he only met you this morning, he could dislike you so much.'

'Jealousy?' Allen suggested. 'After all, he worked for Sir Gerard for quite a long time.'

More and more what Trish was telling him supported his

belief that there had been something wrong with Mr Hall's recent stewardship.

Trish seemed satisfied with his last explanation. She rose and said sadly, 'I really ought not to stay here any longer. I've no doubt that we are under surveillance by the servants, and we must not be seen to be meeting when Sir Gerard is not here.'

She heaved a great sigh. 'Oh, Allen, I do dislike this secrecy, but what else can we do if we wish to meet? The annoying thing is that Harry will be calling this afternoon to take me driving in the Park, and no one objects to me meeting him—or even being alone with him. Quite the contrary. And, pleasant though he is, you're worth twenty of him. He really hasn't a single idea in his head, and being married to him would be like being married to—'

Here her invention failed her and she fell silent.

'To?' queried Allen, teasing her as though they were in Mr Nance's shop.

'I'm sure I don't know. I can't say the village idiot, because he's not an idiot, just not interested in anything which interests me.'

What she couldn't say, but was implicit in everything she had ever said to Allen, was that the sense of excitement which being with someone who was the other half of one's self gave her was quite missing when she was with Harry.

'To be fair to him,' she added ruefully, 'he must think the same of me. I'm not interested in his world, either. For us to marry would be a recipe for disaster.'

Allen could not but agree with her. All the same, the news that she was going out with Harry and would be seen with him in the Park roused a tiny demon of jealousy in his heart. He remained outwardly calm, but inwardly he was filled with the most bitter regret that he could not yet proclaim his love for her to all the world.

He could only hope and pray that somehow, some time, the world would turn and bring that day to him.

Chapter Seven

Once Trish would have thought that to be driven along Rotten Row on a fine summer afternoon by a handsome young man of future title would have been the ultimate of her ambitions—society conquered and the prospect of a wealthy marriage before her.

She would never have thought that when the dream became reality it would be like dust and ashes in her mouth. First of all the appearance of mutual affection which she and Harry gave off was nothing but a sham, and secondly, and more importantly, she was unable to acknowledge publicly the man she loved for fear of depriving him of his livelihood.

More than once she had thought to hint to him that there was no need for him to worry about his future: her fortune was sufficiently large that were they to marry it would easily support them both in great luxury. Even the allowance which she received until she reached twenty-five and gained full control of it would be more than enough to keep them in comfort.

Delicacy, and an intuitive understanding that Allen Marriott was not the sort of young man who would happily live on his wife's fortune, had kept her silent. At some point he would declare himself, and until then she must put no pressure of any kind on him, however much she loved him—and wished to marry him. He would never ask her to run away with him and marry him secretly. Like her, he regretted the necessity to deceive the Schuylers, and to do more than that would compromise their honour completely.

It was like being confronted with an insoluble logic puzzle of the kind which appeared in most magazines these days, usually at the end, away from the stories about Sherlock Holmes by Mr Conan Doyle, or the historical romances of Alice and Egerton Castle.

Meantime there was Harry Norman to consider. He was looking sideways at her, his expression an admiring one—which was something which she did not want. Over the last few weeks his manner to her had changed. To begin with he had treated her as a jolly chum who happened to be a girl, but lately he had become personal, paying her little compliments.

Earlier that afternoon when she had met him in the entrance hall he had exclaimed, 'Oh, I say, Trish, you do look a picture—positively deevy.'

This last word proved that he was now moving in the circle which surrounded the Prince of Wales. 'Deevy' was a high society slang word short for divine, and was the ultimate compliment one could pay to anything.

She had shaken her head briskly. 'There's nothing divine about me, Harry. I'm far too down to earth. You ought to save that word for Gaiety girls.'

'I'm not one for Gaiety girls,' Harry had returned a trifle dolefully. 'They never look as handsome in the street as they do on the stage. Must be the limelight that does it. *You* look your best in the afternoon.'

'Not at night in the ballroom?' Trish had teased. Teasing was a habit she had learned from Allen, and using it against Harry helped her to keep him at arm's length.

Not today, though. He had started as he meant to go on, praising and complimenting her, and laughing immoderately at any mild joke which she happened to make.

Now he said to her, 'How about us taking a walk in the Park? The groom can look after the carriage. It's difficult to talk to you while I'm driving.'

Trish didn't feel that she could refuse him. After all, they were supposed to be interested in one another, and to walk together, laughing and talking, would merely support that useful fiction.

Except was it still fiction?

Once walking along the grass, her parasol up and her hand on Harry's arm, he began unpromisingly, 'I've been thinking, Trish.' Harry announced this extremely gravely, as though to think needed the most tremendous skill.

He paused, apparently waiting for her to answer him. Trish hesitantly came out with something as neutral as possible. 'Have you, Harry? What about?'

'Us, of course—haven't you guessed?'

This was turning into something of a verbal fencing match, since Trish parried this question with one of her own. 'Guessed what, Harry?'

'You don't help a fellow,' he said plaintively. 'I would have thought that you would have noticed. Girls are supposed to, or so I'm told.'

Trish suppressed a terrible desire to say, Noticed what? Instead she said, 'I must be rather slow today, Harry, for I don't quite take your meaning.'

'Don't you? I suppose that shows what a perfect lady you are, and I shan't complain about that! I fear that I've quite forgotten my young lady back home since I met you. She's a quiet little thing, you see.'

'While I'm noisy?' Trish could not prevent herself from riposting.

'Oh, no. Lively is the word. You make a fellow laugh.

What I'm really trying to say is, why don't we make the pretence real? It would please Mother no end. I'd as soon marry you as anyone.'

This naïve utterance set Trish thinking all over again that she could never have married Harry even if Allen had not existed.

'It's not just a matter of pleasing your mother, Harry, nor even yourself. I am quite happy with our present arrangement and have no wish for it to end.'

'You mean that you wouldn't like to marry me? But now that I have been in society I can quite see that Mother was right—Lizzie would never have done as a wife for me. You, on the other hand, possess every qualification—I could scarcely do better.'

Trish stopped walking: perforce Harry had to stop too. She looked him firmly in the eye. 'Harry, I don't wish to marry you. I agreed to your proposed arrangement because I have become very fond of someone my guardian considers unsuitable. Your feelings might have changed, but mine for him have become even stronger. If you feel that we must end the arrangement because you would like to marry me and I have no intention of marrying you, then let this outing today be our last.'

He looked mournfully down at her, rather like a puppy dog who had been struck by a master whom he had thought loved him.

'You really mean that?'

'Yes, I do.'

'Well, I can't say that I'm other than sorry. Can we go on being friends? I like being with you.'

'Only if you promise never to talk of marriage to me again.'

He heaved a great sigh. 'I suppose I must agree. Who is this lucky chap you're dead set on? Do I know him? I should like to congratulate him on his good fortune.'

Trish shook her head before walking on again. 'No, Harry, you can't meet him, and he's not in society. That's all I'm prepared to say. Now drive me back to Park Lane.'

'Very well, but we're still friends, I hope. For I want to keep Mother quiet. If I stop seeing you she'll be sure to find me someone unsuitable—and ugly. You're the first girl who's not ugly that she's ever approved of.'

Well, that was some sort of accolade, Trish thought, stifling a laugh at Harry's artlessness. He's such a good-hearted young man, she told herself sternly, you mustn't mock him, and beside the roués, both young and old, whom you've been meeting in so-called good society, he's a beacon of light.

He's not Allen, though. I wonder what he's doing now.

Allen was reading a letter which had arrived by the afternoon post. It was from his mother, whom he had not seen since he had arrived in London five years ago. The letter's contents surprised him greatly.

Dear Allen,

I have some news for you which I hope will please you. A few months ago I met Frederick Hurst, an old friend whom I have not seen since before I married your father. In truth he was more than my friend, but my parents, seeing how much we cared for one another, forbade me to see him because he was poor, and we lost touch for many years. While we were apart he made the fortune which, when we were young, would have allowed us to marry. His wife died last year, and he has been very lonely—as I have been—with my husband long gone and my son in another country. To cut a long story short, we were married last week.

I beg you to forgive us our haste, but we have already lost such a lot of time together and we did not wish to lose any more. Frederick joked that he was too old to wait for the next century to arrive before he married me! One fortunate consequence is that I now no longer need the annuity which your cousin Gerard settled on me to prevent me from sinking into poverty. I shall write to thank him for his kindness to me—and to you, in enabling you to find work. Wish me happy, dearest son. I know how much you lost because of your father's folly, and I can only hope that one day you will find happiness as I have done—my one wish is that you will not have to wait so long as I did to find it.

                    Your loving mother, Alicia Hurst.

Allen put the letter carefully down. He remembered seeing a painting by Millais entitled *The Order of Release*, showing a soldier coming home from the wars. Well, he was not a soldier, but this was his order of release. The main reason why he had not left Gerard's employment before was because he had not been entirely certain that he would be able to keep his mother in the comfort which Gerard's annuity had provided for her. Now that reason was gone. His mother was provided for by her new husband and his future was his own.

It was the strangest of sensations to contemplate that. He had heard that prisoners, released from gaol, frequently found themselves disoriented, unable to return to the world which they had left. His feelings were the same. He almost felt giddy.

He said aloud, 'I shall have to reconsider my future when this news has had time to sink in.'

First of all, though, he needed to write a letter to his mother, telling her how pleased he was to hear that she had reached harbour at last. He knew that her life with his father had never been a happy one—as his had not been. She had made another for herself after his father's death, and one of his regrets was that, of necessity, they had seen little of one another after he had gone to work for Schuyler's. It was a relief to him to know that she would never be lonely again.

If only I could tell Trish, he thought. But since he had agreed that his relationship to Gerard was to be a secret that was impossible. And even though the obligation to his cousin could be considered to have been cancelled by the fact that his mother was no longer his dependent, Allen's pride would not allow him to reveal it.

His musings were interrupted by Gerard's entrance. His cousin was also holding a letter, and Allen correctly assumed that it was the one of which his mother had written. Gerard's first words confirmed his belief.

Gerard said, 'Am I right in assuming that you have also had a letter from your mother? She said in mine that she was writing to you by the same post to inform you of her marriage and her changed circumstances.'

And then, dryly, 'I see by your expression that you have. Let me begin by assuring you how happy it makes me to learn that Aunt Alicia has married someone for whom, she tells me, she had some affection long ago. He is, it appears, rich enough to keep her in luxury—which relieves me of any worry that she might have been snared by a fortune-hunter.'

'Yes,' said Allen. 'I, too, have had a letter from her. I was about to ask you whether, now that your financing of my mother is at an end, you would wish me to leave your service, seeing that it was originally a condition of your assistance to her.'

He was careful to make his little speech in as indifferent a manner as possible. So indifferent was he, indeed, that Gerard was somewhat nonplussed.

'Yes,' he said at last. 'That contract, too, is at an end. You must make your own decision as to your future.'

'Yes, sir,' he answered, his voice giving none of his true feelings away.

Gerard appeared to be about to say something else, then decided not to. He sat down at his desk and began to read the report on his dealings with Standard Oil, Rockefeller's huge company, which Allen had compiled and had left there for him to inspect.

After a little time he looked up and said, somewhat heavily for him, 'A word with you, Marriott.'

Allen looked up from his work. 'Sir?'

'I have been reading this report. I think that I may have undervalued you, now and in the past.' It was not simply the report which made him say this; he had been both surprised and impressed by Allen's efficiency, his speed of work and his ability to understand immediately whatever was put before him.

'Yes, sir, you did,' replied Allen, stone-faced.

Exasperated, Gerard said, 'Is that all you have to say? Most men would have been both pleased and flattered to learn that from me.'

Allen stared at him. He was suddenly, cynically, sure that Gerard had discovered that he did not wish to lose an invaluable aide—possibly to rivals—and was offering him this sop to persuade him not to leave.

'Would you like me to speak the truth, sir?'

'By all means, Marriott. I am beginning to believe that you rarely speak the truth—whenever you care to speak that is, which is not often.'

'Then, sir, I am neither pleased nor flattered to learn that, for once, your famed intuition let you down, and that you chose to throw me away, condemning me to servitude in a position which was much beneath my talents.'

Gerard stared at him. He felt as though he had baited a mouse and started a tiger!

'Godammit!' he roared at last. 'I can do a great deal for you, Marriott, if you possess the correct attitude! Would you throw that away?'

Composedly Allen said, 'Oh, I have no wish for you to do anything further for me, sir. I am content for the moment to remain as your secretary, and I am perfectly capable of looking after my future myself, and at a suitable time will do just that.'

He paused.

'Have you any new orders for me, sir? If not, I will continue with my present task.'

Checkmate! thought Gerard with a sudden inward grin, his anger dissipating before Allen's impenetrable façade. Hard man that he was, he knew and respected those who were like him. Improbably, his unconsidered cousin had proved to be as hard as himself. Whether he had always been a hard man, or whether hardship and his rage at being undervalued had made him one were moot points, and, to Gerard, irrelevant. He dealt in facts, not unsupported evidence and hindsight. He suspected that the man before him did the same.

He sat down again, saying dryly, 'Well, if you *do* decide to leave me, I would be grateful for a reasonably long notice. My one complaint about Hall's going was that he wished to leave me at extremely short notice, and after such long service that I could not refuse him.'

Allen put that piece of news away in his capacious memory to be thought about later. 'When I leave I shall certainly give you due notice,' being his only comment.

They worked in silence for about an hour, until Gerard rose and announced that Torry was having a bun-fight that afternoon and that he had promised to be present.

'Would you care to come down and indulge in a cup of

tea, Marriott?' he offered—as a form of olive branch, Allen sardonically supposed.

He shook his head. 'Thank you, no. I have a great deal of work before me.'

Gerard thought, a little ruefully, that Allen would have refused this belated invitation even if he had had no work at all before him. He had never before realised how much pride was hidden behind his cousin's silent self-control since the apparent humility Allen always displayed had deceived him.

Once he had gone Allen rose and paced restlessly around the room, reliving his skirmish with Gerard. For the moment, despite what he had said to his cousin, his ability to concentrate had left him. He sat down again, but to no avail. For the first time since he had walked into Gerard's office nine years ago he was on his own, and the world lay before him.

The telephone's harsh bray interrupted his musing. It was Tom Moidore on the other end of the line. 'Is Sir Gerard there?' he asked, nay, demanded. 'If he is I need to speak to him at once. Tell him that the matter is urgent.'

'Urgent enough to interrupt him while he's at one of Lady Schuyler's campaigning bun-fights?' queried Allen.

'Look, Marriott,' roared Tom in exasperation, 'believe me, it's urgent enough for you to interrupt him if he were entertaining the Prince of Wales!'

'In that case…' murmured Allen, and sped to do as he was bid. The reason for his reluctance was that he did not wish to invade the Schuylers' private space rather than that he wished to disobey Tom.

The drawing room was full of men and women. Harry Norman was there with his mother, seated beside Trish, who looked enchanting in a violet and cream tea-gown. Torry Schuyler was enchanting in green and cream.

'If you will excuse me for intruding, Lady Schuyler, but

Lord Moidore is on the telephone and wishes to speak to Sir Gerard. He said that the matter was most urgent and could not wait.'

'Oh, if that is so,' smiled Torry, 'we will excuse you, Gerard, provided only that Mr Marriott will take your place and a cup of tea.'

She had always had a soft spot for Allen, whom she considered a most decent and gentlemanly young fellow— with hidden depths. The shrewdness with which she had run her life as a single woman had not deserted her on marriage.

There was no way in which Allen could refuse her, as he had refused her husband, without looking a boor. He sat down, not far from Trish, and was handed a cup of tea and a tea-cake.

The other young men in the room—there were a few beside Harry—were all superbly turned out and sat with their inverted top hats—their white gloves inside them—at their feet, balancing cups of tea and plates of tea-cakes as to the manner born. Allen had often wondered if they took lessons in it all at public school.

He tried to look inconspicuous, and was succeeding until the young woman next to him—Trish's friend Lucy Chalfont, who was enabling Trish to visit him and Mr Nance— asked archly, 'I take it that you are Sir Gerard's secretary, Mr Marriott. Have you been with him long?'

'Not very long,' he told her, swallowing a piece of tea-cake rapidly. 'About two months now.'

Lucy noted his slight American accent, and continued her interrogation with, 'And how long have you been in England?'

'Oh,' he said, as unassumingly as he could, 'I have worked in Schuyler's head office in London for the past five years.'

'Well, whatever else,' pursued Lucy, 'you have almost lost your American accent.'

'Being from the East Coast,' he told her, 'I never had a strong one. Most people think Americans have a decided twang, but in our part of the States people pride themselves on trying to lose it.'

Trish leaned forward to say, 'Do you think, Mr Marriott, that in the coming century we shall speak more like the Americans—or will they speak more like us?'

Before he could answer Harry Norman said, somewhat aggressively, 'Seeing that it is our language which they speak, it would seem reasonable to me that they will adopt our way of speech completely, hey, Marriott?'

Now this was said after a fashion that expected the answer Yes, but Allen, feeling freer to speak his mind than he had done for years, said, still quietly, 'I think not. There are many influences at work in the States which are sure to change our speech even more. I refer to the American Indians, and even more to the successive waves of immigration from countries other than England. Consequently I think it likely that you will become more Americanised and will adopt many of the new words being coined there.'

This was heresy to Harry, and to most of the others present. Only Torry, an American herself, said thoughtfully, 'I believe that you are right, Mr Marriott. During the years I have been in England I have noticed that many of our livelier expressions have been adopted over here.'

'The twentieth century will be an American one, then,' said a middle-aged man mockingly. 'What a prospect!'

Trish, indignantly defending Allen—and Torry for that matter—said, 'We could do worse, I think. It seems to me that there is a drive in Americans which we appear to lack these days. Perhaps being a young country helps!'

'You have been listening to the Prince of Wales,' remarked Torry with a laugh, trying to defuse the situation a

little, and at the same time ignoring the slur on herself and
Gerard as Americans. 'He thinks that we are growing a
trifle decadent as the end of the century approaches.'

'Everyone thinks that at the end of centuries,' said Lady
Norman decidedly.

Trish said, her eyes sparkling, 'In that case all will be
remedied when the clock strikes twelve on December the
thirty-first, 1899, for, by that logic, we shall immediately
be transformed into babes again, innocently blowing bub-
bles and forgetting our recent wickedness.'

The general laugh which followed this turned the conversation away from Allen and the United States, for which
he was heartily grateful.

Lucy, who had been watching both Allen and Trish curiously, whispered to him, 'Do you like England, Mr Marriott? I hear that American girls are supposed to be very
pretty. Do you think that English girls are pretty?'

Allen said, under his breath. 'I like England very much,
and I like pretty girls, too. There doesn't seem to be much
to choose between the two countries in that department, I
am happy to say.'

Lucy preened herself a little. 'What a diplomat you, Mr
Marriott! Is that why Sir Gerard employs you?'

Allen nearly choked over the remainder of his tea-cake
at this, remembering his recent highly undiplomatic remarks to Gerard.

'I hardly think that can be true. I'm sure he values my
skills with the pen and with numbers much more. I leave
the diplomacy to him.'

Trish, watching him talk to Lucy, was wishing that she
had been fortunate enough to sit by him. Instead, she was
lumbered with Harry, who had become a bit of a bore
lately, what with wanting to marry her and being determined to believe that if he pestered her long enough she
would give in through sheer exhaustion.

She could scarcely bellow across the room at Allen to attract his attention. She wondered what he and Lucy were finding to talk about so animatedly. At one point Lucy grabbed a plate of fancy cakes from a passing footman in order to offer him one, which he took with a slight smile.

That smile, offered to someone else, caused such a fierce pang in Trish's breast that she almost felt faint. And then he looked across at her, when Lucy turned to speak to the man on her other side, and, unable to prevent himself, gave her one of his sweet, slow smiles—which Harry intercepted.

He was not a man often given to insights of any kind, but he was a man in love and he immediately interpreted the smile correctly.

So that solemn lump was the fellow whom Trish preferred to himself! Sir Gerard Schuyler's secretary, no less. Well, you could scarcely get less than that, could you?

Allen was released from what he was beginning to think was an odd sort of bondage by Gerard's return. He rose and, bowing to Torry, murmured, 'I am sure that you will allow me to resume my duties.'

'By all means, Mr Marriott. Gerard can be your able deputy here.'

Although some of the company laughed at this quip Allen was not sure that Gerard appreciated it. He said, when Allen passed him on the way to the door, 'I'll have a word with you later, Marriott. Something rather odd has come up.'

The other odd thing being me coming down to the drawing room, Allen said to himself as he mounted the stairs. Nice to see Trish in her glory, even if I couldn't speak to her. I wonder, however, if that shrewd piece Lucy Chalfont twigged that I am her secret friend, and, if she did, will she be able to hold her tongue? He did not worry about Harry

Norman having discovered their secret because he was unaware that, for once, he had given away his inmost feelings.

Torry Schuyler was bearded by Mrs Chalfont before she
left.

'I'm not reproaching her in any way,' she said confidentially, 'but I'm very sorry that Trish seems to have little
time for Lucy these days. She was always coming over to
spend the day or the afternoon with her, and she's such a
good influence on my girl, who is a little wild. Lately,
though, we've seen nothing of her. I can only suppose that
she has found another friend.'

Torry gave no indication that this was news to her. She
had been under the impression that Trish was spending at
least one day a week with Lucy—or so she had said. If she
were not with Lucy—then where was she? Something,
some nuance of behaviour which had struck her over the
last few weeks, offered her a hint of what might be happening.

Aloud she said, 'I'll have a word with Trish. Give her a
hint that Lucy might like a visit.'

And I might try to find out what Trish is up to!

Harry, on the contrary, wasted no time in hinting to Trish
what was troubling him about her behaviour. He had asked
for her to escort him to the door whilst his mama stayed
behind for a short private talk with Torry and twitted her
about Allen Marriott before he left.

'I never thought you'd develop a pash for such a solemn
lump as Sir Gerard's secretary,' he grumbled at her. 'He *is*
your mysterious lover, isn't he?'

Trish stared at him, aghast. However had he managed to
guess her secret? She had no wish to lie to him—indeed,
she replied hotly without thinking first, 'Allen's not a solemn lump, by no means. It's just that as Sir Gerard's secretary he has to obey the forms.'

'Well, he doesn't ''obey the forms'' by making up to

you and encouraging you to meet him in secret. Perhaps I should have called him a sly lump! Just remember that I can make you Lady Norman one day—he can't.'

Now this was unworthy of Harry, and he knew it. If Trish's secret lover had turned out to be a poor gentleman of title he would not have felt quite so demeaned, but to learn that she preferred a mere pen-pusher to him, Harry Norman, the heir to a baronetcy, was too much for him to stomach.

Trish almost told him as much, but managed to hold her tongue, saying only, 'I don't want to quarrel with you, Harry. I might remind you, though, that I never deceived you in any way. I told you that I already cared for someone else and I thought that you did, too, or I would never have agreed to your scheme. Perhaps we ought to call it off.'

'No, never!' he exclaimed. 'Certainly not. For one thing I hope to change your mind, and for another it would upset my mother—she approves of you greatly, you know, thinks that you are just the thing.'

'But it's not your mother I'm marrying,' said Trish reasonably. 'And I'm sure that there are lots of girls besides me who are just the thing.'

'Mother doesn't think that,' said Harry gloomily. 'She has this bee in her bonnet about the end of the century ruining everything. She thinks that's why most girls are so fast these days and would make unsuitable wives.'

'Well, she'd think me fast if she knew about Allen Marriott, wouldn't she? So you see I'm far from being just the thing, after all.'

There were occasions when Harry thought that perhaps Trish was a little too clever for him, and this was one of them. She had such a terrible way with words—and come to think of it that awful bounder Marriott was just the same, prosing on about how people might speak in the future.

Perhaps that was why she liked him. Harry found words difficult, and was just bright enough to know that he did.

His mother's arrival ended that little conversation. Her adieux made to Trish, she said to Harry once they were safely on the way home in the carriage, 'My little chat with Lady Schuyler was to the purpose that you should ask Sir Gerard if you might speak to Patricia with a view to proposing to her. If she knew that Sir Gerard blessed your suit, she might well be eager to marry you. At present I think that it is only proper maidenly shyness which is holding her back.'

Trish's proper maidenly shyness! What a joke, Harry mourned, when all the time she was meeting that fortune-hunter Marriott on the sly. How little his mother knew of her. For the first time Harry asked himself whether his mother's view of herself as worldly-wise and shrewd was actually a true one if she could be so wrong about Trish.

Lucy's farewells to Trish were equally frank. 'Allen Marriott's your young man, is it? One of the quiet kind with hidden depths, I suspect. I might have known that you wouldn't have chosen anyone ordinary. Don't worry, I shan't say a word to anyone, but you must know how the fur and the feathers will fly when your guardians discover what you are up to. Sooner or later they're bound to, you know. For a start you probably aren't deceiving the servants.'

'Apparently we're not deceiving anyone except my guardians,' returned Trish dryly. 'We might as well hire a sandwich-board man to parade the streets with notices saying, "Trish Courtney and Allen Marriott are meeting secretly—watch out for further news!" That would set the world alight.'

'Oh, you can joke about it...' said Lucy, soberly for her. 'But it isn't a joke, you know.'

It wasn't, and Trish wasn't as brave as she sounded, but

there was no profit in being miserable about her dilemma, so she might as well be cheerful. What worried her was that Allen had so much more to lose than she had if their conspiracy was discovered. In that she was wrong, but, not knowing his changed situation, she was right to worry about him.

One further thing troubled her. It would be difficult for her to join him on his day off for the next few weeks since Lucy and her parents were about to visit Richmond to stay with Lucy's rich maiden aunt, who had a villa there. Now, alas, she had to think up a new excuse to meet him. On top of that the season was growing busier, and Sir Gerard and Torry would expect her to be present at all the major events where she might encounter eligible young men of good family.

But I only want an ineligible young man, she told herself sadly, and what is worse it is growing harder and harder for me to be with him and for us not to... Here she found herself in difficulties, for her imagination would only take her as far as having Allen's arms around her, and him kissing her fervently. She was reasonably sure that there was more to making love than that, and the mere thought of exploring this new country was beginning to excite her.

Like Mr Nance, she was beginning to wonder where Allen got his iron self-control from. One day, when she knew him even better than she already did, she would ask him whether it had been such sweet torture for him as for her—she suspected that it was.

She was not wrong. Allen, alone in the study, working rapidly and waiting for Gerard to return, was asking himself the same question. His father had introduced him to a famous New York courtesan when he was sixteen years old and had told her 'to blood the boy.' Allen would never forget the six weeks which had followed. Weeks which had revealed to him the depths of passion of which he was capable. Deep enough for it to have begun to frighten him.

He had known that his father was a spendthrift, a drunkard, a sadistic bully and a gambler. Then, from what the courtesan had told him during that brief interlude, he became aware that he was also a roué. He had already despised his father for his cruelty towards himself and his mother, and, young though he was, had determined that he would never be like him in any way. As a result his father had despised *him*, shouting during one beating that Allen was more like the cold-blooded, tight-fisted Schuylers than was decent.

Just before his father's death he had become engaged to a pretty young woman whom he'd thought loved him as he'd thought that he loved her.

He had been wrong on both counts. She had thrown him over without a qualm as soon as she and her family had discovered that he was ruined. What had saddened and surprised him was how little it had hurt him. Alone in the world after his father's death, he had engaged in a few brief liaisons, but he had never found anyone whom he had thought he would like to marry—even if he could have afforded to. He had even begun to wonder whether he was cold: whether what he had experienced with the courtesan was an aberration, something which would never recur.

And then he had met Trish—and his whole world had changed. The passion which he thought that he had lost, or that he had never truly possessed, had come surging back. It was as sweet, and, because of his previous experience, it was even more demanding than that which Trish felt for him. Only his self-control, which had been honed by his years of servitude, kept him from taking advantage of her charming innocence.

Gerard's entrance broke a concentration which Allen was finding it difficult to maintain. His cousin's first words were not promising. 'What the devil have you been saying or doing to make my wife so partial to you, Marriott?'

His tone was not unkind: rather it was curious. Stifling an inward grin that he should have caused Gerard to think about him at all, Allen said in his coolest office voice, 'I really can't answer that, sir. I was quite unaware that I have ever spoken to Lady Schuyler in a manner different from the one in which I speak to everyone else.'

Gerard gave a short laugh. 'You should go on the stage, Marriott. There must be a living there for someone who could play the butler, secretary or servant whose calm manner is exactly the same to everyone at all times—a talent which you appear to have mastered. I have to admit that there are times when it annoys me. That was why I was curious when I discovered that Lady Schuyler appears to have some kind of strange admiration for you.'

'Women's intuition?' offered Allen, after a short pause in which he debated with himself whether to say anything at all.

'In that case I should like to know just what it is that she is intuiting! No, don't answer me. Just bend *your* intuition—which I have come to respect—to something which Tom Moidore rang me about earlier this afternoon. It appears that some rather unpleasant rumours about my past and my honesty when I lived in the States have begun to circulate about London society and the City. They could be exceedingly damaging, even though there is not a word of truth in them. As yet, they have not become widespread. It is also, however, not the only problem I am faced with. My treasurer informs me that his latest audit shows that large sums of Schuyler money have gone astray in the past few years.

'In other words embezzlement on a massive scale has been occurring. Now, since all authority for the transfer of money rests with me and my signature, this is a matter which I cannot take lightly.'

He stopped pacing around the room—a habit of his when perturbed or concentrating—and fixed Allen with a hard stare. 'Any ideas, Marriott? Have you come across anything which might throw light on either of these disturbing matters?'

What to reply? I think that I have found something odd in your accounts, but it is difficult to say what, and it would throw doubt on the honesty of an ex-employee whom you valued highly?

Allen hesitated before answering Gerard. 'Do you have an obvious enemy who might profit from the circulation of such rumours—and if they were to be believed could their existence damage—or prevent—your future investments in the United Kingdom?'

'Of course I have enemies—who in my position does not? And certainly my investments and my interests here could be affected. As to which of my rivals might be responsible—who knows? I might ask you if you have heard anything suspicious, but since you appear to live like a hermit, I doubt whether you have.'

'Does that mean that you would prefer me not to live like a hermit, sir?'

Now this was not only impertinent but risky, given his cousin's known temper.

Gerard gave a harsh laugh. 'That was not in character, Marriott, not at all. Your choice, always yours, what you do when off duty. You have no more ideas to offer?'

'For the moment, sir, no. And I have taken due note of your remark about my off-duty hours. It is quite a relief to know that I might do as I please.'

He was risk-taking again, but baiting the bear who was his cousin was a challenge which he could not resist.

Gerard's stare at him told Allen that he was not quite

sure how to take his last sentence. Delivered in his usual
flat tone of voice it could be taken either as humble agreement with a superior—or as mockery. To a man who was
usually ferociously forthright in his dealings with others,
and expected others to be equally so with him, the Mach-
iavellian subtlety which Allen had perfected over the last
nine years was something which he found difficult to deal
with.

He gave a grunt which might have meant anything, and
which would have earned him a rebuke from Torry had she
been present, before adding, 'Your humility is slipping,
Marriott. I have taken due note of what you have just said.'

'Thank you, sir.'

Gerard restrained himself by not retorting, What the devil
for? and somewhat ruefully retired from the field, silently
admitting that this was the second time his cousin had out-
smarted him in the game of wits and words. He was beginning to grasp that he had underestimated Allen even
more than he might have thought. He told himself that once
these wretched problems of which Tom Moidore and his
auditor had informed him were safely over and done with,
he ought to find him something to do which was more
worthy of the sharp intellect which he was beginning to
reveal. An intellect which he had concealed beneath a veil
of humility.

What was more, he might also take the time to ask himself why his cousin should suddenly begin to reveal it at
all!

In a well-appointed room, in a house as palatial as Gerard's, another man was making a similar judgement about
Allen Marriott. Facing him were Mr Robert Hall and an
ex-policeman who had been dismissed for corruption and
who now sold his services to those who needed secret and
illegal business done for them.

'I commend you,' he said, addressing Hall, 'for paying the butler to keep a watch on him and report to no one but you—with what results?'

'He discovered that Marriott was repeatedly visiting the watchmaker Nance, with whom he used to lodge, and that on his full day off he was clandestinely meeting Miss Patricia Courtney there, although he had been ordered by Sir Gerard to have nothing to do with her. We can only conclude that he either intends to seduce her, or to acquire her fortune by marriage.'

'Good, very good. I trust that you have told the butler to keep this information to himself unless we give him leave to inform Sir Gerard?'

'His pay from me was conditional on that, sir.'

'Good, very good again. Now, what of the other business—did you find anything which might lead you to believe that he has discovered any of our—shall we say—business, since he became Sir Gerard's secretary?'

Hall hesitated before replying. 'I discovered nothing substantive, sir, which might prove that—except that when I examined the files on his desk those which might alert him to anything odd were missing. His manner to me was short, as well, but I gather that he is a man of few words with everyone.

'I also discovered, on a visit to Schuyler's head office, that he is regarded as something of a mathematical freak who was far too good for the job he was paid for. More than that, neither the staff at Schuyler's, nor Sir Gerard himself, know that he is a member of the British Horological Institute, where he is highly valued for his maths and his knowledge of clocks and clockmaking and is due to give a paper to the members later this month—an honour not conferred on many, I understand.'

'You are sure that Sir Gerard knows nothing of this?'

'Quite sure.'

'A devious gentleman, Mr Allen Marriott, then, and a clever one. Something which you think Sir Gerard might not know?'

'I am sure of that, too.'

'Better and better.' He fell silent for a moment.

'Norris,' he said abruptly, turning to the ex-policeman, 'I want you to keep an eye on Marriott for me, and report on all his doings.'

He turned back to Hall again. 'In retrospect I think it was a mistake for you to retire from Sir Gerard's employment, although our enterprise was successfully over and I approved at the time. What made you suspicious of Marriott?'

'First of all I assumed—wrongly, I now know—that anyone who was likely to replace me would be a mere penpusher with no other abilities, and then, talking to a friend who works at Rothschild's, I discovered that they wished to employ Marriott. They had found out from work he had done for them when they were on a joint enterprise with Schuyler's that he had a nose for fraud and that Schuyler's was unaware of this. Rothschild's offered him far more than he was being paid at Schuyler's to work for them, but he turned them down.'

'That, in itself, is odd.'

'I agree—unless he thought it might interfere with his relationship with Nance.'

'The butler says that Sir Gerard is always short with Marriott—something else which is odd. Schuyler has many faults, but he has always been courteous to those who work for him.'

'As you well know,' smiled his interlocutor. 'You are not to worry, Hall. I have a plan to dispose of Mr Marriott which you and Norris here will help me to carry out. Until then go about your business as usual and do nothing to arouse suspicion. Marriott may know nothing, but we dare not take any risks.'

After Hall and Norris had gone their master thought that it was fortunate that he would be dining with Sir Gerard Schuyler and his wife in the near future and might be lucky enough to meet this strange young man. Hall had earlier told him that he was a Yankee, and he would employ the Pinkerton Detective Agency in America to try to find out who he was and where he came from.

Chapter Eight

'Oh, Allen, there's nothing better than a fine day on the Thames, is there—with a blue sky and a slight breeze to make it perfect?'

Trish and Allen were on their way to Greenwich by steamer. It would be their last day together for some time and they were determined to make the most of it. They were unaware that they were being watched.

'I have been longing to take you to Greenwich to see the Royal Observatory and the Park,' he had said shortly after she had arrived at Mr Nance's shop that morning. 'You told me recently that you had become fascinated by time, and by the importance of clocks in our lives, so I am taking you at your word. We shall have a jolly trip downriver to the pier at Greenwich Reach, which is not very far from the Observatory. It's the home of time: the place where the world's time is regularised.'

'It's strange, isn't it,' Trish had remarked, 'that the end of the century is making us keep thinking about time. Once again the guests at Sir Gerard's dinner party last night were talking as though living in a new century must mean that everything will have a new beginning and all our problems will be solved.

'I can't believe that January the first, 1900, will be very different from December the thirty-first, 1899—and I can't imagine why everything should change once midnight has chimed.'

'To some extent all dates are imaginary,' Allen had replied. 'Every race and every religion has a different set of dates and times and supposes that everyone else's are incorrect and that theirs is the only true one. On the other hand we do need to agree to the same standard of time around the world if ships and trains and times of the delivery of goods—or people, for that matter—are to run efficiently. That is why the meridian and Greenwich Mean Time are important.'

One nice thing about Allen was that he never patronised her. He had never said to her what one young man had come out with when she had asked him a question about what made motor cars run—'Sweet Trish, don't trouble your pretty little head about that. Girls ride in cars; they don't need to know about their innards.'

Allen had recently shown her a clock's innards, and given her a little talk about how they made it work. Also, once they had boarded the steamer he pointed out to her all the interesting places which they were passing, telling her the names and history of the different docks and waving a hand towards Deptford, where Christopher Marlowe, the poet and dramatist, had been killed in a tavern brawl.

'The Thames along this stretch isn't pretty,' he said, 'it's a place of work, the hub of the world's trade. All the riches from the Indies and the East arrive here—to say nothing of what comes from America now.'

Some of the passengers looked curiously at the pretty girl and her escort who were enjoying their day on the river. The wind grew a little stronger and Trish had to hold her big straw hat on.

'If it blows any harder,' she said, 'I shall take it off and

hang etiquette. I've left my gloves off, and if I'm not careful I shall be eating in the street next.'

'Oh, do!' exclaimed Allen. 'On our way back we can
leave the steamer at one of the stops, to find a place to eat
whelks, cockles and oysters and drink half a pint of porter—a true East End treat. Jellied eels might be on the
menu, too.'

Trish gave a little skip on hearing this. 'I was once told
that you eat cockles with a pin. Is that true?'

'It's the only way to eat them,' Allen assured her. 'And
you'd better give me your gloves. I'll put them in my
pocket; you might lose them otherwise.'

Years later Trish would remember everything about that
happy day. They went ashore by the pier at Greenwich
Reach and strolled along King William's Walk towards
Greenwich Park, where the Royal Naval College stood in
all its eighteenth-century glory, golden in the morning sun-
shine. The Royal Observatory was proud on a hill high
above them.

A number of well-dressed people, together with a sprin-
kling of ragamuffins running about and shouting, were enjoying the splendours of the summer's day.

'That's Flamsteed House,' Allen told her, pointing to the
Observatory. 'It was designed by Sir Christopher Wren especially for the first Astronomer Royal, John Flamsteed,
who was appointed by King Charles II to make observa-
tions which would help to make safe navigation possible
when ships were out of sight of the land. To do that it was
necessary to make an accurate map of the stars—which was
why it was put high on a hill above the smoke of London.'

Trish gazed in admiration at the beautiful mellow brick
building and its central octagon with a tall window in each
wall which Wren had designed to allow the astronomers to
observe every part of the heavens. Above one of the domed
towers which surmounted the octagon was what looked to

be a flag-staff, except that it flew no flag. Instead, at the staff's base was a large round ball. Above that was a cross-bar.

'Whatever is that?' she asked, pointing at the ball.

'That's the Time Ball,' he told her. 'At five minutes to one o'clock it rises halfway up the pole, three minutes later it rises to the top, and then, exactly at one of the clock, it drops down again. The master of every ship leaving the docks on the Isle of Dogs opposite to Greenwich then sets the ship's chronometer by it. Later, when he is out at sea, he can use it to calculate longitude exactly.'

'But why is that important?' Trish asked.

'Because only then can a ship avoid running ashore, or on sandbanks, or pile up on the rocks with fatal results. The most famous disaster occurred in 1707, when Admiral Sir Cloudesley Shovell, three ships and two thousand men ran aground and perished in a storm. One of the consequences of that was that a prize was offered to anyone who could make a device from which longitude could be calculated at sea—a prize which a clockmaker called John Harrison won. He is one of Mr Nance's heroes. He says that there should be a statue of him in Trafalgar Square alongside Nelson's. Nelson saved the nation from being invaded in 1805 and Harrison saved the lives of a great many sailors—but no one knows about him, more's the pity.'

'Is anyone inventing anything as important as that now?'

'Oh, yes. Electricity changed everything recently, and I'm sure that there will be even more changes in the future.'

'And have you seen Harrison's clock?'

Allen shook his head. 'I'm afraid not. I've seen drawings of it, of course. When we reach the Observatory I shall have a suggestion to make to you—but that can wait. We shan't be able to go in to the Observatory. Entrance is at the invitation of the Astronomer Royal, and I'm nowhere near being important enough to be honoured by him.'

They walked through the park along the avenue leading to the bottom of the hill, which they mounted, rapidly at first and then more slowly when the hill grew steeper as they neared the top.

Three-quarters of the way up Allen suggested that they stop for a moment, rest on a bench and admire the view of the Thames and the City which lay far below them. Or rather Trish admired that view: the view which Allen was admiring was Trish herself, violet eyes glowing, lips parted a little, her cheeks rosy with the effort of walking up the hill in her fashionably long draped skirts which trailed along the ground.

'Thank goodness that bustles have gone out of favour,' Trish told him. 'Imagine having to drag that up the hill behind one! You know,' she added thoughtfully, looking at him, 'although I think women's clothes make it difficult to take any exercise, I don't think men's are much better. It may be *de rigeur* for you to have to wear a frock coat in the morning, but on a day like this it must be most uncomfortable.'

'Most,' agreed Allen. 'I'd be better off in rolled-up shirt-sleeves, but imagine the furor that would cause! I should most likely be locked up for disturbing the peace by being dressed in an immoral fashion while escorting a young society lady in a public place.'

This came out in his best mock-pompous fashion, which was only a slight exaggeration of the manner which he adopted with Gerard. It set Trish laughing, and in this happy and relaxed mood they made light of the rest of the hill and rapidly reached the gates of the Royal Observatory and the cobbled courtyard which stood before it.

By the gate was a large twenty-four-hour clock—something which Trish had not seen before. Allen had taught her to find beauty in clocks, and this clock, while not exactly beautiful, was certainly interesting, with the roman figures of twelve at the bottom of the dial and of twenty-four at the top.

'Did you bring your pendant watch and its little key along with you, as I suggested?' Allen asked her.

'Of course,' Trish told him with a merry face. 'The master commands and the slave obeys—just like the clocks!'

'Minx,' he said, and leaning over he kissed her on the cheek. 'Now, when twelve o'clock approaches slip your watch off, take out the key and the moment that the hand of the clock reaches twelve at the bottom of the dial where six normally is, correct your watch by it and the perfection of Mr Charles Shepherd's handiwork will mean that your watch is, for that moment at least, absolutely accurate.'

They had ten minutes to wait, so first Allen showed her the spot through which the prime meridian passed, and which since 1851 had determined the basis of calculation of the world's time. After that they admired an even better view of the river and the City than the one they had seen on the way up the hill.

The river was full of shipping. It was one of London's most busy highways, Allen told her. 'In the old days, before roads were improved, it was the main one. Kings and queens were rowed up and down the river. Henry VIII had a palace here, and like some of our other kings he visited Greenwich often in order to escape the smoke and unpleasant smells with which London was afflicted.'

'Several hundred years later we come here by steamer—and the smoke and the smells are no better!'

Back at the clock, ready for midday to arrive, Trish held her watch at the ready and obeyed Allen's whispered instructions. A pair of portly gentlemen were also inspecting their gold hunters for the same purpose.

'Why don't you set your watch now?' Trish's voice was almost accusing.

'Because I thought that we could have two experiences

here, not one. I shall set my watch by the Time Ball at one o'clock.'

Trish's cheeky answer to that set several of the spectators laughing. 'But you're not the master of a ship about to sail to the Indies, are you?'

'One o'clock is the same time for me as for him,' Allen retorted grandly, 'even if I'm not standing on the deck of a steamer.'

Nothing daunted, Trish twitted him again. 'Oh, you always have an answer for everything. My old nurse used to say, "Don't be so sharp or one day you'll cut yourself."'

'Not with my watch, I won't!'

They laughed together. One of their hearers snorted contemptuously at their obvious pleasure in each other and the day, but most of them smiled encouragingly at the handsome pair.

'We'll take a little walk around the building while we wait for one o'clock,' Allen suggested. 'If you've still an appetite for walking, that is.'

'Always,' said Trish. 'Although I've been asking my guardian if I can buy a bicycle. Lots of girls I know ride bicycles. Lucy Chalfont for one.'

'By the sound of her Lucy Chalfont has everything new and daring.'

'True,' agreed Trish. 'Until I told her about us and our secret she thought I was a real old stick-in-the-mud.'

'But not now?'

'No, not now. She's quite jealous—especially after she saw you that day she came to tea with her mama.'

They were still laughing about Lucy when a young man, flashily dressed, wearing a curly-brimmed bowler hat and carrying a silver-topped cane, stared at the pair of them before saying familiarly to Allen, 'Well, if it ain't you, Marriott, got up like the dog's dinner! Got a girlfriend now, have you? Thought what with one thing and another you was always too busy to have one.'

'You wrong me, Parker,' said Allen gravely. 'I have the honour to present to you a good friend of mine, Miss Patricia Courtney, who I am showing the sights of Greenwich. Miss Courtney, this is an old friend of mine, Justus Parker.'

'And who better than you to show her Greenwich, eh, Marriott?' said Mr Parker, staring even harder at Trish. 'S'pose you know, Miss Courtney, that Marriott here is that rare bird, a gentleman amateur who knows as much, if not more, than the professionals. Old Nance got a real bonus when you walked into his shop, eh?'

Trish had already gathered by his clothes, his manner and his speech that Mr Parker had nothing to do with the high society of which she was a part. Allen confirmed this by saying, 'Mr Parker is Asprey's chief horologist and has forgotten more about clocks and watches than I have ever known.'

'Up to a point, old chap, up to a point. I'm not the high-flyer you are, by no means. I s'pose you know, Miss Courtney, that Marriott is going to present a paper to the British Horological Institute. All about the future: can't wait to hear it.'

Trish turned to Allen, who had begun to say, 'Come now, Parker, my paper is purely speculative...'

'Is this true?' she asked him. 'That you are to give a paper?'

'Well, yes.'

It was the first time that she had ever seen him awkward or embarrassed.

'Have you told Sir Gerard?'

'Emphatically, no. It is none of his business what I do in my spare time.'

Trish nodded. She had known what a secret person Allen was, hiding his talents from all the world—except perhaps

herself—ever since he had asked her to say nothing about
his heroic conduct at the railway accident. Not for the first
time she wondered what lay behind his decision to hold
himself aloof from Gerard, given that his heroism and his
mathematical prowess, to say nothing of his mastery of
horology, could—if revealed to Gerard—have brought him
nothing but honour and praise.

Allen gained unexpected support from young Mr Parker.
'Quite right, too,' he said emphatically. 'Never let the
bosses know too much about you, eh, Marriott. Still clerk-
ing for that Yankee bigwig, are you?'

'In a manner of speaking,' Allen admitted.

'It'll all change in the new century,' Mr Parker declared
confidently. 'We shall become more like you Yankees, with
very little difference between master and man. For my part
I can't wait to see it. Peace and plenty, they say, as well.
Peace and plenty in the twentieth century—no more wars.'

'So they say.' Allen's response was a dry one. He wasn't
prepared to shake young Mr Parker's confidence in the future, particularly when everyone else seemed to share it!

'Mustn't bore Miss Courtney, though,' Parker offered.
'Waiting to see the Time Ball drop, are you?'

'Oh, you're not boring me,' Trish told him cheerfully.
'I'm not one of those young ladies whose only interests in
life are small talk, playing the piano badly and doing a great
deal of ugly embroidery. I must admit that until I met Allen
I'd never thought of clocks being interesting, but the more
I learn about them the more I wish that young ladies were
encouraged to know something about the practical side of
life.'

'Oh, I can see that you've netted yourself a New Woman,
Marriott! Better watch her or she'll be fastening herself to
the railings of Greenwich Park or trying to storm the Royal
Observatory itself.'

'Oh, I doubt that. I really do, Parker. From all I know

of her Miss Courtney has a lot more sense than to behave like that.'

'So you say now, old fellow, so you say now. But we all know that marriage is quite a different thing from courting.'

He pulled out his watch. 'Mustn't rant on, though. The Time Ball is due to fall any moment now.'

They all turned towards the domed tower where the Time Ball was just beginning to climb up its pole. Allen fetched out his watch, which did not need a key but had a button on its top. Time slowed while they waited for the Ball, which was now at its highest point, to fall again. When it did the watching spectators gave a loud hurrah.

'That's it, then,' said Mr Parker cheerfully, putting away his adjusted watch. 'Nice to have met you, Miss Courtney. Must leave you, though. Two's company, three's none, eh, Marriott?' And he gave Allen a great nudge and a wink.

'Very true,' responded Allen, as though young Mr Parker had said something very wise and witty. Mr Parker responded by waving his stick at them and walking away.

'What a cheerful young man,' Trish said.

'And a hard-working one,' Allen told her. 'Don't be put off by his airy manner. He's ambitious, is young Mr Parker.'

'And are you ambitious, young Mr Marriott?' Trish quizzed him.

'More than you might think, young Miss Courtney. More than you might think.'

'And more than almost middle-aged Sir Gerard Schuyler thinks,' retorted Trish. 'What do we do now?'

'I suggest that we walk down into Greenwich for lunch. We can try to find a restaurant, or even a barrow which sells shellfish so that you can enjoy the delights of mussels, winkles and cockles.'

Allen took her hand in his. 'But first I think we'll look

for a shady place where we can sit down away from other people and have a little rest. Come.' And he walked her down the hill after they had both taken one last long look at Flamsteed House and the Time Ball high above it.

Halfway down the hill Allen led her off the path towards a small stand of distant trees. Beneath them was one of the few benches in the park. On the way there they passed young couples, dressed in their holiday clothing, lying side by side on the grass, their arms around one another.

Would Allen ask her to lie beside him on the grass? If he did would she agree? Surely not, must be the answer to both questions! The mere thought excited Trish, though, and when, once they were almost alone, he lifted her hand to his lips and kissed the back of it very gently, the shivering sensation of delight which passed over her was strong enough to make her fear—if that were the right word—that she could deny him nothing.

If Allen noticed the shiver he said nothing—but he thought a great deal. He already knew how strongly Trish was attracted to him—as he was to her—and had told himself sternly that he must go carefully with the innocent creature which she undoubtedly was.

On the other hand he also believed that she was more than ready for a most important question, and after that for some gentle lovemaking, and where better than here, alone, in the shade of the trees, with the Observatory high above them and the River Thames taking its blue-grey way in the valley below? Here Time was their friend and ally, not the enemy it could be at Park Lane, where every moment they might spend together was perforce a snatched one.

To begin with they admired the splendid view, and Allen quoted Spenser, '"Sweet Thames, run softly, till I end my Song..."'

'Poetry as well as clocks,' marvelled Trish. 'I would

never have had such an interesting time if I had been out with Harry. He talks a lot, but he doesn't say very much.'

Allen laughed at this joke for a moment, before his whole manner changed and his face assumed the gravity with which Gerard had become familiar.

'My darling,' he said, taking her right hand in his, 'before we go any further there is something important that I must say to you. I love you very much and I believe that you love me, so will you marry me?'

Trish closed her eyes before she murmured, her voice shaking with emotion, 'You know I will, Allen, but what will Gerard say?'

'I have to admit that that is a problem for us. Since our worldly situation is unequal I am bound to be branded a fortune-hunter until I am able to offer you more than I can at present. I must therefore ask you another question: will you wait for me? I know that I am expecting a great deal from you by demanding such a thing, but you know how matters stand.'

'I will wait for you forever, Allen, you know that.'

'Then I am doubly blessed, and would wish to bless you,' he said humbly, raising her hand to his lips again, this time to kiss her palm not once but several times, before trailing tiny butterfly kisses on to her wrist and then up her bare arm to the elbow, where her silken sleeve began.

Trish looked down at his dark bent head, rapt, scarcely breathing, enjoying once more the state of delight which the mere touch of his mouth brought her. She gave a long shuddering sigh when he stopped, lifted his head, looked into her eyes and asked, his voice as soft as he could make it, 'Did you like that?'

'Oh, yes,' she breathed.

'Good.' And taking her in his arms he drew her gently towards him, saying, 'Then perhaps you might like this,' before kissing her on the mouth.

Again the kiss was as gentle as he could make it, although merely to hold her close to him with her soft breasts against his hard chest, and the sweet scent of her strong in his nostrils, roused him immediately.

Allen drew a deep breath, for he must not frighten her. He must subdue his rising desire to crush her to him, to make her his, to act in lust but not in love. Every instinct which he possessed told him that seduction would be easy, for by all her bodily signs she was as roused as he was.

After their long kiss he opened his eyes to find her face flushed, her mouth a swollen rosebud, the pupils of her eyes dilated, large and black surrounded by violet, and knew that she would offer him no resistance, nay, would willingly cooperate with him.

He must not yield to temptation after he had proposed marriage to her. To violate her innocence, however much she might wish him to, would be to degrade her. It might at the worst expose her to the world's contempt if the inevitable end of their loving should occur and she conceived a child. Not only would seducing her be the act of a careless cad, but it would also justify every contemptuous thought which Gerard Schuyler had ever had about him. His own honour demanded that he should restrain himself lest he destroy hers.

He lifted himself away from her a little, only to find that, having opened her eyes, she leaned forward to take his face in her hands and kiss him on the mouth as gently as he had kissed her. Allen could not prevent himself from responding to her initiative. It was so typical of her.

The kiss lengthened and deepened until she drew away from him, looked earnestly into his eyes, and said, artlessly, he was sure, 'I shouldn't have done that, should I? It was very forward of me. My mother always said men don't like forward girls.'

What could he say to her? That many men liked forward

girls? That he loved her regardless of whether she was forward or not? Or even, My dearest love, I don't think that
you have the remotest notion of how a truly forward girl
behaves.

Instead he said, 'My dearest love, I certainly don't think
you forward. What I do think is that I want to make gentle
love to you, and if you make it back to me, as you have
just done, I like that, too.'

Trish's eyes glowed; indeed, her whole face glowed.
'Yes, please,' she offered to both his statements.

'Oh, Allen,' she continued, a mixture of love and des-
peration in her voice, 'do other people feel like this? That
they want to be one with the other? Oh, I know that we
can't be out here, and I'm not even sure what being one
with another means. I only know that I love you and want
to be with you always, and I can only hope that it won't
be long before we can marry.'

'And I hope that as well,' he agreed. 'But we must be
good as well as patient, although God knows it will be very
hard for both of us. I wish most desperately to marry you,
but until we are able to marry we may only be gentle with
one another, like this.' And he kissed her again.

This time it was the hollow of her throat which he celebrated, the tender mauve of it in the shade of the trees.
She shuddered again, and the shudder alone roused him
even more. Allen shook his head, and said hoarsely, 'I wonder if you would like being stroked,' and ran his hands
gently up the sides of her neck until he reached her face,
where he held her head gently between his hands and kissed
her again.

For some moments they kissed and stroked one another's
face, neck, arms and hands. Allen could not resist putting
his hands around Trish's tiny waist and then running them
up, up to her shoulders, gently flicking the silk over her
small round breasts on the way. This produced even further

shudders from Trish, and a gasping moan which excited Allen even further: to the degree that he drew back immediately lest he lose his fragile self-control.

Trish looked at him with huge blind eyes.

Allen gasped, 'Enough for now,' and kissed her chastely on the brow.

'Yes,' breathed Trish, but she hardly knew what she was saying. She took his large right hand in her two small ones and they sat side by side, saying nothing until Allen, who had now cooled down, said 'Time to go, I think.'

Like Adam and Eve leaving Eden at the end of Milton's great epic poem, Allen and Trish felt that they were abandoning Paradise for the mundane world outside. Time had stopped for them—but was running again, faster than ever.

'I feel hungry,' announced Trish, 'for the first time in weeks.'

Allen's hunger was of quite a different nature, but he did not say so. Instead he came out with, 'We'll cure that when we reach Greenwich.'

They did. Allen found not a barrow but a little eating house with lace-curtained windows where he introduced Trish to the delights of the shellfish which ordinary Londoners took for granted.

The café's owner, a large woman with a jolly face, made a fuss of them. She fed them oysters, mussels, cockles and winkles together with a large wooden platter of bread and a dish of butter. As promised, Allen ordered porter for them to go with their second course of jellied eels. Trish daintily drank a small amount of it from a large tankard.

'Well?' queried Allen, his face amused.

'Not as horrid as I thought that it might be,' conceded Trish. 'I think that I might even manage a little more.'

'Good girl!' he said, drinking down his own porter, thinking again how different she was from some of the finicky society women he had seen in Park Lane—and how much he loved her because she was.

It was when they left the café that he had the strongest impression that he was being watched: strong enough that he looked around him, but among the crowd of people filling the pavement he could see no one who looked at all suspicious.

He laughed at himself a little for imagining that a clandestine watcher might wear a placard announcing what he was doing. It was no laughing matter if he were being watched. This was the second time in the week that he had had the impression of unknown eyes boring into his back, and it was not a pleasant one. He said nothing to Trish, and when they travelled back on the steamer towards Central London, and the stand where Trish would take a cab back to Park Lane, he put his right arm around her shoulders as they stood by the rail and defied the gods to harm them.

The gods were kind to them both on the journey home, and when she left him he watched her go, longing for the day to come when they would not need to part when it ended.

Her face glowing with the memory of those few brief, but glorious moments when Allen had put his arms around her and made gentle love to her, Trish encountered Torry Schuyler in the entrance hall at Park Lane.

'You and Lucy have enjoyed yourselves today, I see,' remarked Torry.

This was the one result of her secret life with Allen which Trish most disliked: lying by implication to someone who had always been kind to her. She said nothing more than an appreciative and breathless, 'Oh, yes.' A brief sentence which, of itself, was the truth—but a truth designed to deceive.

Torry, who knew perfectly well that Trish had not been

with Lucy, said cheerfully, determined not to give away her own secret knowledge yet, 'I would be grateful if you could see your way to a rapid change of clothing and come down to tea. I have just been informed that Lady Norman has arrived and is in the green drawing room—Harry is apparently closeted with Gerard.

'I could do with your moral support if nothing else.'

'Of course. I will be as quick as I can.'

Ringing for her maid, having her hair brushed, and changing into a filmy tea gown whose pinks and mauves complemented her violet eyes left no time for Trish to sit and savour her memories of her trip to Greenwich Observatory. She was a little puzzled as to why Torry should be so urgent in her request to join her downstairs.

Lady Norman rose when she entered the green drawing room, and greeted her effusively, kissing her on the cheek, holding her at arm's length when she had finished, and exclaiming, 'You look more charming than ever these days, my dear. I believe that I know the reason for that,' she added.

This confused Trish a little. Lady Norman, however, was referring in her arch way to the number of times on which Harry had escorted Trish to the season's most prestigious events.

There were no other visitors but the Lady, and no sign of Harry—presumably he was still closeted with Gerard. Trish accepted a cup of tea, but refused anything to eat: the memory of the whelks and oysters she and Allen had enjoyed was still with her.

As at all afternoon tea parties they talked of inanities. Trish often wondered at Torry's patience on such occasions. She knew that her guardian was a clever woman, who had written a temperate but pointed book on the disabilities which women suffered—among them the lack of the right to vote. It was scarcely a topic, she thought, smiling to herself, which would interest Lady Norman, who was quite content with her own position in society and would have agreed with Queen Victoria that women ought not to hanker after more rights than they already possessed.

Lady Norman saw Trish's smile and mistakenly thought it a reaction to the topic under discussion, which was who would and who would not be invited to Lady Leominster's reception, one of the last which would be held before the season ended.

'Oh, I gather by your expression, Miss Courtney, that you and Sir Gerard and Lady Schuyler have already been invited. Her guest list does rather separate those who matter in society from those who do not. Harry and I have, of course, already received our invitation.'

This last came out in what Allen had once described to Trish as the society woman's preening mode—something adopted when the speaker thought that she had scored a point over someone else. Lady Norman's whole life consisted in scoring such points, and doubtless she would expect Harry's wife to join her in the game.

The thought that before the season began she might just have taken Harry seriously, even married him, made Trish feel quite faint. It also told her how far she had travelled both emotionally and intellectually since Allen had rescued her from the Birmingham/London train wreck.

Torry, though, knew that Trish's smile probably had little to do with anything which might preoccupy Lady Norman. Her own reaction was to turn the subject, and beg Lady Norman to consider joining one of the many committees with which she was involved.

'Oh, my dear, no,' responded the Lady archly. 'You do such good work on them, I know, but they are not my sort of thing at all. Not at all.' She paused, looked at her watch, and said, 'I am sure that we ought to have heard something by now.'

In her innocence Trish wondered to what she was referring, and almost as though he had heard her the butler entered, and said, 'Your pardon, Lady Schuyler, but Sir Gerard asks that Miss Courtney will have the goodness to join him in his study.'

Lady Norman's face glowed with anticipation. Trish looked at Torry, who said gently, 'Indeed, I am sure that Miss Courtney will be only too willing to oblige Sir Gerard.'

Light suddenly dawned! Trish looked from Torry's grave face to Lady Norman's beaming one and back again. Harry had undoubtedly been seeking Gerard's permission to ask for her hand in marriage. She had not the slightest desire to go upstairs simply in order to refuse him—but there was no help for it.

'Very well,' she said, and rose to follow the butler, who for some reason the moment they were out of the room abandoned his stiff face and was now giving her an odd stare which she could not interpret—other than that it was not friendly. And why should that be?

She had little time to address this problem—or rather time had shrunk again: one moment she was in the green drawing room and in the next she was facing Gerard, who was alone.

He advanced towards her, smiling a little.

'My dear, I am happy to see you look so blooming. I am also happy to inform you that I have just been speaking to Harry Norman, with whom you have spent many afternoons this summer. He has asked me for my permission to offer for your hand in marriage, and I was pleased to consent to his wishes. He is, as you know, a good young man, with a large fortune, and will succeed to his father's title in the fullness of time.

'Should you decide to accept him I shall be delighted to

give you both my blessing. He is waiting for you in the upstairs drawing room.'

'Do I have to see him? I don't want to marry anyone yet.' Trish was disturbed by how frantic she sounded, not at all her usual equable self.

Gerard's smile did not exactly disappear, but it grew a little strained.

'Come, come, my dear, you have virtually encouraged him all summer in the belief that you are interested in him by going everywhere in his company, and it is a little late to change your mind now.'

Trish stood stock-still and stricken. The innocent masquerade which she had embarked upon with Harry had turned into something not quite so innocent after all!

There was no way in which she could avoid a confrontation with him other than by telling Gerard what she had thought was the truth 'But Harry knows that I am not interested in marrying him, nor is he interested in marrying me. We are good friends, nothing more.'

Gerard said, 'That may have been true in the beginning, but Harry obviously believes that the friendship between you has matured into love.'

'As far as I am concerned, that is not true,' returned Trish bluntly.

'Nevertheless, my dear, I think that you must do him the honour of seeing him and allowing him to press his suit,' said Gerard gently, since he could tell that Trish was genuinely distressed.

'Very well.'

Trish could not fault Gerard for wanting her to consider Harry's offer carefully. After all, that was his duty as a guardian, and Harry was considered to be one of the catches of the season. He passed all the tests of eligibility which Trish's world considered important.

Gerard's relief was patent. 'Good,' he said approvingly.

'You at least owe him the opportunity to make his offer to you personally.'

He paused before resuming with, 'I am not putting any pressure on you to accept his offer, you understand, merely ensuring that you give it your proper consideration.'

'I shall certainly do that,' Trish assured him fervently.

Nevertheless, entering the upstairs drawing room, where she found Harry sitting in an armchair pretending to read the latest issue of the *Illustrated London News*, she felt quite sick with worry.

He rose to his feet, smiling, throwing the magazine down on to a side table.

'Darling Trish,' he said, 'Gerard has told you that he is permitting me to offer for you. Do say yes, I beg of you, and you will make me the happiest chap alive. I promise to be a good husband—kind and faithful and all that.'

He seemed to have forgotten that she had already told him that she wished only to be his friend, not his wife— he probably thought these were the female whim-whams of a girl faced with marriage!

'Oh, Harry,' she said sorrowfully. 'I told you that I wished to be your friend and nothing more, and I have not changed my mind since then. I'm sure that you can find another girl better suited to you than I am.'

'No, no, dear Trish. It's all my fault,' he went on, his face shining with a mixture of love and excitement, 'for being straightforward and blunt, isn't it? I really ought to have gone down on my knees and offered you endless devotion as well as marriage, but when you came in everything flew out of my head.'

Trish reflected sadly that this was a common occurrence where Harry was concerned. His enthusiasm outran his common sense—particularly when he was with her.

'It's nothing to do with that, Harry. You could have been

Cinderella's Prince arriving with her glass slipper and I would still have refused you.'

'But it's such a suitable match for us both, do admit.'

'No, I don't admit it at all. Most unsuitable. You wouldn't like having me for a wife.'

'Why ever not? I know I should!'

Trish cast wildly about her for something convincing to say. 'Well, I should want to do all sorts of things you—and your mother—wouldn't approve of—'

He interrupted her indignantly. 'I'm sure you wouldn't.'

'But I would... I would like to join the Suffragettes and campaign for Votes for Women, and throw water at important people and misbehave in the gallery of the House of Commons...'

His perplexity was evident. 'You don't do any of those things now—why should you do them when you are my wife?'

'Because I should be much more free to do as I please—married women are, you know. And then I shall...buy a bicycle and ride it down Piccadilly. You wouldn't like that—you told me so once. As well as make all sorts of unsuitable men friends—I've always envied Violet Kenilworth and Lily Langtry.'

Trish was referring to two women famous for their liaisons. She was secretly appalled at the series of lies which flowed from her in her efforts to discourage Harry. Fortunately they seemed to be working.

'No, you're quite right,' he conceded sadly. 'Mother wouldn't like any of that at all—she'd expect to live with us when we were married, you know, and she would be very upset if you carried on like that. I couldn't bear her to be upset.'

He frowned. 'You're sure that that's how you would go on? You're not just teasing me?'

Trish shook her head. 'Dear me, no. I've been thinking

about it a lot lately.' Another thundering lie, but unfortunately these days lies seemed to be working better than the truth!

'That's that, then. I can see that it wouldn't do at all. I suppose some men wouldn't mind, but I would. If you change your mind about your behaviour when we're married, do let me know—if I haven't changed my mind about wanting to marry you, that is, and fancy someone else.'

He was so doleful that for the first time Trish felt unhappy at behaving in such a way as to make him unhappy. But if her happy days with Allen had taught her anything it was that she would make a most unsuitable wife for such a cheerful ass as Harry Norman, however well-meaning he was in his feckless way.

And to have to live with Lady Norman didn't bear thinking of.

They both stood silent and awkward before a situation for which no rules of etiquette existed.

'I suppose I ought to leave after wishing you all the best in the future. You know where to find me if you change your mind,' Harry finally came out with.

Trish's answer was heartfelt. 'And I wish you all the best. The only thing which I regret is that we ever set out to deceive your mother and the Schuylers.'

'I suppose you're right.' Something struck him. 'This fellow Marriott that you fancy. Would you behave so wildly after you married him? Or has he let you know he wouldn't mind?'

'We haven't got as far as that yet. I've only told you how I feel at the minute.'

This evasive answer appeared to offer Harry some hope. His face brightened immediately, but he said no more before the door closed behind him, leaving Trish with the difficult task of telling Gerard that she had, after due consideration, refused Harry's splendid offer.

* * *

Trish returned to her rooms to change again for the evening. She was beginning to find this constant attention to her clothing and her hair more than a little tiresome. She was finally arrayed in all her splendour to attend the dinner party which Gerard was giving that night when there was a rap on her door.

It was Torry Schuyler—like herself, already dressed in what she had once jokingly referred to as 'my war-paint.' War-paint or not, she looked splendid and a little formidable.

'Gerard tells me that you refused Harry Norman's proposal this afternoon. I cannot say that I am surprised. I wondered if you might like to talk about it.'

They were seated in armchairs opposite to one another in Trish's little sitting room. Trish considered for a moment before answering. Torry's voice had been kind, not critical, but she felt a little hesitant about saying anything which might later be held against her.

'I hope you will believe me when I tell you that, while I quite like Harry as a friend to go about with, he is not at all the kind of man whom I would wish to marry—and that was why I refused him. I thought that he understood that all I wanted was friendship, and I believed that that was what he wanted, too. I was sorry to learn that he had changed his mind.'

Torry nodded. 'That was what I thought might be the reason why you refused him. I told Gerard that you probably valued him as a friend. He was a little upset that you refused him, but he agreed with me that the decision must be yours and that we ought to put no pressure on you to reconsider.'

'That was kind of you both,' said Trish gratefully.

Torry was brisk. 'No more than we ought to be. And now let us forget it. By your expression when you came in you had enjoyed your day out.'

'Yes, I did.' Trish offered no account of where she had been, and Torry allowed the omission to pass. She spoke briefly of their guests that evening, ending, 'Gerard would have liked Mr Marriott to be present tonight in order to meet Mr Jordan Foster, with whom he might need to do some work—Mr Foster being sometimes Gerard's business collaborator and sometimes his rival—but it was Mr Marriott's day off and he had made other arrangements, he said, which could not be altered.

'Gerard did not make an issue of it—he thinks highly of him as a secretary, although, apparently, not very highly of him as a person. I wondered what you think of him—he is nearer in age to you than to Gerard and me.'

This last question came out artlessly, almost as though it were an afterthought, and it was a difficult one for Trish to answer.

'He is always very polite, and my maid tells me that he is most considerate in his dealings with the servants. I have also gained the impression that he does not consider Gerard as a person any more highly than Gerard considers him.'

This was saying everything and nothing. Torry nodded. 'My opinion exactly. I also believe that he is a very deep young man and that there is more to him than appears on the surface. Nevertheless I like him—which surprises Gerard. I tell him that it is women's intuition working, to which he replies, "Pish tush!" Not in those words, of course, but that is his meaning.'

Trish began to laugh. Without thinking she rose from her chair, walked over to Torry and kissed her on the cheek, saying, 'You know that you are really the mother I never had. My own mother was an invalid and it was not her fault that she could never do very much for me.'

The real reason that she had kissed Torry was because she had been kind about Allen. Later, brooding over this conversation, Trish wondered if Torry's intuition had given

her some hint of her own feelings for Allen, and she spent
her time during dinner and afterwards trying to discover
whether there was any foundation for this suspicion.

Torry, however, said and did nothing out of the ordinary,
leaving Trish to feel vaguely discomfited without finding
any valid reason for being so!

Allen entered the Schuylers' Park Lane home around
eleven of the clock. He had no wish to use the front door
and be bearded by the butler, who obviously disliked him.
He walked through the empty kitchen, yawning gently and
blessing the absence of the staff who had retired for the
night after their long day.

He almost had his hand on the green-baize-covered door
which led to the Schuylers' living quarters when it opened,
and Timson, Gerard's valet came in.

Allen had always considered Timson a bit of a mystery.
He ghosted around the house like a knowing servant in a
novel by Henry James, so portentous was his expression.
He had rarely spoken to Allen, who was that hybrid, someone who was neither servant nor master. Timson didn't
have much to do with the other servants, either.

Tonight, though, was different. About to pass him, Allen
found himself being addressed by Timson in the voice
which was peculiarly his own. A voice which always carried subtle overtones of double meaning—even when he
said yes or no.

'Ah, Mr Marriott, late home, I see. You look tired.'

This was no less than the truth. Allen had spent his time
since Trish had left him working on an old clock which Mr
Nance had been unable to repair, and which, after a deal
of patience and internal bad language, he had been able to
subdue—Mr Nance's word for a solution to a difficult problem.

Allen nodded. Timson continued as though Allen had not

responded in any way. 'I think that it might make you a little happier to learn that this afternoon Miss Courtney refused Mr Harry Norman when he came to propose to her. In my opinion, she was most wise not to accept him.

'Good night, Mr Marriott. Sleep well.' And he ghosted away.

Thunderstruck, Allen stared after him.

What in Hades was all that about? Was Timson in his oblique way wishing him well with Trish? Surely not.

But it was a thoughtful Allen Marriott who took Timson's words to bed with him that night.

Chapter Nine

'You are telling me, Norris, that this young fellow Marriott not only continues to conceal his other interests from Sir Gerard, but is also still meeting his ward on the sly—having been expressly forbidden to have anything to do with her!'

'So the butler informs me. What is more to the point is that I have been recommended to Sir Gerard, who also needs some work done for him. He has apparently become aware that something odd and financially damaging has been going on at Schuyler's and wishes to discover who is behind it. Naturally I did not inform him that I am employed by you to do something quite different, and I accepted his offer with pleasure!'

Norris's interrogator began to laugh. 'Did you, indeed? Better and better. It occurs to me that we may be able to provide him with an answer which will leave us in the clear but which Mr Allen Marriott might not like. Keep me informed.'

'Indeed—the thing which will please you most is that Sir Gerard has asked me to keep my appointment a secret from all his staff, including his secretary.'

Norris dismissed, his employer leaned back in his chair

and read again the report which had arrived from Pinkerton's that morning and which had caused him some amusement and some bemusement.

All unknown to everyone, Allen Marriott was none other than Sir Gerard Schuyler's cousin! And the fact that he had never acknowledged him in any way—not even to his wife—told an interested observer that Gerard Schuyler must have some reservations about him, particularly since the butler's report had hinted at hostility between the pair of them.

The rest of the season was sweet torture for Allen and Trish. Unable to meet secretly very often because of Trish's involvement in its increasingly hectic pace, they were confined to seeing one another only when they passed on the stairs or in corridors. Occasionally they were both present at dinner on the few occasions when the Schuylers dined alone, or when Gerard required Allen's attendance because he wished him to meet one of the guests.

Now that she was almost inaccessible, he thought ruefully, Trish had never looked more beautiful. For her part the sight of Allen seated opposite to her, grave and calm, quite unlike the lively man with whom she had laughed and joked, and who had made such gentle, lyrical love to her, was unbearably hard when she had to pretend not to know him well.

One way in which they could communicate was by letter, their names and addresses carefully printed. Allen had decided that print was safer than handwriting because it was highly likely that the servants would examine their correspondence before it was placed on the table in the entrance hall. He had the strongest feeling that he was being watched—not only at Park Lane, where he knew from what Trish had overheard that the butler was spying on him, but when he left it. However much he tried, though, he was never able to detect anyone in the act.

He told Mr Nance of his suspicions on one of his evening visits after he had finished putting the final touches to the paper he was due to read at the British Horological Institute. He never took anything that belonged to his life as a horologist to Park Lane because he was certain that his rooms there had been searched more than once.

They were drinking coffee together before Allen left to return to Park Lane. Mr Nance heard him out, then thought for a few moments, his old face sad.

'What makes you believe this, Allen?' he asked. 'Your intuition—or do you have any evidence?'

'I have a little evidence.' And he told Mr Nance what Trish had overheard: that the butler was spying on him at Park Lane on behalf of Mr Hall, for what reason he was not entirely sure.

'But there's more to it than that,' he added. 'I have the strongest sense of being watched in the street, so strong sometimes that the hairs on my neck stand on end. Now that cannot be the butler, for I always leave him on duty at Park Lane. You might, I suppose, call what I am experiencing intuition. Also, I am having bad dreams which I cannot remember when I wake up.'

He shook his head violently. 'That all makes me sound frightfully namby-pamby, doesn't it? There is no one else I would willingly confide in but you—indeed, my situation is such that there is no one else but you I *can* confide in. I don't want to worry Trish by speaking of it to her, even though I'm afraid that someone may also be watching her.'

'I can quite understand how disagreeable this must be,' said Mr Nance. 'You know, Allen, in my long life I have acquired some odd friends. Would you like me to make some discreet enquiries of them for you?'

'Only if it will not endanger you.'

'You sense danger, then?'

'I fear so.'

It was the old man's turn to shake his head. 'I am willing to undertake that risk,' he said.

What impressed Allen the most was that Mr Nance was considering what he had told him seriously. He had thought that the old man might dismiss what he had to say and try to reassure him by suggesting that he was feeling unhappy now that he was not able to see Trish so often, and was translating that unhappiness into the sensation of an un-named, unidentifiable menace.

They looked together at the big clock over the mantel-piece. Allen rose reluctantly. 'Time to go,' he said. 'One more thing. If you feel that you might be putting yourself into danger, drop your enquiries at once, I beg of you.'

'You are my true friend,' responded Mr Nance, as gently as ever. 'For my true friend I would do anything. You are not to worry about me. Worry about yourself and Trish, if you must.'

Allen stopped on the way to the door. 'There is one other thing which might or might not be important. This is for your ears only, not to be told to anyone. Something has happened which supports my belief that there have been criminal goings-on at Schuyler's and that it may be con-nected with my predecessor, Mr Hall. Trish overheard him bribing the butler for information about me. Had *I* over-heard them talking I might have gone to Sir Gerard about it, but I don't want to involve Trish in this. They would probably say that she was a silly girl who had misunder-stood them, and Sir Gerard would jump to all the wrong conclusions about why she should have imagined it.

'Somehow, though, I have the feeling that it might be connected with my vague sense of being menaced. Why I should think this, I don't know. I've no reason to believe that there is a vast conspiracy against me involving spies and criminals, and I can't believe that Mr Hall is stalking me in the street! What I do know is that I am on the verge of a complete understanding of what might be wrong with Schuyler's accounts. Up to now I had very little hard evidence to offer Gerard, which would make what I might say to him sound like vague whim-whams.'

'Oh, I don't think they're whim-whams,' responded Mr Nance. 'Just try to forget them and sleep well tonight. I know that's a useless piece of advice, but I feel that I have to offer it to you.'

Allen was thinking about his discussion with Mr Nance when he reached Park Lane. Sir Gerard was entertaining that night, and he knew that some of the servants would still be in the kitchen.

He was on his way to the stairs when the drawing room door opened and his employer came out, escorting a heavy-set man and his fat wife who were apparently about to leave.

Gerard's face brightened when he saw Allen. 'The very man! I have twice hoped that I might introduce my new secretary, Mr Allen Marriott, to you when you came to dine, Foster, but both times I was entertaining you on his day off, when he had made other, and binding, arrangements. He comes quite apropos tonight, however.

'I have the honour, Mr Marriott, to present you to Mr Jordan Foster and his wife. I have spoken of him to you a number of times, Foster, and now he has the privilege of meeting you.'

Allen mumbled something duly humble out of which crept the words, 'Honoured, I'm sure,' as he bowed.

'I understand that you're the young fellow who's taken over Hall's position. His is a hard act for you to follow, as I am sure you understand.'

Allen managed to say, 'Indeed, sir,' without his face losing its usual appearance of impassive severity.

'I gather that you are to take the minutes of the first meeting of the consortium which is to bid for the next Underground Line, now that it seems that the Central Railway is sure to be a success when it opens. There's a great deal of enthusiasm already for the Tuppenny Tube, as it has been named, since every journey on it, long or small, will only cost tuppence. It will be exactly the thing to usher in a new, democratic century.'

It was plain to Allen that Jordan Foster and his wife were fellow Americans, but neither of them possessed, or had chosen to adopt, the manners and habits of the British among whom they lived, as Sir Gerard and Lady Schuyler had done. Indeed, they were both by dress and speech almost caricatures of the uncivilised Yankees who turned up in bad plays, not at all like the people among whom he had lived in the United States.

He recalled that Foster had made his money in copper and that it was rumoured that his wife had been a barmaid in a mining camp. She certainly had the remnants of great good looks of a brassy order.

'I shall look forward to being connected with such a noble enterprise, particularly one which furthers those ideals dear to all good American hearts,' Allen agreed, still duly humble.

He saw Gerard look sharply at him and wondered for a moment if he had overdone things for once. His cousin, however, said nothing, and concentrated on bidding his guest goodnight.

The footman arrived with Jordan Foster's overcoat and his wife's wrap. The butler saw them to the door. Allen bowed gracefully in their direction and made to retire. Gerard, however, signalled for him to remain and ushered him into a side-room, not the drawing room where Torry was waiting for him.

'You will remember, I hope,' he said coldly, 'that it greatly benefits Schuyler Inc. for us to remain on good terms with Jordan Foster. Whether we like the man or not is beside the point.'

'Oh, I am in absolute agreement,' said Allen earnestly. 'That is why I tried very hard to please him by emphasising my devotion to the noble motives which so obviously inspire his business ventures.'

There, he *had* overdone it, he was sure. He waited for Gerard's inevitable explosion, but when it came it was not at all what he had expected.

His cousin gave a great burst of laughter and clapped him on the back. 'Couldn't have put it better myself,' he finally gasped. 'I only beg that you will spare me the edge of your tongue—not, I think, that Foster was aware that you were roasting him.'

Allen's control never faltered. 'Who, me?' he asked, eyebrows raised a little haughtily. 'I never roast anyone. Every word I ever utter is always heartfelt, I do assure you.'

He had again wrong-footed Gerard, who stopped laughing to stare at him. 'I do believe that you mean what you say,' he came out with at last, 'incredible though that might be. Go to bed, man, you look done in. Being humble must be wearing work.'

Allen bowed. Neither by word, deed or facial expression would he cede Gerard anything. 'Thank you, sir. Yes, I am a little tired. Very gracious of you.'

He made his way up the stairs, aware that Gerard's eyes were boring into his back. His own laughter was silent, but…heartfelt all the same. Very few men ever succeeded in dancing Gerard around, but it seemed to come naturally to him.

One day, though, he would go too far—and what would happen then?

Allen was doomed to meet Jordan Foster again, and more than once. After Allen had taken the minutes of the consortium's meeting about the Underground, Gerard invited Foster and his wife to a small dinner party at which he asked Allen to be present. Almost unconsciously he was using Allen more and more, not only as a secretary but as someone with whom he might discuss matters of policy.

Unaware of their secret meetings, he thought that Allen had taken his orders not to associate with Trish very well—another point in his favour.

'It's probably a bonus that I never know exactly what he's thinking,' he told Torry in Trish's presence. 'If I can't tell then neither can my competitors. He'd be a great man to keep a secret and no mistake!'

Trish smiled to herself when she thought of all the secrets which Allen was keeping. Her only worry was that one day Gerard might discover the most important of them all—that she and Allen were disobeying his express orders. Not that they had been alone together very much since their visit to Greenwich. By accident, however, they managed to spend some time together in the library on the morning of the dinner party.

She was sitting at the map table examining a huge folio of Piranesi prints of fearsome and imaginary dungeons and prisons. Mr Nance had spoken of them one day when he and Allen had been talking about strange works of art. He had travelled in Italy as a very young man, and he had never forgotten being shown them by a friend he had made there. The very name had intrigued Trish and she had asked Gerard's librarian about him. He had told her that the library possessed a book of his etchings which some eighteenth-century traveller had brought from Italy, and he had left it out for her to inspect.

She had been meaning to look at it for some time, but her life had grown very busy and had given her little spare time in which to visit the library. At the back of her mind that morning had been the hope that the librarian would not be there and that she might meet Allen.

Both wishes were to be fulfilled. Dr Ryan wasn't there, and she had been looking at the mysterious drawings for some time, wishing that someone would explain them to her, when Allen walked in.

His face lit up at the sight of her.

'Well met—and no one could have accused us of having planned this meeting,' he said softly, 'since I had no notion that you were here.'

He walked over to where she sat. 'I see that you have found the Piranesi etchings of which Mr Nance spoke.'

Trish stood up in order that he might be able to inspect them, too. 'True,' she said, smiling at him, 'for once we are innocent—unlike these drawings, which make me shiver because they seem so menacing, although nothing terrible is happening in them.'

'That is because Piranesi has drawn them in such a way that you almost see the suffering people who are not there—which is far more powerful than showing them being tortured—your mind does that for you.'

Trish looked at him. 'How do you know so much, Allen? You are quite unlike most of the men with whom I am acquainted. Harry, for instance, appears to know nothing. He has a good seat on a horse and that's about it!'

Allen shrugged and looked a little uncomfortable. 'Oh, I make no claim to universal knowledge. Far from it. But my life was a lonely one until I met Mr Nance and then you, and I filled it by reading and studying anything I came across which interested me. Robert Louis Stevenson, the novelist and poet, once wrote, ''The world is so full of a number of things, I'm sure that we should all be as happy as kings.'' Some of the things in the world comforted me and became my friends. They also made me think.'

He had never said very much about his past life, and that he had chosen to tell her a little of it showed how much he was beginning to trust—as well as to love—her.

'Stevenson may be right,' Trish said, 'but despite that, many people are unhappy.'

Allen smiled. 'I think happiness has to be earned,' he told her. 'It's not a right, and in any case it's hard to be happy if you're penniless and don't know where the next meal is coming from. My life was not hard after that fashion, and consequently it has been relatively easy for me to find happiness. The people I dislike are those whose life is comfortable and who spend their time complaining about how bored and unhappy they are.'

Trish said quietly, 'Some women are unhappy because their lives are aimless—particularly young society women who have not been educated and whose sole purpose in life is to find a husband. What happens to them if they don't? Or if they have very little money, are unable to earn a living and are condemned to be maiden aunts and spinsters, forever dependent on the bounty of others.'

Allen smiled a rueful smile. 'It can happen to young men, too,' he said. 'But I agree, such women are in a worse case than men.'

Trish said spiritedly, 'Women should be educated just like men. I'm sure that I should have liked to have been.'

'Spoken like a true Suffragette, Trish. Are you going to join the movement?'

'Don't tease, Allen, although I suppose I deserve it for teasing Harry by suggesting that he wouldn't want to marry me because if I did become his wife I should immediately begin to tie myself to railings and do all the things which Suffragettes do.'

'And will you do that when we are married, my darling?'

They were standing close together now, and only the thought that someone might enter and find them in a compromising position was stopping Allen from taking her in his arms.

'No, indeed. For one thing, I am not sure that it will answer. It does seem rather odd to me that you try to prove that women are responsible people who deserve the vote by behaving irresponsibly! There must be a better way— though I can't think of one.'

Allen, in his saner moments, would have agreed with her immediately, but standing opposite to her, looking at her charmingly indignant face, her violet eyes flashing at him, her mouth set in a determined line once she had finished speaking, was doing odd things to him. He would never have believed that he could be roused so quickly.

A few moments passed before it took him all his self-control, hardened over the years, to reply to her, saying, 'Logic rarely determines these matters, my darling.'

'I suppose not. Speaking of other things, Torry has told me that you will be present at the dinner party tonight. Another occasion for us to meet quite innocently.'

Before he had time to answer her they heard the sound of footsteps advancing along the corridor outside. Allen moved quickly away and vanished through the door to the office before the main library door opened and Dr Ryan entered to find her alone and apparently absorbed in studying Piranesi's disturbing drawings, with which she occupied herself until dinner time neared.

Allen was still in Trish's thoughts when she had finished dressing for dinner. She was wearing her pale mauve toilette and was trying to read the latest number of the *Illustrated London News* when Torry visited her.

'I thought that we might have a quiet word together before we join Gerard. I should have spoken to you earlier, but we were late returning home. This is something which I have been putting off, but Gerard made a remark this afternoon which made me think that I ought to raise it with you as soon as possible.'

Goodness, whatever could be exercising Torry, who looked a trifle embarrassed before she began to speak? Could it possibly be something to do with her and Allen?

It was.

Trish tried to be as calm as Allen always was. She asked Torry to be seated—largely because she thought that it might ease the tension from which they were both suffering.

'I hope that what I have to say won't distress you overmuch. Perhaps I ought to begin with a question which I hope you will feel able to answer truthfully. Have you been secretly meeting Allen Marriott?'

Now this was clever of Torry, for she surely knew that Trish would not give her the lie direct. Nor did she.

'Since you put it like that,' said Trish, still calm, 'I am compelled to tell you that I have.'

'I thought that you and he were strongly attracted to one another.' Torry felt that she ought to explain further. 'And something which Lucy Chalfont's mother said to me made me suspicious. That, added to the way in which you look at one another.'

'Oh, dear,' murmured Trish, still calm. 'Are we so obvious?'

'Not to most, I suspect. I am bound to ask you whether you think you are being wise—and whether you are being fair to Mr Marriott. I recently learned that Gerard told him that he was not to have anything to do with you—and, after all, we—and you—know very little about him.'

Trish kept her composure with difficulty. 'I have found out a great deal about him,' she said, 'now that I have got to know him better.'

'Gerard was fearful that he might be after your fortune,' Torry said. 'He also thinks that Mr Marriott is too clever for his own good and perhaps might treat you in such a way that marriage would be inevitable—leaving you with no choice but to marry him.'

Trish's struggle not to say anything which she might later regret was plain to see. 'That he might seduce me, you mean. Do you think that?'

'I'm bound to say no, except that you are very young and he is not only older than you but, as Gerard says, deep. I must ask you to reconsider, to stand back a little, perhaps. I must repeat: you know very little of him. That he has persuaded you to meet him in secret is not a good sign.'

Trish was hamstrung by the fact that Allen did not wish her to tell anyone of his life with Mr Nance, or of his heroism in the railway accident, nor of his high standing in the British Horological Institute.

All that she could say was, quite simply, 'I know that he is brave, that he is clever and that he is good and kind. He has never said anything wrong to me, or given me the slightest reason to believe that he wishes to ruin me for his own ends.'

'Nevertheless,' said Torry reasonably, 'these are merely your impressions of him. Without hard evidence to support your beliefs they must only remain those of an inexperienced girl. I wish that you had spoken to Gerard and me before you embarked on a campaign of deceit with him. Gerard's bark is worse than his bite, you know. Before we married that might not have been true, but he has changed

very much since then. If you and Mr Marriott would confide in him, I believe that he might listen to you.'

'I think,' said Trish slowly, unwilling to give any of Allen's secrets away, 'no, I am sure, that Allen would find it
difficult to confide in Gerard. That is the impression I have
gained from being with him over the summer.'

Gerard had said something similar to Torry—'I don't
know whether I like him or not, but I'm damned sure that
he dislikes me.'—so she did not argue with Trish.

There was nothing more which Trish could say; she
could only listen to Torry beg her again to give up seeing
Allen and reconsider her current behaviour. When Torry
had finished Trish said simply, 'Are you going to tell Sir
Gerard about us—that we are meeting secretly and have no
intention of stopping? You must understand that I am
twenty-three years old, and were it not for Father's will
making me dependent until I am twenty-five neither you
nor Gerard could prevent us from meeting quite openly.'

'Did he tell you that?'

'He had no need. I am well aware of my legal position.'

Torry could only admire Trish's dignity and composure.
She had never once raised her voice, and in this discussion
had shown a maturity which Torry had not known that she
possessed. She was compelled to admit how much Trish
had changed since knowing Allen Marriott—and for the
better.

As simply as Trish, she said, 'No, I shall not tell Gerard,
unless circumstances insist. But I still wish that you would
reconsider.'

It was plain by the expression on Trish's face that she
had no intention of doing any such thing. She said in a low
voice, 'You must know that I have never enjoyed deceiving
you. My deception was undertaken solely in order to protect Allen. From what he has said he is alone in the world,
and I believe he values his employment here, although we

have never discussed that, or anything to do with you, Gerard or Schuyler's. I do know that for Gerard to dismiss him would mean that he might have trouble finding another position. For him to go voluntarily would be quite another thing.'

Yes, Trish had changed.

Torry shook her head regretfully and rose to leave. 'Very well. You are of age, and I can only trust that when you are with him you will exercise the good sense which I am sure you possess. Now, let us put this behind us. Mr Marriott will, as you know, dine with us and the Fosters this evening, and nothing personal must be allowed to cast a shadow on the gathering.'

Trish bowed her head and said, 'Good manners alone will see us through, I'm sure. And Aunt Torry—as I used to call you—I do not think any the less of you for raising this matter with me, and I hope that you will think no less of me and trust in my good sense.'

'My dear,' exclaimed Torry, coming over to Trish and kissing her on the cheek. 'I won't allow this to come between us. Now let us go down together and wait in the drawing room for Gerard and the others as though we had not a care in the world. And remember, I am now deceiving Gerard, too!'

Jordan Foster and his wife were in the drawing room with their hosts when Allen walked in that evening. He tried not to look at Trish too much, since not to look at her at all might be as betraying as doing the other thing!

Torry gave him a brief smile; Gerard merely said to the Fosters, 'You remember me introducing my secretary, Mr Marriott, to you the other evening, I'm sure.'

'Of course,' said Jordan Foster, 'the fortunate successor to Mr Hall who later made such a good fist of keeping the minutes at the last meeting of the consortium.'

Allen bowed his head and said meekly, 'I was merely doing my duty, sir, but thank you all the same.'

Gerard, exasperated as usual by Allen's humility, said brusquely to Foster, 'Paying Marriott a compliment is like throwing water into the Thames—it sinks without trace. I have to say that, good though Hall was, Marriott surpasses him by far. He has an eye like a hawk for anything dubious in a document or a report, and with his mathematical skill ought to have ended up as an accountant or treasurer—he could probably have commanded a fortune.'

To say that his hearers were astounded when Gerard came out with this oddly worded compliment would be to understate matters. The person most surprised was Allen himself. For once he lost his perfect control to the extent of flushing slightly.

The most delighted person in the room, however, was Trish. Did this bode well for the future? Might not Gerard withdraw his opposition to Allen's having anything to do with her if he really valued him highly?

Jordan Foster said jovially, 'I think that's the first time I've heard you be so enthusiastic about anyone, Schuyler. You should be flattered, young man.'

Allen gave him the cool smile which Trish knew so well. 'Oh, I am,' he said. 'Immensely flattered.' He tried to avoid Gerard's eye and wondered what it had cost his cousin to praise him. Instead he saw Torry's eye on him with an expression on her face so speculative that he wondered at it.

Now what was all that about?

Fortunately for his own composure the butler arrived at that moment to inform them that dinner was served, and he duly took his place beside Trish at the end of the procession into the dining room. Mrs Foster was seated next to him, and while the first course of asparagus soup was being served asked him how long he had been working for Sir Gerard.

'About three months as his secretary,' he told her. 'Before that I worked in Schuyler's offices first in New York and then in London.'

'Thought you was a Yankee when I first heard your voice. Come from the East Coast, do you?' asked Jordan Foster before he picked up his soup spoon.

'Yes, sir.' Which was all the information which Allen was prepared to offer to him.

'Thought so. Was you ever at university there?'

There was no help for it, and with Gerard listening he was compelled to tell the truth.

'I was fortunate enough to go to Yale.'

'No surprise to me. Can always tell a university man.'

Allen was not sure whether this was a compliment or not.

He thought it odd that Foster was being gracious to him—but possibly that was the consequence of Gerard's unexpected praise. He wished most sincerely that the spotlight would move away from him, which a few minutes later it did.

One thought struck him which brought a small smile to his face. He had kept his answers short to conceal his own past and his own secrets. How many of those around the table had secrets to hide besides himself and Trish? He knew that Gerard was concealing the fact that they were cousins, and he was sure that he had other secrets to hide.

And Jordan Foster—what was he concealing behind his mask of clumsy joviality? There had been a certain something in Foster's coarse voice when asking about his past which made Allen uneasy. Why should he care about the origins of a humble secretary? Unless, perhaps, he had notions of bribing him away from Gerard—which with a man of Foster's kidney was always a possibility.

He became aware that Mrs Foster was speaking to him again.

'Tell me, Mr Marriott, as an American living in England, have you discovered the secret behind the beautiful complexions of English girls? Miss Courtney, now, has the most exquisite colouring, and as far as I can tell is wearing no artificial aids—as I am sure you must have observed.'

Yes, Allen had observed. Given implicit permission by Mrs Foster to look at Trish, he smiled at her across the table before saying to Mrs Foster, his face as grave as ever again, 'It's the rain.'

'Oh, my, the rain, Mr Marriott! However do you make that out?'

'Well, in the States we have a lot of sun, but here in England the sun is in short supply and, as Shakespeare once said, ''The rain it raineth every day,'' so that the complexions of English girls are always fed and watered by it, whereas our girls are not so lucky—except in some of the Eastern States—and have to submit to their skins being baked by the sun.'

'Oh, my, Mr Marriott, aren't you clever! Mr Foster, I'll have you know that Mr Marriott is as clever as Sir Gerard said he was. He knows all about English girls' complexions.'

Gerard looked up from his place at the head of the table.

'Does he, indeed! Is that what you do on your day off, Marriott? Inspect girls' complexions?'

'Among other things,' returned Allen smoothly, trying to avoid Trish's eyes again. Her amusement was visible. Later he was to tell her that Mrs Foster had asked him to admire Miss Courtney's perfect complexion. 'She said that she was sure that you were using no artificial aids, and I was compelled to agree with her.'

Trish would give a little laugh. 'I'll have you know that

you were both wrong. My cheeks were so flushed this evening that I used a little *papier poudre* to cool them down.'

But at the time she simply offered him her enchanting
smile, saying, 'I'm sure that Mr Marriott always researches
any problem most carefully, however slight the problem
might be.'

Allen bowed his head in response. 'I always try to be
helpful, Miss Courtney.'

Mrs Foster, who had decided that she liked this young
man who seemed to combine the best characteristics of the
European as well as the American male, said enthusiasti-
cally, 'Oh, I'm just so sure you do. Tell me, Mr Marriott,
what is it you like most about English girls—or perhaps
you find that they don't compare well with American ones.'

Allen scarcely knew whether to laugh or to cry. He had
come to this dinner party determined to be as self-effacing
as possible. But instead the rotten luck of the draw had
landed him next to a woman who was determined to make
him the centre of attention by asking him the kind of question which ensured that he could not remain anonymous.

'Oh, they are both beyond compare,' he told her, 'but in
quite different ways. English girls are shy while American
girls are more forthcoming. I find the difference most in-
triguing—or I probably would if my duties left me much
time to examine them at length.'

Jordan Foster gave a dry laugh. 'You should have been
a diplomat, Marriott. Leave the lad alone, Mother, you've
teased him quite enough. This wine we're drinking is pretty
good, Schuyler. Had it specially imported, did you?'

'Yes. Tom Moidore recommended me to a vineyard near
Bordeaux. He's by way of being a connoisseur.'

'And now you're by way of being one yourself. You
never do things by half, do you, Schuyler?'

Allen thought that Gerard was not best pleased with this
compliment, and although this was the second time in as

many weeks in which he had entertained the Fosters to dinner he gained the impression that his cousin did not care much for their company. He was probably cultivating it because it was good for Schuyler's rather than because he liked them.

Foster later re-opened the two main subjects for discussion these days: the possibility of a Transvaal war and the vexed question as to whether the twentieth century began on the first day of January, 1900.

'Big mistake if the Government decides on war,' he offered. 'The British ought to take a leaf out of our book, eh, Schuyler, and let the Boers have their democratic freedoms. I have the feeling that the great British Army might meet its match in a pack of Boer farmers running around the countryside, even if they don't have much in the way of arms or artillery. None of this bodes well for the next century, I must say.'

Gerard said, a trifle wearily, 'Oh, as for the next century, I suppose it will take care of itself—whatever date we choose to begin it on. Marriott, here, would probably tell you what he told me—that all dates are imaginary and since we make them up ourselves it's up to us to decide when the twentieth century starts, not some imaginary rule. I have to say that I agree with him.'

Foster stared at Allen, who tried to look modest whilst eating his Nesselrode pudding. 'Got an original mind, has he? I suppose that's one way of looking at it—particularly since he's a bit of a time and date man himself.'

This last statement had Gerard looking interested, and Allen trying not to. Gerard raised his thick black brows at Foster, who added hastily, 'Him being your secretary must mean that he's into dates, eh? Most important in our business.'

Now why should he think that Foster had been lying when he offered that explanation? Allen ate his pudding carefully and slowly, at the rate which the late great British Prime Minister W.E. Gladstone had recommended as being good for the digestion—each mouthful being chewed thirty times in a minute.

His mind was working nearly as busily as his teeth. Could Foster have made that remark because he knew of his connection with Mr Nance and horology? If so, how did he know of it—who could conceivably have told him? Had he made the remark unthinkingly? Or had it been a slip of the tongue? Or had he made it deliberately? If it were any of these things, what precisely did any of them signify? He had offered Gerard an explanation which could hold water, but the very speed with which he had made it was in itself suspicious.

If it were Foster who was having him followed then he would, of course, know not only of Mr Nance and his shop, but also of his secret meetings with Trish. Furthermore, the only reason he could think of to explain such surveillance was that Foster had something to do with what he suspected had been criminal interference in Schuyler's interests and thought that he, Allen, might possibly discover how they had been managed if he were half as clever as Gerard had been claiming.

Was it conceivably possible that he was somehow connected with Robert Hall, whom he had found examining his papers and who had suborned Gerard's butler to keep an eye on him? Was it also possible that Foster was responsible for the unpleasant rumours about Gerard of which Tom Moidore had spoken?

All of this, he thought, eating cheese and biscuits as the meal ended and drinking rather more wine than usual, required a great leap in logic on the basis of what might conceivably be an innocent remark whose meaning he had misunderstood.

Why did he think he hadn't—other than the famous

Schuyler intuition, which he might have inherited through his mother? Finally there was another possibility to consider. Did Gerard mistrust Jordan Foster?

And what was he going to do about all these suspicions? If there were anything he could usefully do, that was!

While he was musing dinner ended and the ladies were leaving them to their port. Allen remained behind. He would much rather have gone with them to have a further opportunity to sit opposite to Trish rather than fuddle himself with a drink which he did not care for.

Jordan Foster apparently had no such qualms about drinking. He never passed the decanter on when it reached him until he had recharged his glass. His conversation grew ever more confidential and ever more coarse.

He spoke brutally and rudely of the men whom he and Gerard had met during the development of the Central Line and the creation of the new consortium.

'Pretty filly, your Miss Courtney,' he finally offered. 'Got m'son Ellsworth coming over shortly—would like him to take a look at her. Gather there's money there. Mother said that the rumour was that young Norman had offered for her and been refused. Good thing that. It's highly likely such a high-stepping lass might prefer a red-blooded American with some go in him—such as my Ellsworth—to one of your effete English gentlemen. Let's drink to that, eh?' And he winked first at Allen and then at Gerard.

On hearing this sneering reference to Trish, Allen felt his self-control on a knife-edge. He would have liked to ram Foster's words down his throat. Instead, quite involuntarily, his hand tightened around his glass of port with such force that it shattered—sending a red stain like blood spilling across the damask cloth.

'Your pardon, sir,' he exclaimed to Gerard.

'Accidents will happen,' he said hastily. 'Not used to port, I take it, Marriott.'

'Not really. I don't drink often and wasn't aware how much it was beginning to affect me,' returned Allen, lying with as much tact as he could muster, keenly aware that Foster was staring quizzically at him. He was suddenly sure that Foster had spoken slightingly of Trish quite deliberately in an attempt to get some reaction from him, and he silently cursed his temporary loss of control.

On the other hand if Foster *had* taunted him deliberately then it was further proof that he knew of his secret meetings with Trish, and, more importantly, it was evidence that he had set a spy on him.

But to what end?

Thinking about that could wait. The butler, with a scornful stare at Allen, set one of the footmen to trying to repair the damage to the cloth. Another fetched a fresh glass for him and poured him more port, which he drank in order not to betray how much Foster's light words had affected him.

'I should go easy on the port,' Gerard advised him, 'if you aren't used to drinking.'

Allen set his glass down. It was true that he didn't drink often, even though he had discovered long ago that he had a hard head, but the dreadful consequences of his father's self-indulgence were always with him as a warning not to overdo things. Nevertheless he smiled somewhat blearily at Gerard and Foster as though the drink had got to him, and said, equally blearily, 'I have had a hard day, and with your permission, Sir Gerard and Mr Foster, I would like to retire.'

'Permission granted,' said Gerard brusquely. 'The last thing I want in the morning is a secretary with a bad head.'

Relieved, Allen walked through the drawing room, bowing to all the ladies before he left them.

'What a charming young man,' gushed Mrs Foster, once

he had gone. 'Handsome, too, don't you think?' she asked, appealing to Trish for support.

'Oh, yes,' agreed Trish trying not to look at Torry. Later she was to agree with Allen that the dinner had been an exercise in avoidance: not saying what one really thought and never looking in certain directions in case one betrayed that interesting fact!

'Quite handsome—and charming, too, if you like the quiet sort.'

'Ah, but when he does speak he's worth listening to,' said Mrs Foster, revealing to both her hearers that she was not so silly as her appearance and manner might suggest.

Torry remarked on this to Gerard when they were at last alone together in their bedroom.

Gerard smiled. 'Not surprising,' he said. 'No one who was a successful madam in a brothel in a mining camp could possibly be a fool.'

'Agreed,' said Torry, 'and as a rider to that, no one who is as circumspect in everything he says and does as Allen Marriott is could possibly be a fool, either.'

'No need for me to agree to that,' returned Gerard, who was now safely in bed, 'and for God's sake hurry up, my dear; the only thing which can wash away the effects of an evening with Jordan Foster is having you beside me. You might add to your verdict on Master Marriott that he's also as artful as a wagon-load of monkeys but not as noisy. I'm damned certain that he wasn't drunk tonight, although he wanted us to think that.'

'Really?' queried Torry as she finally ended up in Gerard's arms, even though she knew perfectly well exactly how artful Allen was—and Trish, too.

'Really,' repeated Gerard—and put out the light.

Chapter Ten

The dinner with the Fosters was one of the few occasions when Allen and Trish had been able to meet publicly. To meet privately grew ever more difficult. On the other hand they had begun to enjoy a lively correspondence with one another. Trish, being romantically-minded, thought that it was like living in a novel by Samuel Richardson, or one of the other eighteenth-century writers, when lovers seemed to have endless time with nothing to do but write to one another.

Allen received her thoughts on the Fosters by third post the next day: Miss Trish Courtney to Mr Allen Marriott.

What a comic dinner party that was last night! When the ladies retired Mrs Foster did nothing but sing your praises. This was more than a little embarrassing for me because I'm sorry to have to tell you that somehow Torry has found out that we have been meeting secretly. She asked me point-blank if we were and I could not lie to her. The remarkable thing is that although she advised me to think carefully about what I was doing, and was a little worried about your intentions, she says that for the time being she will not tell Gerard!

She also suggested that we inform him that we
have been meeting and throw ourselves on his mercy,
but I pointed out to her that since he had expressly
forbidden you to see me this might mean that he
would dismiss you for disobeying him.

Fortunately she did not notice—or I don't think that
she did—that I was unable to eat very much. Between
the pleasures of loving you and the pains of worrying
about our distressful situation I seem to have quite
lost my appetite again.

You didn't seem very hungry, either.

Until we exchange glances again—for that is all
we can exchange—I remain,

Your loving Trish.

Allen to Trish:

My darling heart, the only thing that I'm hungry for
is you!

Things were a bit sticky for me when the ladies
had gone. Jordan Foster is not a good advertisement
for the charms of the American man, and between
embarrassment over that, and worries that I might say
or do the wrong thing, I fled the dining room pleading
tiredness and an inability to drink port without it having a bad effect on me.

I know that this was cowardly, but there are limits
to what a chap can take—as Harry Norman would
say—and this chap has taken quite a lot lately. I was
sorry to learn that Lady Schuyler has found us out.
Fortunately Sir Gerard complained to me the other
day that she has a soft spot for me, and I can only
hope that somehow or other we shall work our way
out of our present impasse before she feels it necessary to tell Sir Gerard about us.

Mr Nance says that he misses your cheerful voice as well as your talent for washing the dinner and tea pots. I have to say that these are not the things which I miss when I am not with you in Piccadilly—or anywhere else for that matter.

My darling, it grows harder and harder for me to be away from you—I never thought that I would find someone who seems like the other half of myself. Do be careful when you are crossing the road. When you all drive off in Sir G's motor car I pray to the god of roads—whoever he might be—that you don't have a horrible accident.

For the present my love goes with you.

Your own Allen.

Trish to Allen.

Dearest Allen,

How I long for the summer to end—something which I never thought that I would do—but at least when the season is over and we retire to Padworth I may see a little more of you, even though we shall have lost our happy days together in Mr Nance's shop. None of the men whom I am meeting attracts me in the slightest, so you are not to torture yourself by thinking that I am flirting with them in your absence. On the contrary, I seem to have gained a reputation as a cold fish, and even Harry has given up trying to corner me in remote parts of the ballroom.

One of the things which I miss most is watching you at the work-bench, and another is our happy talks when we went out together, to say nothing of going to see Marie Lloyd—Covent Garden is not a patch on her! As for our day at Greenwich, everything about it is written on my heart.

I have not even had the pleasure of learning how

you went on when you gave your paper to the British Horological Institute. I know how hard you worked at getting it just right, and though I wouldn't have understood a word of it—or even been allowed to be part of the audience—I should have loved to hear you give it. Do tell me what happened—I'm sure that it must have been a success.

I never thought that loving someone and not being able to be with him in all the ways which matter would be painful. Don't forget me, I beg of you, while you are so busy working for Gerard. He called you a treasure the other day, when talking to Torry and me, but added that you are very deep. I'm not sure whether that was meant as praise. When we can talk to one another again you must tell me. Until then I am your own Trish.

Give my love to Mr Nance and tell him I am longing to see him again soon. I shall have to think up an excuse to visit his shop. Lucy writes that she will be out of town until the autumn, so we shall be lost to one another for some time yet.

All my love, my own heart. The days are long without you. I know you said when we were in Greenwich Park that you wished us to marry, but that until you could afford to keep me properly we must wait, since you do not want to be accused of fortune-hunting. Dear Allen, you must know that I would willingly marry you with or without my fortune, but I also know that I must respect your wishes, even though obeying them is so painful.

Goodbye for the present, my love.

Trish.

Allen to Trish

I, too, long for our separation to be over, and for that happy day to arrive when I shall be able to tell you in person how much I love you. Until then we are confined to words on paper, which are not the same thing at all. I burn with jealousy when you leave for yet another grand ball because I cannot bear to think of you on the dance floor in the arms of another man.

Mr Nance sends you his best wishes and begs us both to be patient, for he is sure that everything will come right for us in the end. I must not complain overmuch because I can still see you every day— tantalising though that is.

You asked me in your last letter how I fared when I read my paper to the British Horological Institute on Tuesday. I was in a rare old state of nerves before I gave it. Mr Nance kept offering me encouragement in the cab all the way to Clerkenwell, where the Institute meets in the upstairs room of a public house. He would have fed me brandy when I got there if I had let him!

The first shock was that Lord Grimthorpe, our President, was going to be the chairman. He is a very fierce old man with a dreadful reputation for being rude to everyone—even the Prince of Wales if he speaks out of line! The original chairman for this meeting had fallen ill and he had taken his place—he doesn't always attend the meetings. Since he dislikes clocks being powered by electricity I was somewhat fearful as to how he would react to my paper, which is enthusiastic about it. He is famous as the man who designed and built Big Ben.

Fortunately, years ago, he was a friend of Charles Babbage, who built the difference engine which I suggested might be revived and powered by electricity, so he was willing to give me a hearing, and in the end my paper was received with great enthusiasm, even though Lord Grimthorpe snorted at me that I had 'a touch of the H.G. Wells,' which was not intended as a compliment!

One thing we were agreed on, and that is in disliking this ridiculous notion that the coming of the new century will solve everything. I thought of you when he was blustering away about it. A number of well-known figures came up to me afterwards to discuss some of my ideas, and I have the feeling that something important might yet happen which would eventually enable us to solve our problems over marriage.

Mr Nance was fit to burst, particularly when someone in congratulating me remarked on how much I must owe to him, which is nothing less than the truth, and instead of letting him buy me brandy before the paper I plied him with whisky after it! The only thing missing was your presence, if not at the meeting, then afterwards. My life is only half lived when you are not with me—you give it point and purpose. I never thought that I would ever meet anyone who would share my enthusiasms, and now that I have I can't wait for you to be with me always.

Adieu, my own dear love. You also share my heart and mind, and I hope that, one day, you will share more than that.

Until then I am ever your own Allen.

The correspondence, once begun, was continued with great enthusiasm on both sides.

Trish kept Allen's letters in a pretty lacquered Japanese box which her mother had given her when she was a girl, and Allen put Trish's in a small locked safe which he kept in his room, where he hid anything which he did not wish a spy to find. He always carried the last one she'd sent him in the inside breast pocket of his jacket and thought of it as a talisman, or the equivalent of the favours which knights of old were given by their beloved.

He was carrying it when he visited Mr Nance, shortly before Gerard was giving the dinner party which was to be the crown of his season. He had invited the Prince and Princess of Wales, their immediate entourage and several important friends to visit Park Lane. Their Royal Highnesses' agreement to attend was enough to silence the rumours of which Tom Moidore had spoken.

For Allen this had created a great deal of work, as it had for Gerard's whole household. The only person taking everything in his stride was Gerard himself.

'You look tired,' Mr Nance told Allen when he visited his shop. 'Sit down and have a cup of tea before you try to do anything. Sir Gerard driving you hard, is he?'

'No harder than he drives himself.'

He didn't tell Mr Nance that seeing Trish every day without being able to do more than smile in her direction was taking its toll of him.

'I have some news for you from my dubious friend,' Mr Nance said. 'He tells me that the word is that you *are* being watched, by an ex-rozzer called Norris. He's not exactly sure who is employing him, but rumour says that it's a Yankee bigwig. My informant isn't sure which Yankee bigwig because he's been given two possible names. One is that of Jordan Foster and the other is your employer.'

'By ''rozzer'' you mean policeman, I suppose,' was Allen's dry—and only—comment.

Mr Nance nodded. 'London slang,' he said briefly.

Allen was thinking hard about the significance of what Mr Nance had told him. Could it possibly be that this man Norris was watching him for both Foster *and* Gerard? No wonder he felt the back of his neck prickle every time he walked London's streets!

'Helpful?' enquired Mr Nance, brief again.

'In the sense that it confirms what I feared, yes. On the other hand I've been confronted with a bit of a puzzle.'

'About your employer possibly having you followed?'

'Yes. I'm not surprised about Foster, though. He said something at a recent dinner party which led me to believe that he knew more about me than he ought to if all that he knew of me was legitimately learned.'

'Well put,' said Mr Nance, smiling. 'I'll tell my friend to carry on keeping his ears and eyes open for you.'

'How can I ever thank you enough for all that you have done for me?' said Allen fervently.

'I have done very little, alas, for you will not allow me to do more,' was Mr Nance's answer to that.

'You have already done more for me than you know,' said Allen quietly. It was Mr Nance who had restored his confidence and belief in himself from the very first moment he had walked into his shop.

It was worrying to think that Gerard might be having him watched, too. Was he doing so in collusion with Foster, or were they each quite unaware of the other's activities? And, if they were, what did that tell him about Norris— and Gerard?

'By the way, a letter arrived for you yesterday. I think it is from Rothschild's.'

Allen had given Mr Nance's address to Rothschild's, pre- ferring any mail from them not to go to Park Lane. The letter was brief: it offered Mr Allen Marriott a position with them which would pay him double what he was getting from Gerard—an offer which was a huge advance on their previous one. They understood that he had given a paper to the British Horological Institute and complimented him on that.

He put it down thoughtfully. His debt of gratitude to Gerard had been paid. His mother's remarriage had freed him. To accept Rothschild's enhanced offer would enable him to marry Trish without the accusation of fortune-hunting being levelled at him. Why, then, was he hesitating?

He did not need to ask himself twice. It was the unfinished business at Schuyler's which was holding him back. What Mr Nance had just told him proved that he was somehow connected with it after a fashion which he did not completely understand. Until that was cleared up he could not leave.

He was about to tell Mr Nance of the offer, and why he could not immediately accept it, when the shop doorbell rang and Mr Nance left him to serve his customer.

Only it was not a customer. Mr Nance returned almost immediately, followed by an ill-dressed man who looked about him with the air of one who always sizes up his surroundings in case he has to take leave of them suddenly.

Mr Nance said, 'This is a messenger from the friend of whom I have just spoken. I think that you should hear what he has to say.'

The man nodded, sucked his stained teeth, and said, in a Cockney accent so thick that Allen could barely understand it, 'Aye, last night as ever was he was stopped by a couple of fellers and knocked about something cruel. He was told to leave off busybodying about who was after a young chap who was working for Schuyler's, it was no business of his'n, and if he didn't do as he was told it would be the worse for him. He wanted to warn you and the young chap you was helping—' he nodded at Mr Nance '—to let well alone, or you'd be for it as well.'

'Max,' said Mr Nance agitatedly. 'You're speaking of Max Stein. Is he badly hurt?'

The man nodded agreement. 'Took him to hospital, I did. He'll live, but he's lost most of his teeth, has two black eyes and a broken arm. Insides damaged, most like.'

He looked closely at Allen. 'Is this the young feller? Looks harmless enough to me.'

Mr Nance and Allen stared at one another. Allen said, 'If I'd known that this was likely to happen I would never have told you about being followed and allowed you to put your friend in danger.'

'Aye, you're being follered all right,' grunted the man, 'by a rozzer thrown out of the force for being bent. Won't say his name. Tain't safe. Bye-bye, gents, keep your noses clean, and p'raps they'll let you alone.'

He put a large and dirty forefinger by his own nose and ambled out of the workroom.

'He means Norris,' said Mr Nance. 'That's the ex-policeman Max told me about. And who did he mean by "they"? What in the world have you become involved in, Allen?'

'I believe that Schuyler's is being defrauded on a large scale. The man behind it must be very powerful if he can attack someone whom you hinted was a big man in the criminal underworld. I can hardly credit Sir Gerard with organising this—it's not his style at all—even if Norris is working for him as well as the mystery man behind this brutal attack. What I do know is that you must not ask any more questions of anyone about me or my doings—I should never forgive myself if I put you in real danger.'

Mr Nance opened his mouth to argue with him, to say that he would not be deterred even by such threats as these, but he closed it again when he saw Allen's face change. Again, although he did not know it, Allen's expression, when he was roused or angered, was formidable. He looked exactly like his cousin Gerard, whom he otherwise barely resembled. It served to put Mr Nance off his stroke.

'Well, yes,' he assented, much against his will.

Allen smiled, and became the man whom Mr Nance had

always known: the cheerful, quiet man who never raised his voice or used his will to dominate others.

'Good. Then that's understood,' he said. 'Now let us talk of more pleasant things. Did I tell you that Sir Gerard is about to entertain the Prince of Wales to dinner?'

Mr Nance shook his head. 'No—and shall you be present at the dinner?'

'Oh, no. But I—and the rest of the senior staff, including the chef—will be presented to him before the dinner. Sir Gerard says that when the Prince visits anyone he is always insistent that those who work hard to ensure his pleasure are thanked by him personally. It is one reason why he is popular.'

'Unlike the Queen,' commented Mr Nance, 'who hides herself away at Windsor and is seldom seen by her people.'

'Exactly. Sir Gerard's great friend, Lord Moidore, who has known the Prince since they were young men together, says that he has the rare talent of knowing how to charm people when he meets them—unlike his late father, the Prince Consort, who, although clever, was awkward with people. He says that the Prince of Wales would have made a great diplomat—if only his mother had allowed him the opportunity to be one. Sir Gerard agrees with him.'

Allen had seldom spoken before of the great men who were Gerard's friends and frequented his Park Lane home.

'And what does Mr Allen Marriott think of Sir Gerard Schuyler—or of Lord Moidore, for that matter?' asked Mr Nance. He had never questioned Allen about his Park Lane life, but the disturbing events of the day had made him curious.

If Allen was privately a little shy about discussing his cousin with someone who did not know of the relationship no one would have guessed it.

'Hard-working, clever and ruthless would describe both of them. Sir Gerard never expects of me more than he is prepared to give of himself. Lord Moidore is smoother and more civilised, but they are great friends precisely because, at bottom, they are like one another.'

If Mr Nance thought, as he did, that Allen displayed some of the attributes of his employer and his employer's friend, he kept that thought to himself. The shop bell ringing ended their conversation. Mr Nance left to answer it and Allen slipped on his canvas apron and started work on a small watch, not unlike the one which Trish had bought on the day she had found him in the shop.

When Allen had told Mr Nance how hard those who entertained the Prince of Wales had to work he had spoken no less than the truth.

'Everything is being washed, polished and rearranged to within an inch of its life,' was Trish's somewhat disrespectful comment to Allen in one of her letters to him. 'And I hope that includes you. You mustn't look shabby when you are presented.'

He wasn't going to, for Gerard insisted on Allen having a new evening suit in which to be presented to the Prince.

'Your current one would shame a counter-jumper in Selfridge's; it has grown quite threadbare,' was his unkind comment one morning, 'and I'm not having the Prince think that I am paying you starvation wages. I shall count it as a legitimate expense so you may have it put on my bill at Simpson's.'

'Do I have to be presented?' Allen asked in his most humble tones—so humble that Gerard knew that he was being roasted again.

'Well, since I understand that even the sous-chef is to be favoured, you can hardly be left out. And after all, you *are* my cousin.'

'But the Prince doesn't know that—unless you are prepared to make a grand gesture and publicly admit the relationship to him after tacitly denying it to everyone else for the last nine years. That would make a talking point for your staff and no mistake!'

'Marriott,' enunciated Gerard, in the voice of someone who would brook no nonsense from anyone, 'there are times when I wonder why I put up with you. I never had to endure this kind of insolence from Hall.'

'A different kind of insolence, perhaps?' queried Allen. 'I dare swear that you put up with me because you'd be hard put to find anyone who could do my job half as well. Think of it as the price you pay for that!'

Gerard drew a deep breath, glared at him, and then began to laugh.

'Words fail me,' he came out with at last.

'Try "Aw, shucks,"' suggested Allen. 'It's a good old Yankee saying which seems to fit the bill.'

'That will be all, Marriott,' bellowed Gerard. 'Get out of my sight and carry on with the task of seeing that the Prince's visit goes off without a hitch. I might even give you a rise if it does.'

Laughing to himself as he retired to consult with the butler, Allen suddenly realised that not only had his fear of Gerard disappeared, but the dislike in which he had held him had vanished as well. More than that, he had succeeded in talking to his cousin as though they were equals—and had got away with it again!

He was still smiling when he reached the entrance hall in time to meet Trish, who was just leaving the drawing room.

'Oh, Mr Marriott,' she exclaimed, for the benefit of any eavesdroppers. 'How pleasant to meet you! I suppose that you are busy overseeing all the arrangements for the Prince of Wales's visit.'

Then, in a lower voice, 'What is amusing you, Allen?'

'Sir Gerard,' he told her, 'has just insisted on buying me

a new evening suit in which to be presented to the Prince, who will doubtless have the opportunity of admiring it for at least three minutes. He considered my previous one would bring shame on the noble house of Schuyler and result in his being despatched at the double to Tower Hill and execution.'

Trish could not help herself. On hearing this she gave way to a disgraceful fit of the choking giggles which was witnessed by Timson, who had ghosted into the hall while they were speaking.

'Might I fetch you a glass of water, Miss Courtney?'

Before she could answer him, he turned his solemn face towards Allen in order to say, 'A word to the wise, Mr Marriott. If I might take the liberty of advising you, you really ought to be more careful when you address Miss Courtney in public lest you reveal more than you intend to. What you might say to her in private, of course, would be quite a different thing.'

Like his cousin a few moments ago, Allen began to laugh. He stopped in order to ask, 'Have you any more useful tips to offer me, Timson? I am always open to advice from anyone.'

Timson thought for a moment. 'If you really mean that, Mr Marriott, then I might suggest that you take great care of what you say in the presence of the butler, although I believe that that piece of advice might be, shall I say, re-dundant, since you take such great care to say little to any-one—Miss Courtney excluded, of course.'

He bowed in Trish's direction. 'Always begging your pardon, Miss Courtney, if I appear to take a liberty in speaking of these matters. I always act only with the best of intentions.'

Allen said, 'I'm sure you do. Forgive me if I leave you both. I have a great deal to do, and, as a dying Prime Minister once said, "so little time to do it."'

His bow to Trish—and to Timson—was impeccable.

Trish, scarlet in the face, muttered, 'I shall see you this evening at dinner, I believe, Mr Marriott,' and consented to be led by Timson back into the drawing room, where a jug of water and glasses always stood on a side-table. Allen watched them go, suddenly sure that he had at least one ally in Park Lane, even if it were only Gerard's eccentric all-knowing valet.

His dear girl was also of the same opinion. She allowed Timson to pour her a glass of water and drank it down under his concerned eyes.

'Do you know everything which goes on here, Timson? Everyone's secrets? And do you have any of your own?'

He bowed to her, a touch of admiration on his face. 'Yes, to both questions, Miss Courtney.'

Before she could make any kind of answer he continued somewhat hesitantly, his eyes wary, 'I think, Miss Courtney, that you ought to advise Mr Marriott to watch his back. I think that it would come better from you than from me, even if you do tell him that I passed on that piece of information.'

Fascinated, Trish stared at him. 'Could you not be more specific, Timson?'

'I fear not, Miss Courtney—I have no real evidence to offer you. Only things circumstantial, as the lawyers say. You should both be cautious.'

Trish said, 'Have you spoken to Sir Gerard of this, Timson?'

He shook his head solemnly. 'No, and for the same reason which I have offered you. Sir Gerard is not a man to whom to utter whim-whams and speak of cobwebs, as Mr Marriott well knows. By the by, you might pass on my compliments to him on the paper he gave to the British Horological Institute. I understand that it was very well received.'

'And you haven't told Sir Gerard of that either, I suppose.'

'Indeed not, Miss Courtney. Had Mr Marriott wished Sir Gerard to know of it he would have informed him of it himself. Will that be all?'

Trish's answer was worthy of Allen himself. 'I think that has been quite enough, Timson, don't you?'

'If you say so, Miss Courtney, if you say so.' And Timson ghosted out.

An old nurse of Trish's had often said to her when she was too young to grasp its meaning, 'More know Tom Fool than Tom Fool knows.' Well, she and Allen certainly seemed to be a pair of Tom Fools so far as Timson was concerned.

Fortunately Timson seemed to be as close-mouthed as Allen—which was just as well, seeing that he obviously knew even more than he had hinted at to them! She would certainly pass on his message to Allen that he was in some sort of danger...

Trish gave a little shiver—what sort of danger could Allen possibly be in?

Chapter Eleven

Regardless of who might see them together, Trish ran upstairs to the office where she knew that Allen would be working. She passed Gerard on the landing, but, careless of whether he saw her or not, she opened the door and ran breathlessly in.

'Whoa! Steady on!' Allen exclaimed, as though he were gentling a frightened horse. 'Whatever is the matter?'

'Timson,' Trish gasped. 'He told me that you must be careful—that you are in danger.'

Allen walked around the desk to take her in his arms in order to calm her. He also was careless of who might see them.

'Just now? Did he tell you that just now? In those words?'

'Not exactly. He said that I ought to advise you to watch your back.'

'Did he, indeed? Did he give you any precise information as to why I should?'

Trish stood back from Allen a little. Under his comforting hands she realised that her shivering was taking on a different nature—and here, in Park Lane, that would never do!

'No, he said that he hadn't any. "Only things circum-stantial" were his words. Oh, and he knows about us and has said nothing to Gerard.'

'Very good of him, I'm sure.'

'You don't seem terribly surprised, Allen. *Are* you in danger?'

Allen hedged a little. He did not wish to alarm her; nor did he wish to lie to her. 'I might be, but I'm not really sure why.'

'And what sort of an answer is that?' exclaimed Trish indignantly. 'If you are in danger then I must know—I am not a child.'

'Of course you aren't,' returned Allen forcefully, 'but, as Timson told you, it's all supposition and I have no real notion of who might have it in for me, as they say over here.'

Now, after the recent attack on Mr Nance's friend this was not quite the whole truth, but it was true that Allen was not absolutely certain who was after him. He thought that it might be Jordan Foster—and Hall—but he had no proof.

'You will be careful, won't you?' Trish said. 'For my sake, if not your own.'

This came out so feelingly that Allen put his arms around her again and kissed her on the cheek as a reward for her loving kindness. He dared do no more in this place of danger, where they might be discovered together any minute.

'I promise that I will try to be careful,' he said, giving her another chaste kiss, 'trust me, Trish.' He kissed the dimple on her right cheek and then released her before he was tempted to do more, or worse, or better—it depended on how you looked at it.

'I'd better go,' Trish said. 'I don't trust myself with you in here.'

This wrenched a laugh from Allen. His eyes were still

shining when she left him by the library door, although by the time that Gerard walked in a few minutes later he had reverted to his normally impassive self, with nothing about him to betray that he had been cruelly tempted to surrender to the demands of love…

What he did have to surrender to were the demands of the preparations for the Prince's visit, which was now almost upon them. He visited Gerard's tailor and was measured for a new suit, which was made for him with the utmost despatch as soon as the tailors realised that he would be wearing it to be presented to the Prince of Wales.

Allen had to confess when he finally tried it on that it was a great improvement on his previous one. He thanked Gerard, only to receive a curt, 'Think nothing of it, Marriott. Consider it to be the equivalent of a footman's uniform—and I couldn't have you looking shabbier than they do!'

Well, whatever else he was—or wanted to be—Gerard was scarcely fit for the *corps diplomatique*, Allen thought with an inward grin. He was far too downright. He wondered what Trish would think of him when she saw him in his new magnificence—or Mr Nance, if he ever did.

Things seemed to have quietened down recently. He knew that he was still being watched, but whoever was responsible was doing no more than watch. Perhaps they were waiting for the Prince's visit to be over! This was an odd thought, and, although Allen did not know it, a true one. Norris and Hall's employer wanted it safely out of the way before he brought off his coup.

Allen had written to Rothschild's asking for time to think their offer over, saying, truthfully, that he was having some problems in his private life which he wished to solve before making a final decision. They wrote back agreeing to keep the post open for the time being, but urging him to make his mind up soon.

Even Torry, that model of an equable grand lady, was exercised by the Prince's visit. Everything, she had decreed, must be perfect. On the great day itself she and Trish helped the housekeeper to fill the house with flowers. She and Trish also spent hours deciding what to wear.

'I shall be glad when tonight is over,' she confessed to Trish when they were drinking coffee together, after the flowers had been arranged to her satisfaction. 'I know that it's a great honour, but no one ever thinks of the work which it entails. Violet Kenilworth told me that the Prince's long visits to them have nearly bankrupted them—fortunately for only one evening we shan't have to worry about that!'

Violet, Lady Kenilworth, was a great beauty who was the Prince's current mistress. She would be present at the dinner party since the Princess of Wales, with the perfect manners and tact for which she was famous, turned a blind eye to her husband's liaisons. This was partly because it was what duty said a Princess of Wales ought to do and partly because of her husband's great kindness to her. She herself was noted for her kindness and her consideration to those about her. She was Torry Schuyler's friend as Gerard was the Prince's.

'Tell Mr Marriott that he need not worry about how the Prince will treat him when he is introduced,' Torry said, being kind in her turn to Trish. 'The Prince is noted for his perfect behaviour in such situations as these.'

'I don't think that Mr Marriott worries about things like that,' said Trish, 'but of course one never really knows how other people will react, does one?' Privately she thought that it seemed that Allen had more to worry about than being presented to the heir to the throne.

'And you know that you've no need to worry because

you have already met him,' Torry said, 'and since unlike some past Royal Princes he does not prey on pretty girls. Make sure that you are dressed and ready to receive the Prince in good time. He usually arrives at such functions as these on the dot, but one never knows.'

The afternoon was spent readying the dining table for Royalty and for Gerard's other guests, who included all the great names who surrounded the Prince. Among others Tom Moidore would be there, and Jordan Foster.

'Unfortunately,' Torry said, 'since Lord Fotheringham has had to cry off through illness, Gerard has asked Lord Grimthorpe and his wife to make up the numbers. He was originally asked, but refused because he had a prior engagement. When Fotheringham withdrew, however, quite by chance Gerard heard that Grimthorpe's engagement had fallen through, so he sent a messenger post haste to secure him for tonight and keep our numbers correct.

'I'm not sure whether I'm happy about his presence. He really is the rudest man, but he's also clever and many people think that his rudeness is amusing. I gather that the Prince does.'

Torry was so involved in telling Trish of her news that she failed to notice the expression of consternation which passed over Trish's face when she was told that Lord Grimthorpe would be a guest.

Whatever would Allen think? And, more to the point, would Lord Grimthorpe recognise him and say something tactless?

Goodness me, thought Trish agitatedly, I must warn Allen. Nevertheless it was some little time before she could leave Torry without appearing rude herself, and when she did, it was another gallop up to the office, praying that Gerard had not come back from the City.

He hadn't, so for the second time in a few days Trish shot into Allen's office, bursting with news.

'Allen,' she exclaimed. 'Have you heard? Lord Fother-ingham has cried off through illness and Gerard has invited Lord Grimthorpe instead.'

No, Allen had not heard.

'You're sure?'

'Quite sure.'

'Of all unfortunate things—and *I* can't cry off now that Gerard's bought me this new suit. I shall just have to hope that he doesn't recognise me, or is talking to someone else when I'm presented to the Prince. At least forewarned is forearmed.'

They looked at one another and they both began to laugh—ruefully.

'Oh, dear,' Trish said. 'I never thought that keeping secrets was such a difficult thing to do.'

'You know what the old rhyme says, ''O what a tangled web we weave, When first we practise to deceive!'''

'It really is depressing,' Trish mourned, 'that so many of my old nurse's sayings seem to have a great deal of truth in them. I didn't believe her at the time.'

'That's because you're older and wiser,' Allen said, 'and now that you've grown up you have real secrets while small children don't.'

'Does everyone have secrets?'

'Yes, but not all of them are deep or serious. Some are like Lady Kenilworth's.'

'Goodness, what's hers?'

'That she dyes her hair with henna because she is turning prematurely white.'

'Now how in the world do you know that?'

'Because her lady's maid and one of our footmen are walking out together. She told him and he told the butler and I happened to overhear them.'

Trish thought of Timson and how much he knew about them all, and came to the conclusion that it was impossible to keep secrets from one's servants even if one could keep them from one's equals.

She told Allen so, and they had another rueful laugh.

'I mustn't keep you from your work,' Trish told him, and, leaning over his desk, she kissed him on the nose, 'and I'm sure that Torry has much more for me to do before she sends me off to be dressed to within an inch of my life!'

She was gone as rapidly as she had come, leaving Allen feeling as though she had just given him a drink of water in the desert which seeing her so rarely had made of his life.

Torry Schuyler followed her own advice. She was ready and raring to go quite some time before she was due to join Gerard to greet the Prince.

Careful not to destroy the perfection of her appearance, she sat down and picked up the post which she had not had time to open. The first letter was addressed to her in a hand which she did not recognise. Curious, she opened it and turned to the end. It was from Alicia Hurst—now who could she be?

Even more curious! She turned to the beginning and be-gan to read. The more she read the more her eyes opened in surprise. Reaching the end, she sank back into her easy chair, a subtle smile on her lips and spoke aloud.

'Well, I never! I would never have thought that!'

Edward, Prince of Wales, known as 'good old Teddy' to most of his subjects, who loved his zest for life, of which his mother disapproved, 'arrived on the dot,' as Torry had put it. All Gerard's other guests had arrived earlier, and were seated in the drawing room waiting for him. When one of the footmen came in and informed them that the Prince and his suite were being received by Gerard in the entrance hall they dutifully rose to greet him. Those members of Gerard's staff who were to be presented to him, including Allen, were already standing to one side.

True to form Lord Grimthorpe, a huge man with a scarlet face, muttered to Lord Leominster, 'I do object to all this hocus pocus directed towards a man because he happened to be born in the right bedroom!'

Leominster, not usually noted for either his brain power or his on-the-spot repartee, muttered back, 'I wonder why you came if you feel like that!'

The entry of the Prince saved him from one of Grimthorpe's fabled verbal explosions. While it was true that the Prince was always conscious of his Royal birth, he nevertheless possessed a warmth of manner and appearance that was in marked contrast to the cold severity which his mother always displayed in public. Now in his fifty-eighth year, he had put on weight and a certain amount of gravitas, but despite that he bore little personal resemblance to his long-dead father, the Prince Consort—another count against him in the Queen's opinion.

To her he was Bertie; to the disrespectful of society he was known behind his back as Tum-tum, though no one dared call him that to his face.

He was talking animatedly to Gerard when he entered, his beautiful wife beside him and two members of his staff in the rear. Most of the guests were already known to him and he nodded acknowledgement to them as they were briefly presented to him as his companions at dinner.

Allen had seen the Prince before, but not at such close range, and he acknowledged his future sovereign's strange charm. While waiting he had taken care to stand back in the shadow of Gerard's librarian, Dr Ryan, in the hope that Lord Grimthorpe might not see him. What he did not notice was that one of the Prince's staff had given a great start upon seeing him, and had spent much of the time since he had arrived in gazing surreptitiously at him.

'And now,' said Gerard, 'at your request, sir, I have the honour to present those senior members of my staff who have helped me to ready my home in order to receive you.'

Allen was to be the last to come forward, immediately behind Dr Ryan. On hearing Gerard mention his name he bowed to their Royal Highnesses, aware that Trish's loving eyes were on him—and hoped that Lord Grimthorpe's knowing ones were not.

No such luck! Gerard had scarcely had time to introduce him to the Prince, nor the Prince time to acknowledge him, than Lord Grimthorpe, his eyes, popping out of his head, exclaimed in his bull roar of a voice, 'Why, if it ain't Electricity Marriott! What's he doin' wastin' his time as your secretary, Schuyler?'

Gerard could not conceal his surprise, nor the Prince his amusement. Grimthorpe, ever alert, registered both reactions.

'Never say you didn't know, Schuyler, that young Marriott here is such a whiz in the horology line, both practically and theoretically, that he could name his own price with any firm in England? He's so highly thought of that he gave a paper to the British Horological Institute. On top of that,' he continued, his loud and domineering voice informing everyone in the room of all Allen's secrets, 'a friend of mine at Rothschild's tells me that he is a whiz at maths, too, and that they're willing to offer him a fortune if he'll go to work for them.'

The Prince's interest was plain. Allen bowed his head after first looking the Prince straight in the eye and then offering his beautiful Princess a slight rueful smile. What he did not know was that, although he valued his own mental and physical accomplishments, he had no idea of the effects of that smile on women of any age.

He had, unknowingly, already won Torry Schuyler over with it, as well as Lucy Chalfont, who could quite understand why Trish was attracted to him, and it was a part of his attraction for Trish herself.

The Prince, intrigued by the whole situation—for one of the penalties of being Royal was that it was only rarely that anything amusing or untoward ever happened in his presence, everything being blandly arranged beforehand—said genially to Gerard, 'Is this true, Schuyler? Were you unaware of this young fellow's accomplishments?'

Before he could answer, Torry, standing by Gerard's side in front of the Royal pair, breached protocol by answering for Gerard, who she could see was, for once, nonplussed, indeed shocked, by Grimthorpe's confident announcement and Allen's silence in face of it.

'Of course my husband and I are aware of Mr Marriott's remarkable background. After all, is he not Sir Gerard's cousin, the son of his father's sister, and therefore happy to assist him in his business interests!'

This was shock number two for Gerard, who was quite unaware of his sister's letter and its remarkable contents which had informed his wife who Allen really was. He could only conclude that his wife had been mind-reading. As for his conclusions about Allen—*they* were unspeakable!

'As usual,' he said, controlling himself with some difficulty, 'my wife has the right of it. I fear that Lord Grimthorpe has leaped to an incorrect conclusion without checking his facts with me first.'

'And not for the first time,' said the Prince genially, not believing a word of what he was saying, but willing to go along with Torry's statement, which he was sure was a fiction. Oh, no, not the bit about young Marriott being Gerard's cousin—that was obviously true enough—but that his accomplishments were known to Sir Gerard and his wife when they, equally obviously, were not.

As for the young man himself, who had behaved with perfect calm propriety whilst the storm had raged over his head, what a true member of the Schuyler family he undoubtedly was, being both clever and devious. The Prince had not missed Allen's small smile at his wife.

The Prince used his own smile on Grimthorpe, who was grinning with delight at the brouhaha which he had started. Rightly or wrongly he had made his mark on Gerard's dinner party. Even the footmen standing at the door were listening, their ears undoubtedly flapping at the prospect of passing on this delightful piece of gossip to the servants' hall.

'A small apology, perhaps?' the Prince continued, raising an eyebrow at Grimthorpe. Grimthorpe, never one to be at loss, bluffly offered it.

'Sorry, Schuyler and Marriott, didn't quite know the form!'

Since, though he was a clever man, Grimthorpe was something of a licensed buffoon—the Prince encouraged several among his entourage to be that—he knew that he would still remain in favour, and at the least he had made that damn'd Yankee Schuyler have to think twice. Like the Prince, he didn't believe that Gerard had known of his cousin and secretary's exploits.

Exploits! Now there was a word he should have used, but too late now, dammit. No matter, the cat had successfully been thrown among the pigeons and the air cleared for good and all! The Schuylers should be grateful to him.

Allen stood back when the Prince had finished speaking, but he was not immediately given his *congé* for the small grey man behind the Prince now leaned forward to whisper something urgently in his master's ear.

The Prince nodded, and said quietly in order that only

those immediately about him could hear him, 'Yes, but we must avoid further embarrassment for Mr Marriott. Later, I agree, later.'

He looked at Allen, and said, 'I must speak to you again after dinner, sir. Mr Beauchamp has informed me of something which I would wish to raise with you and Sir Gerard privately. Pray arrange to be in attendance in the dining room when all the gentlemen except Sir Gerard, Lord Moidore and myself retire to join the ladies in the drawing room after dinner.

'Before I release you, may I say that your silence under provocation has been admirable. I am given to understand from what Mr Beauchamp has told me that your conduct on another occasion was more than admirable, but we will speak of that later.'

Allen bowed and walked away. He knew to what the Prince was referring, and it was plain that all his secrets—but one—were secret no longer. He wondered what Trish had made of the revelation that he was Gerard's cousin, and what she would think of them both for concealing that from her.

After that matters proceeded normally. There was a universal and polite pretence that nothing untoward had occurred. The only persons who were not surprised by Grimthorpe's revelations were Jordan Foster—who knew that Allen had at least one other secret not disclosed—and Tom Moidore, who had not only long been suspicious of Allen's seeming meekness but had also given him far more credit for high intelligence than Gerard had done.

He was also of the opinion that Allen and Trish were in love, but he had said nothing further of that to Gerard. It was none of his business and Trish Courtney was no fool.

Trish, for her part, had sat listening to Grimthorpe's comic tirade, a smile on her face until Torry had announced that Allen was Gerard's cousin, when it had disappeared for he had never breathed a word of that to her!

Suddenly many odd things about his relationship with Gerard were explained, but the most extraordinary thing of all was why it had been concealed so carefully—and why Gerard had been so cold and hard to someone who was his cousin!

She was so distracted that she could scarcely eat her dinner. She had been seated next to Tom Moidore, with Jordan Foster opposite to her.

'You are not to worry, Miss Courtney,' Tom told her, reading her white face correctly. 'Mr Marriott is what Americans call a cool customer, and is well able to look after himself. Surprisingly enough I believe that you resemble him in that yourself.'

Trish turned startled eyes on him. 'I'm not quite sure what you are trying to tell me, Lord Moidore.'

He smiled at her, and she could see the handsome young man he had once been long ago. 'Oh, I'm sure that you are. I have reason to believe that there may be yet another revelation to come concerning your young admirer, and that you have knowledge of it.'

Trish began to tremble. 'I assure you that neither of us have ever done anything discreditable.'

'Oh, I'm sure of that, too—even if you have been meeting in secret.'

This eased the pressure on Trish. She began to laugh. 'And you shouldn't be saying that to me, either.'

'My dear Miss Courtney, I am doing you the honour of treating you as a highly sensible young woman. I am only sorry that Sir Gerard denied his relationship with young Marriott for such a long time—I assume that he thought that he had good reason for doing so, because by rights he ought to be here at table with us, not waiting like a servant for the Prince to speak to him later, when dinner is over.'

Trish, who had heard nothing of the Prince's command to Allen to wait on him again after the meal, began to tremble once more. Tom saw it, and put his large old hand on her small young one for the briefest of moments.

'I told you not to worry,' he said gently, 'and I meant it.'

Jordan Foster, watching them, wondered what that aristocratic ass Moidore was saying to Trish Courtney and what she was saying to him. Was it about young Marriott? He could not make up his mind whether the evening's revelations were a good or a bad thing for him. It was possible that Schuyler would be sufficiently annoyed on learning that Marriott had been concealing so much from him that he would be prepared to believe that it also meant that he was dishonest—if only in revenge for being brutally snubbed for so many years.

As for Allen, he was in ferment. Gerard had despatched a footman to tell him to wait in the small drawing room, not the large one to which the ladies would retire after dinner when they left the men to their port. He had barely had time to sit down when Timson entered, followed by a footman carrying Allen's dinner, a bottle of wine and a glass on a large tray.

He laid the tray on the table, which he dragged from its position behind the sofa, bowed and left. Allen stared at it. He had never felt less like food. On the other hand he had never felt more like getting drunk. He picked up the opened bottle of red wine and poured a large measure of it into his glass. He looked up to find Timson's beady eye on him.

Recklessness being the order of the night, he said roughly to Timson, 'For God's sake, man, do me the favour of drinking with me! There's a tray of glasses on the sideboard yonder and you can save me from becoming totally legless by sharing the bottle with me. And then you can inform me why I am being favoured by your presence.'

Timson said, 'Sir Gerard thought that under the circumstances you ought not to be left alone.'

'And I'm sure that you know what those circumstances are,' said Allen savagely.

Timson gave him his most conspiratorial smile. 'Oh, yes, indeed, sir. I knew that you were Sir Gerard's cousin even before you arrived here to be Sir Gerard's secretary. Lady Schuyler, on the other hand, only found out late this afternoon, when she received a letter from your mama—in time to save you and Sir Gerard from even greater embarrassment. Very fortunate, was it not?'

Allen took a great swig of wine. 'Fortunate indeed. Tell me, Timson, who was it who advised my mother to inform Lady Schuyler that I was Gerard's cousin—and if you don't drink some of this goddamned wine with me I shall tell Sir Gerard who it was and you may take the consequences.'

'In that case, sir…' And Timson ghosted over to the sideboard, picked up a wine glass and poured himself an even larger bumper.

'Your health, Mr Allen—which should be your true title here—and good luck to you in all your many ventures. I gather that, since he does not know of it, Lord Grimthorpe did not enlighten my employer about your secret *affaire* with Miss Courtney.'

Allen gave a great moan and poured himself more wine. 'Any more of my secrets which you would like to share with me, Timson? Don't be coy. Spit everything out.'

'Well, Mr Allen—' and Timson gazed at him over the top of his wine glass '—there *is* the matter of the railway accident…'

'Now how the devil did you know about that? And while you're at it, do sit down. If there's anything I dislike it's a wordy know-all towering over me!'

Timson obediently sat down opposite to him. 'If you insist, Mr Allen. As to the railway accident, I fear that it would not be politic to reveal how I came to know of it. I have been wishful to congratulate you on your courage, but again, prudence held me back. May I add that I don't think that you ought to drink any more? You are still to have an audience with the Prince.'

'For my sins, Timson, for my sins. And allow me to inform you of something else. Again for my sins, unlike my late and unlamented father, I have a very hard head. It's a trait I share with the Schuylers, not the Marriotts. One bottle of wine is hardly likely to overset me completely, and, since I am sharing it with you, I shall certainly manage to pass as the sober, competent drudge that Sir Gerard thought I was.'

'Now there was an odd thing,' said Timson thoughtfully, refilling his glass. 'That Sir Gerard should misjudge you so completely. Not usually his way at all, not at all.'

'Good God, Timson, never tell me that I can enlighten you for a change. My father was the most idle, worthless, gambling drunkard who ever mistreated his wife and son, threw away a fortune, committed suicide and left his family penniless. I have the misfortune to look like him, and every time my usually shrewd cousin set eyes on me he saw my late, unlamented father, not me. And since he disliked my father intensely—and rightly—he has spent the last nine years waiting for me to go the same way that he did. I have remained sober and industrious as much to spite Gerard as for any other reason!'

'Not quite, Mr Allen, not quite,' said Timson. 'If I may take the liberty of remarking that you are very like Sir Gerard in character and there was never the slightest danger that you would go to the bad. May I advise you to eat your dinner? The guinea fowl is excellent and does not deserve to grow cold.'

'Oh, very well.' Allen poured out the last drops of the

Chateauneuf du Pape—Gerard had ordered the best in his cellar for him—and began to eat his dinner.

He looked across at Timson. 'Have you had your dinner? If not, you may share this with me.'

'Very kind of you Mr Allen, but I dined some time ago. You know, when you arrived here the staff thought you stand-offish because you were a quiet man. Your consideration for them—something not many show—soon won them over.'

'Except for the butler,' Allen said, picking up the guinea fowl's leg and beginning to gnaw at it—something which he could not have done if he had been dining with the Prince.

'Oh, him!' Timson shrugged his shoulders to show what he thought of the butler.

A companionable silence followed, and if Gerard had sent Timson to Allen in order to ease the pangs of waiting to be quizzed by the Prince again he had certainly succeeded. He had even stopped Allen from worrying about Trish, and how she would respond to his relationship with Gerard and the fact of his concealing it.

He hoped that she was enjoying the guinea fowl, too.

Tom Moidore's kindness restored Trish's appetite and her *savoir faire*. She enjoyed her dinner, and when the ladies retired to the drawing room she was able to join in their idle chat without betraying how much she was worrying about Allen's coming audience with the Prince of Wales.

'What an interesting young man Mr Marriott must be,' said the Princess to Torry, 'and he has the most charming smile. Not many men who had their personal life held up for public inspection would have behaved with such perfect self-control. Your husband is to be congratulated on his cousin.'

'Yes, he is, isn't he?' agreed Torry, not giving away the interesting fact that she had only learned of the relationship at six-thirty, shortly before their Royal Highnesses' arrival. Trish, indeed, took the opportunity to say rapidly and quietly to Torry, while the other women were listening to Violet Kenilworth's amusing recital of her meeting with the Shah of Persia, 'I suppose that you learned that Allen was Gerard's cousin when he was appointed to be Gerard's secretary.'

Torry decided to be truthful. 'No, indeed. I had not the slightest notion until I received a letter today from his mother, who was under the impression that I knew of it. She was thanking me for my kindness to him—thanks which I did not deserve. Not that I was ever unkind, you understand, but my manner to him would have been very different if I had known of the relationship.'

She decided to be even more truthful. 'What I can't understand is why Gerard should have been strongly opposed to your friendship with him, seeing that he is not only hardworking, clever and good, but is also a member of the family. Gerard is not usually irrational, but if I am honest I must confess that he has been so in his treatment of Mr Marriott.'

Lady Kenilworth's comic turn, in which she'd related how the Shah had offered to buy her from her husband in order to install her in his harem, had come to an end. Torry and Trish, neither of whom had heard a word of it, dutifully laughed with the rest.

Trish, indeed, looked at her pendant watch—which the Princess had already admired—and judged that it was highly likely that Allen would soon be having his audience with the Prince. Her judgement was almost immediately vindicated when the gentlemen, minus the Prince, their host and Lord Moidore, joined them to drink coffee and indulge in even more idle chat.

The men's arrival meant that the chat was now about the coming war with the Transvaal and the end of the century. No conversation in either high or low society could last very long without the year 1900 cropping up in it. Trish had become light-headed enough to wonder if it might turn up in the Prince's audience with Allen!

Chapter Twelve

Allen had just polished off a dish of lemon soufflé when the door opened and the butler informed him that the Prince of Wales was ready to receive Mr Marriott in the small drawing room.

He found the Prince seated in a large armchair, puffing on a cigar; a glass of brandy was on a table at his elbow. The grey man stood beside him. Gerard and Tom Moidore were seated opposite to him. A chair for Allen had been posted where all four could see him.

'Ah, Marriott. You are as punctual as I expected. Pray take a seat.' And he waved a hand at the chair. 'I decided to spare you further embarrassment by arranging for Mr Beauchamp to ask you his question in private. My one request is that you will answer it truthfully.'

Allen bowed his head, and said quietly, 'I will do my best, sir,' before sitting down.

'Excellent. Beauchamp, the field is yours.'

The grey man said, his voice as low as Allen's had been, 'I believe, sir, that I owe my life to you. Two months ago I was travelling to London on the Birmingham to London train when it met with an accident. I was in one of the first-class carriages and, although fortunate to survive the crash without any other injury, I was trapped in it, unable to move and consequently quite unable to save myself.

'I had been there for some little time when a young man, with great difficulty, climbed into my compartment, freed me and then lifted me towards the door. He had smashed the window in the door and, again with great difficulty, manoeuvred me through it and to safety. I was unable to assist him because I was too shocked. After that he climbed out himself and entered several other compartments in order to rescue any who were trapped. Shortly after that I was told that he brought out a young woman and her lady's maid immediately before the train fell down the embankment, killing and seriously injuring those who were still inside it.

'The young man disappeared before he could be adequately thanked. I believe that you are the young man who saved me, and that I now have the opportunity to do what I was unable to do then and belatedly express my heartfelt gratitude to you. If I am mistaken, you will forgive me, but I do not think I am.'

Allen said, still quiet. 'No, sir, you are not mistaken. I accept your thanks, but I was only doing my duty as a young and active man who had been fortunate enough to escape injury.'

Beauchamp shook his head, and was about to say something further when Tom Moidore, who had leaned forward the better to hear him, said forcefully, 'Good God, Marriott, it must have been you who saved Trish Courtney! Why in the world did she say nothing of it, nor you, either? Nor did you come forward later, when asked.'

Allen's perfect calm remained unbroken when he answered Lord Moidore's two questions.

'Miss Courtney said nothing because I asked her not to tell anyone about my part in the accident. She felt that she had a duty to obey me because she believed that she owed her life to me. I had no wish that what I had done should be made public. I didn't come forward afterwards because I had nothing useful to add as to the cause of the crash. The thought of being lionised for doing what any decent person ought to have done was distasteful to me.'

Mr Beauchamp said gently, 'I can understand that, but not only did you risk your life several times, I also understand that others were saved because it was you who took charge and organised the rescue parties. On top of that you climbed into the locomotive's cab to try to rescue the driver, even though you were warned that such an act would be highly dangerous. I think that your conduct went far above and beyond the call of duty.'

Gerard, who had been listening intently to Beauchamp, as had the Prince, said, 'This occurred at the end of your holiday, Marriott. You also said nothing of this to me. Why not?'

'I have already told you, sir. It was my business and no one else's.'

Allen looked straight at the Prince, in order to address him and none other.

'Your Royal Highness, I am a very private person. Circumstances have made me so. I would ask you to understand and not criticise me for that. You, sir, of all people, know by bitter experience what the harsh light of publicity can do to one. I wished to retain control over my own life—not cede it to others for a few hours' entertainment. If it were wrong of me to ask Miss Courtney to say nothing then I apologise to you and to her—and to Sir Gerard. But it was never a part of my duties to inform him of my private life outside them. And that goes for those details of it which Lord Grimthorpe made public this evening.'

There, he had said it at last, and Gerard might make of it what he would.

The Prince said, his voice even more guttural than usual,

'Well spoken, Marriott. Yes, I can quite understand why you wished to remain anonymous. There are times when I wish that I could be anonymous, but my position does not allow me that privilege. I trust that your cousin will respect your wishes—as I do. Now, Beauchamp, you have thanked this young man, and his response was a gracious one. I suggest that it is time for us to join the others.'

He turned his head to look as straight at Allen as Allen had looked at him. 'Have you dined, young man?'

A little bewildered by this question, Allen replied. 'Thank you, yes. Sir Gerard arranged for a meal to be sent to me.'

'Excellent. Then it is my wish that you join the rest of the party in the drawing room.'

He rose and signalled to those remaining to follow him, and, when Allen stood back, said, 'No, no, you will walk with me and tell me about the paper of which Grimthorpe spoke so cavalierly. I shall probably not understand a word of it, but no matter, that is the duty—and the punishment— of Princes: that they spend their time listening to the incomprehensible and must answer as though they are the master of every subject raised in their presence!'

The upshot was that when the Prince walked into the drawing room he was deep in conversation with that nonentity Sir Gerard Schuyler's secretary. Once seated, he then introduced him to his Princess and ordered Allen to tell her of his part in the famous train crash which had briefly entertained England earlier in the year.

Tom Moidore walked over to Trish and said, his face amused, 'My dear Miss Courtney, I have to assume that that young man of yours suborned you into keeping silent over his bravery in rescuing you. You make a fine pair of conspirators, I must say! How did he win you over? No, don't answer me—I have to believe, having seen him at work this evening, that should he wish to do so he could win anyone over—if he cared to, that is.'

Trish was defensive. 'You are not to blame him for keeping quiet. I quite understand why he did.'

'I agree with you, but one thing is plain to me, if not to everyone. Your young man has the pride of the devil and a will of steel behind his quiet manner.'

Trish's smile was pure delight. 'But he does not show it, does he? I know him well enough to know that he is good and kind as well. He was quite alone in the world when he came to be Gerard's secretary, with no family and few friends, other than Mr Nance, that is.'

If Tom Moidore was surprised to learn that Gerard Schuyler's cousin was alone in the world he did not show it, instead he murmured, 'Mr Nance?'

Trish immediately told him about Mr Nance and his shop in Piccadilly, and Tom Moidore, that collector of strange facts, listened to her with grave interest, as did Torry, who had come up to them.

'That is where you went when you were supposed to be with Lucy Chalfont!' she exclaimed, before she could stop herself.

Tom Moidore was more amused than ever by this further revelation.

Trish said defensively, 'Allen was working there on his day off. He's wonderful with clocks and watches and does all the fine work for Mr Nance now that his eyes are not what they were. Mr Nance wants him to take over the shop when he retires. He was very kind to Allen nearly five years ago, when Allen first arrived here and was quite alone in London.'

Gerard's wife privately made up her mind to have a stern word with Gerard before he performed his husbandly duties that night. Whatever could have possessed him to be so unkind to that poor lonely young man who was so devoted in his duties to him and to everyone else? He deserved better. What was odd was that this behaviour was not typical of Gerard, who usually looked after his family.

The Prince finally let Allen go with a last kind word. He, too, had learned of Mr Nance, and had listened to Allen's brief résumé of his paper with every sign of interest— which might have deceived Allen had he not earlier heard the Prince's disclaimer!

After that he was accosted by all those who wished to keep the Prince's favour by favouring someone whom he had favoured. From being outside of society and looking in Allen was now inside it, and was the sensation of the moment to be acclaimed in everyone's dining room and ballroom as Gerard Schuyler's cousin and the unknown hero of the train wreck who had saved Patricia Courtney and Hugh Beauchamp among others.

He was rapidly beginning to feel rather as though a large steamroller had passed over him, and he had an overwhelming desire to go upstairs to his room and pull the bedclothes over his head. He had heard some of the women servants in Park Lane come out with the phrase 'I could do with a nice lie-down,' and now he knew what they meant! He could see Trish talking animatedly to Tom Moidore, but the very idea of going over to them made the 'nice lie-down' seem even more imperative.

He was used to being quiet and private, and the thought that every eye was on him was daunting in itself. If only he could be left alone. Lord Grimthorpe, however, never left anyone alone. He had just been informed by Beauchamp of the railway accident and Allen's part in it, and he buttonholed him even as Allen made his first tentative steps towards Trish and sanity.

'Sorry about all that earlier this evening,' he boomed jovially. 'Didn't mean to create quite such a large tohu-bohu…'

Allen could not resist the opportunity thus presented. He interrupted the noble Lord's confident roar with, 'A small one would have been better, perhaps?' suggested with apparent sincerity.

'Exactly.' And then, 'You're roasting me, dammit! Beauchamp told me that you were a dark horse in every way, and so you bloody well are. Butter wouldn't melt in your mouth, eh, but I bet that it would dam'd well freeze. Heard about you and the train—regular Renaissance man, eh?'

This torrent of words, far from exhausting Allen, invigorated him. The weariness which had previously afflicted him disappeared. He even managed a grin.

'Oh, I thought that description was reserved for you, m'lord.'

'Grimthorpe to you, Marriott. You deserve that for your insolence.'

The laugh with which he followed this last sally turned every head in their direction. Satisfied by the effect he had produced, Grimthorpe strode off, leaving Allen to Trish, who had come over to congratulate him.

'The evening is yours, Allen. No one can talk of anyone or anything else.'

'You know how little I value that,' he told her half under his breath.

'I do, but Tom Moidore said that you had the pride of the devil, by which I think he meant that you are content to be yourself without troubling about what others think of you.'

Again her insight surprised him, but before he could say anything she told him, her voice as level as she could make it, 'And if Gerard reproaches you for keeping what you were doing from him, then you have every right to reproach him for shutting you out of his family and leaving you to be alone in London. He was not to know that you would find a friend and patron in Mr Nance—and I shall not hesitate to tell him that if he says anything critical of you in front of me.'

'Dearest love,' he murmured, 'you are not to trouble yourself about me. I came to terms long ago with my position as an outcast. Better so. I am my own man, not his nor any other's.'

'All the same, my darling, he had no business warning you off me when all the time you were his cousin.'

'I was also the poor relation who might become importunate,' he offered. 'After all, I didn't cause tonight's commotion, and I'm rather looking forward to what Gerard will have to say to me in the morning.'

Trish's expression changed to one of pure mischief before she said, 'The next person who is going to make a fuss of you is Lady Kenilworth. I can see her coming towards us over your shoulder. Promise me that you won't be unfaithful to me—she has the reputation of being a man-eater, and by the look on her face you are the man she wishes to eat tonight!'

'God forbid,' he said fervently. 'Trish, my darling, you do realise one thing. Gerard is going to find it difficult to keep us apart after tonight's revelations. I've suddenly turned into the industrious apprentice who also happens to be his cousin. I've already been invited to two dinner parties and one reception when all I really want is to be alone with you, without deceit or secrecy to spoil things.'

'Oh, dear, I shan't be able to take immediate advantage of Gerard's having to give way,' Trish told him ruefully. 'I'm due to spend a few days with an old schoolfriend, an engagement I couldn't cry off without causing her distress.'

'Never mind, when we do meet again it will be all the sweeter for having been lost to one another for a little time.'

Allen could say no more, for Lady Kenilworth was on him and Trish was compelled to relinquish him to her, but he carried the thought of meeting after parting with her until the evening was over. Once released from the Lady, Allen approached Torry and asked to be excused.

'Of course,' she told him. 'You look exhausted. Don't let Gerard bully you tomorrow morning. It's his fault that Grimthorpe nearly wrong-footed him over you tonight, not yours. Sleep well.'

After that, Gerard's buttonholing him as he left with the words, 'Report to me first thing tomorrow morning, Marriott. I need to talk to you,' had little effect on Allen, other than to cause him to reply,

'Oh, yes, sir, without fail. I think that I might have a few words to say to you, as well.'

He didn't wait for an answer, but made his farewell to the Prince and the Princess of Wales. The Princess, like Torry, thought that young Marriott looked as though he needed the benefit of a good night's sleep: a nice lie-down, in fact!

'Your confounded secrecy made me look like a dam'd fool last night, Marriott, and only a piece of blind luck allowed my wife to save me from becoming a laughing stock for not knowing of your prowess. Whatever could have possessed you to keep silent about your part in the railway accident and then persuade Trish Courtney to do the same?'

Gerard would have liked to use the edge of his tongue on his cousin and secretary, but the revelation of first his intelligence and then his courage prevented him from doing any such thing. One could scarcely reproach overmuch someone who had behaved as Allen had done, and one could understand—and forgive—Trish Courtney for falling in love with the man who had saved her.

Allen said quietly, 'I will give you the answer which I gave the Prince of Wales last night: it was my business, and no one else's. I can now remind you—as I could not last night—that it was you who insisted as a condition of my employment that I should not reveal my relationship to the Schuyler family.'

'Well, I was wrong,' admitted Gerard bluntly, 'and a fair roasting I got from my wife last night for treating you as I did. Let me say at once that I shall continue to acknowledge you and, what's more, I can no longer insist that you stay away from Trish Courtney.'

He paused, gave a wry smile, and added, 'From something further my wife said to me last night I believe that you have not obeyed my orders over that, either! In the meantime you will continue to be my secretary, but last night's revelation that we are cousins must change your way of life here. In future, among other things, you will dine with the family.'

'There is no need for that, sir.'

'For God's sake,' bellowed Gerard, 'give way a little yourself, Marriott. Torry and Tom Moidore both agree that you have the pride of the devil and that in many ways you are more like me than I am like myself. I don't see the resemblance, since I'm noisy and you're quiet, but since neither of them are fools there must be something in what they say. What I have to do in future is find work for you in which you can use your hidden talents. I'm not having Rothschild's poach you from me!

'Now that's over, let's get down to some work.'

I suppose I really ought to give way gracefully, if only because I'm being allowed to pay court to Trish. Another thought struck Allen and he began to smile; he couldn't help it. Of course he was like Gerard. He was both strong-minded and single-minded, and when he wanted something he went after it with all the mental and physical resources at his command. Nothing was allowed to stand in his way. He was devious, too—like Gerard. The only difference between them was that he was able to stand back and examine himself critically while Gerard never could.

'What the devil's so amusing?' Gerard barked at him as Allen's smile grew.

'Just that although my name isn't Schuyler, and I've spent the best part of ten years detesting the very sound of it, I seem to be more like the Schuylers than the Marriotts.'

'And thank God for that,' Gerard said fervently. 'The last two generations have all been wastrels. You've a lot to thank your mother for.'

This was typically Gerard in its savage bluntness, and Allen could not prevent himself from laughing. Unwillingly at first, Gerard joined him.

Wiping his eyes, he said, 'I think that I misjudged you because of your name and your father, and I must ask you to forgive me for that.'

'Willingly, cousin, willingly.'

'Shake hands on it then, cousin.' And Gerard offered Allen his.

Later Allen thought wryly that that should have been that. He had been vindicated, his years as the industrious, uncomplaining apprentice had paid off, Gerard had accepted him, he was free to ask Trish to marry him in earnest, and he had been promised a future career at Schuyler's greater than the modest one he already possessed. Gerard had said nothing of Mr Nance and his interest there—but that was for him to work out.

All in all everything seemed set fair. But he forgot that the gods like to play dice with men, and they were not yet finished with Allen Marriott.

Before the heavens fell in again he told Trish of Gerard's change of heart when he drank coffee with her in the library before she left to stay with her friend.

'Lord Grimthorpe did you a good turn, after all,' she said

softly, thinking that the lines of strain were already being erased from his face.

'Helped by the Prince of Wales of all people.' Allen gave a short laugh. 'It's funny, really, like a true democratic Yankee I've always thought of the British Royal family as an anachronism and I couldn't understand why Gerard respected him. Now I know. The Prince isn't clever as the world counts cleverness, but he understands men and women, that's for sure. I still think that Britain could do with a little more Yankee-style equality, though—perhaps the next century will see that happen. Gerard says that the British are slowly becoming more like us.'

Trish put her hand out to cover his.

'I'm glad Gerard was kind to us both. I'm sorry we can't take advantage of it at once.'

'Never mind, I shall be here waiting for you when you return.'

How the gods must have laughed when he said that, but that morning nothing marred their happiness.

Allen even took her in his arms and kissed her goodbye as though they were parting for years and not for one short week.

'But you will come down to see me off,' were her last words. 'Torry thought that you ought to. I gather that she had a few words with Gerard last night.'

Allen gave her his slow smile, not rueful now. 'Gerard told me that she had dressed him down royally—in the nicest possible way. I think that she's like the Prince. She doesn't nag him so much as wear him down with sweet reasonableness in that gentle voice.'

How wise he was, and how much he saw, thought Trish as she waved goodbye to him from the motor which was taking her away—and how long the week apart from him would seem.

* * *

The week seemed impossibly long to Allen when his day's work was over, but during the busy day time flew by him. Whether it was Gerard's altered—and kinder—manner to him which did the trick he was not quite sure, but half-way through it he pinned down the wrongness in Gerard's records and immediately began to write a short report to him.

He now had no doubt that Hall had been involved. He suspected that it was Jordan Foster for whom he had been secretly working, but he had no proof of that.

On the morning when he was ready to present his findings to Gerard he found him at his desk in their office-cum-study—which was odd in itself, since he usually arrived after Allen had started work. He looked up, his face grave, when Allen arrived with the folder containing the report which he had finished writing after dinner the night before.

'Don't go to your desk, Allen—take a seat opposite to me. I have something serious to discuss with you.'

It was the first time that Gerard had addressed him by his Christian name, which was surprise enough: what he said afterwards was even more amazing.

'I will be completely frank with you. I told you some time ago that massive embezzlement on a large scale had been occurring at Schuyler's. What I did not tell you was that details of my plans had also been steadily leaked to some of my competitors, to their advantage. I then took action, of which I did not inform you, to discover who could be the culprit—or culprits.

'I hired an ex-policeman named Norris to look into the business—again I did not inform you.'

He stopped. 'What are you smiling at, Allen? Nothing that I have said is even vaguely amusing.'

How to tell Gerard that he knew all about Norris—and the other man for whom he was working? He decided to say nothing for the moment. By Gerard's manner something more was on the way.

'A stray thought, sir, nothing more.'

'Well, don't harbour stray thoughts when I am telling you something important—and by the way, when we are alone you may call me Gerard.'

'Yes, Gerard,' he said in his usual meek manner—with its underlying mockery.

By now Gerard was used to Allen's ways and he smiled himself before he continued.

'I now have to tell you that last night, after dinner, Norris came here in a state of great excitement and told me that he had found my traitor...'

He paused again, his eyes hard on Allen's face, which remained impassive. Gerard was not to know that Allen was thinking that, after all, since Gerard already knew of it, he need not be the one to report Hall's treachery. On the other hand the report he was carrying would help to pin down his guilt.

'That is good news, Gerard, is it not?' And he held up the file. 'I was going to give you this this morning. I think that I have worked out how the swindle was done and who did it. Added to Norris's information it should sink our traitor for good and all.'

Gerard stared at the file which Allen had placed on his desk.

'I hadn't given you the traitor's name, Allen, and you act as if you know it—no, don't answer me, let me finish. Norris told me, and offered proof, that the traitor is you.'

If Gerard had thought that this news would rob his cousin of his poker face he was wrong.

'Did he, indeed, Gerard? And what was your response to that? Before you tell me I have to assure you that I am *not* your traitor, however many pieces of paper Norris has given you to prove it. But then, I would say that, wouldn't I?'

Allen's voice was as steady as ever but his brain was whirling madly. He had secretly considered this possibility—that he might be set up, or framed, as the Americans had it, for Hall's villainy—but had dismissed it as fancifully absurd, something out of a dime novel.

But, after all, dime novels were inspired by men like Jordan Foster and Robert Hall, were they not?

Gerard's answer was as blunt as ever. 'Before you came here to be my secretary I might have believed what I was told. I might even have thought that you were seeking revenge on me for my denial of our relationship. But I have come to know you, and although the other evening's revelations were something of a surprise to me they were not totally so. Your modesty about your heroism was another factor. If you say that you are not the villain who has stolen my money and my secrets I shall believe you, for, like Tom Moidore, I think that you are almost painfully honest. I have no doubts whatsoever about your integrity.'

This was surrender indeed! Allen said, 'You are taking quite a risk in saying that. Let me repeat again that I am innocent in this matter. When you examine the file before you I believe that you will discover that your late secretary, Robert Hall, was involved in a conspiracy against you and that I can prove it. He was bribing your butler to pass useful information on to him.

'I have other information to give you which may lead you to the man who is behind Hall. My friend and patron, Mr Nance, had enquiries made which revealed that Jordan Foster was having me followed by an ex-policeman named Norris. He also told me that you, not knowing of this, had hired the same man to make your enquiries—which made it even easier for him to frame me for the crime. Once I

knew that Norris was playing a double game, I redoubled
my own secret investigation into your records…'

He was interrupted by a bellow of laughter from Gerard.

'What a priceless pair of devious Schuyler schemers we
are, young Allen! And if Jordan Foster is the man behind
Hall then that makes sense, too. He stands to profit most
by damaging me. It's as good as a play, it really is. All of
us keeping secrets from the other…'

Allen laughed with him, before saying, 'If you believe
my denial, and once having read my report I cannot believe
other than that you will, you will also agree that Hall and
Foster are the swindlers. Have you a plan of action? How
do we frame the framers?'

Gerard thought of his unregenerate youth in the States,
when he had tiptoed around the edges of legality, of his
knowledge of the various ploys employed by the criminal
underworld and the police in order to trap people.

'A sting,' he said at last. 'That's it. We must set up a
sting.'

'A sting?' Allen echoed.

'Yes, it's a way of cheating the cheats by providing them
with a false story. I think I know how to do that, but it
would involve you having to do something unpleasant, perhaps even dangerous, since I would have to act as though
I believed Norris's report and dismiss you. I would tell
Norris that I will not bring a criminal prosecution against
you because of our relationship and the consequent scandal
it would cause.'

Allen thought that he could see the essence of Gerard's
plan.

'I see. If you dismissed me the plotters would think that
they had won and would relax their guard, having achieved
their objective. You, on the other hand, would continue
your investigations with my secret help.'

'True, but you would be left exposed until I had succeeded—if I were to succeed, that is. If you think that I am asking too much of you, then we must think of something else.'

Allen's face betrayed nothing of his inward turmoil. Either way he was in a false position. If Gerard did nothing then, although he might retain his place with Gerard, the true criminals would remain unpunished and there would always be a secret stain against his name. At the worst Foster might even tell the Press, or his friends, that Allen was the swindler who had robbed Gerard.

On the other hand if Gerard appeared to dismiss him but was unable to trap the true criminals the secret stain would still remain. He thought that he preferred the second alternative, which gave him a stronger chance of being cleared since it offered them a chance to trap Foster.

'I'll do it,' he said at last. 'I can go to Mr Nance and work in his shop.'

'Good. It's a sacrifice for you, I know, but what else are we to do?'

He pulled a piece of writing paper towards him. 'To protect you and your reputation I am going to write a statement outlining our plan. I shall lodge it in a sealed envelope with my solicitor and in case anything happens to me you can ask for it to be published.'

'You think that, if cornered, Foster might resort to murder?'

'Perhaps—a wise man covers all contingencies, so you must be careful yourself.'

Gerard wrote rapidly for some moments, then tossed the letter over to Allen for him to approve of it, which he did.

'And you trust me to do this?' Gerard asked, his dark face serious.

'I have to, and I don't think my trust in you is misplaced.'

'Nor do I,' said Gerard, sealing the envelope, 'think that I am wrong to trust that you are telling me the truth.'

He looked wryly up at Allen.

'Marriott, you're fired. You will leave Park Lane before the evening—and I shall inform Norris of your dismissal immediately. But I shall also make sure that I arrange for his every movement to be watched before the day is out.'

He thrust out a hand. 'Good luck, Allen, and I beg of you, don't do anything reckless yourself.'

Allen took the proffered hand and shook it, saying, surprise in his voice, 'Why ever should you think I would?'

'Because in your shoes I would, and if Moidore and the rest are telling the truth, we are very much alike. If you wish to get in touch with me use the telephone. You will be my new English broker, Jack Mullens—no one will think it odd that I spend a lot of time on the phone with him.'

'I shall go to Mr Nance's shop off Piccadilly, and take up my old rooms there,' Allen said, 'and curse the man who sacked me. I shall say nothing to him of our plan. For his own safety the less he knows the better. He has already been threatened with violence because of his connection with me.'

'Agreed. Good luck, Allen. I shall try to flush out Foster and Hall and put an end to this wretched business as soon as possible. In the meantime you must go downstairs and look unhappy.'

His own manner melancholy, Gerard added, 'Torry isn't going to like it a bit when she hears that I've sent you away, but we daren't tell her, or Trish, the truth, either. Their ignorance will ensure their safety.'

With that the cousins parted, friends and allies at last.

Chapter Thirteen

Mr Nance's first words to Allen when he arrived, carrying his luggage and asking for his old rooms back, were made more in sorrow than in anger. 'Turned you away, did he? You would never have left in such a rush of your own accord.'

Allen's reply was equally sorrowful. 'I'm afraid that's true, but I'd rather not talk about it.'

He didn't want to lie to the good old man, and he knew that Mr Nance would honour his request for silence.

'Well, you know that there's always a home for you here, and I must say I'm glad to see you. I've a tricky job on the bench which is proving too much for me. You've no need to go applying for a new post straight away. I'll put the kettle on. You'll feel better after a cup of tea.'

Mr Nance was right; it really was like coming home. The only thing missing was Trish. He and Gerard had decided that he would not leave her a letter; Torry would have to tell her that he had been dismissed.

He spoke of his unhappiness about this to Gerard when he rang him on the following afternoon. Gerard was experiencing mixed feelings about Allen's absence.

'They've sent me an idiot called Barstow to fill your

place,' he moaned. 'I might as well be doing the job myself.'

On the other hand he was much happier when he spoke of the progress of the sting.

'Your information about Norris was quite correct,' he said jubilantly. 'My man tells me that he's working for Foster, no doubt about it. I've a man on Hall as well. He's been living high on the hog, as we crude Yankees say, far beyond what his pay here could have provided for him, however much he had supposedly inherited. I suppose part of what he stole from Schuyler's is responsible for that. A high-up friend at Scotland Yard has done some investigation for me and discovered that a large sum of money was paid into his bank account just before he resigned from my service. With luck it shouldn't be long before Hall and Foster are behind bars and you're back in Park Lane.

'I invited Foster and his ugly wife to dinner last night and told him that I had turned my ungrateful cousin and secretary away. When he asked why I looked mysterious and said that I preferred not to answer. Have you found anything out at your end?'

'Nothing,' said Allen, grinning to himself as he listened to Gerard. He had long known that his cousin was at his jovial and piratical best when involved in this kind of dubious action, 'but then I didn't expect to.'

'Trish is home tomorrow,' Gerard finished. 'I suppose I shall get it in the neck when she finds you gone—in mysterious circumstances.'

'It can't be helped,' Allen told him. 'It must look as though I was turned out within the hour and unable to write to her.'

'True,' Gerard conceded. 'Ring me up tomorrow evening; I hope to have more news. Everything looks promising at the moment.'

Allen had a delightful vision of a maddened Trish, all

dainty Pekingese, hurling herself at the equally maddened
solid bulldog which was Gerard. It accompanied him all
the way back to Mr Nance's shop, and he even managed
to enjoy his evening meal before he retired to his solitary
bed to dream of his dear girl back with him again.

'I don't like it.' In his palatial city office Jordan Foster
was talking to Norris. 'I don't know why, but I feel in my
bones that there's something odd going on with Schuyler.'

'Well, he *has* fired Marriott. He booted him out first
thing in the morning and paid my bill into the bargain,
writing ''with thanks'' on it.'

Foster strode restlessly to the window to look out at the
busy street below. 'All the same he refused to prosecute
him—not like Schuyler at all. He's a hard bastard and I
can't believe that he'd hold off just because the man he
thought had rooked him was his cousin. Where's Marriott
gone?'

'Back to Nance in his place off Piccadilly. My informant
says that he's acting as his mechanic while Nance minds
the shop.'

'I still don't like it. The only thing which would make
me happy would be to dispose of Marriott altogether. That
would end the matter. Could that be arranged, do you
think?'

Norris made a face. 'For a price, yes. It's bound to cost
you. What sort of disposal did you have in mind?'

'A bungled robbery in which the old man is left injured
and Marriott is unfortunately killed. The police wouldn't
question that overmuch, and if Schuyler is suspicious about
whether Marriott is guilty or not it would leave him with
precious little to work on. Whoever does for Marriott can
loot the shop to make it look as though robbery were the
object and Marriott's death merely an unfortunate consequence of his resistance.'

Norris said, 'Are you sure that you want me to arrange this? It could be dangerous if anything went wrong.'

'It's your job to make sure that nothing does go wrong. See that it's done as soon as possible. In this business every day might be vital. Oh, and say nothing to Hall about this. He's been well paid and the less he knows the better.'

Norris shrugged his shoulders and left. If he thought that Foster was tempting fate somewhat, he didn't say so. The man paid well and, given his piratical mode of operations, would doubtless need more of Norris's special brand of assistance in the future. After all, what could go wrong? Everything had gone well up to now, and Foster's doubts could be discounted as those of a man who, needing others to carry out his dirty work, fretted about whether that work had been efficiently carried out or not.

Well, he needn't worry: Norris prided himself that he had never let any of his paymasters down yet.

Trish returned to Park Lane in a state of high excitement at the prospect of seeing Allen again. The moment she entered the house she started up the stairs in order to see him in the office before she changed out of her travelling clothes.

She had barely gone up two steps before the butler said behind her, 'Oh, Miss Courtney, if you are hoping to see Mr Marriott in the office I think that I ought to tell you that he no longer resides here. Sir Gerard dismissed him shortly after you left.'

All Trish's good manners—as well as her joy—deserted her on the instant.

'What?' she exclaimed. 'Can that possibly be true?'

'Very true,' smirked the butler. 'Sir Gerard threw him out of the house at nine in the morning with orders not to return.'

He didn't tell Trish that, shortly after Allen's dismissal, Norris had rewarded him well for information passed on.

Trish said no more, simply turned on her heel and ran up the stairs again—if Gerard was in the office he had some explaining to do.

Gerard was sitting at his desk, gloomily trying to make Barstow understand something which Allen would have grasped immediately—a tedious task which he thought that he ought to have been spared.

Trish glared at the unfortunate Barstow, even though it wasn't his fault that he had usurped Allen's place.

'Could I speak to you privately, Gerard?' she asked.

Gerard, who knew perfectly well why she had arrived so precipitately, sighed. It was bad enough having to nursemaid Barstow, without trying to deal with a rampant Trish arrived to defend her man.

'If you must,' he said. 'I am quite busy.'

'I'm sure that you could find me five minutes of your valuable time,' Trish riposted nastily.

'Oh, very well. Barstow, go into the library and try to remember what I have just been telling you.'

'Yes, indeed, Sir Gerard,' Barstow gasped, only too happy to be relieved for five minutes of his demanding employer.

'What is it, Trish?' asked Gerard, who knew perfectly well why Trish was bearding him in his holy of holies.

'Now, Gerard, you know quite well why I am here. Is it true that you have dismissed Allen during my absence?'

'Yes, I am afraid I have.'

'But why? You always told Torry and me that, whatever else, he was a perfect secretary. Is it because of me? If that's the reason, I take it very ill.'

'No, Trish, it is nothing to do with you, and I really can't be explaining to you why I have dismissed him. It is sufficient to say that I have.'

'No, it isn't,' said Trish hotly. 'Not only is he your cousin but you also know that he and I love one another and that we hope to marry soon.'

'That has nothing to do with the matter, and I really can't discuss business matters with you, Trish, you must understand that.'

This interview was somewhat worse than Gerard had expected when he had discussed the possibility of it with Allen. He had known that Trish was high-spirited, but he had not recognised how strong-willed she was beneath her charming manner. He had thought that if he were pleasantly firm she would soon give up and accept Allen's dismissal as given. This now looked unlikely.

'But it's not simply a business matter, is it, Gerard? He's your cousin and my young man. Couldn't you have waited until I returned?'

'No, Trish, I couldn't. There were important business reasons involved which meant that I had to act immediately. I'm afraid that you'll have to accept that—for it's the truth.'

Which was, in a way, no lie—although the 'business reasons' were not the normal ones which Trish—or any other listener—might have thought that they were.

Trish could see that it was useless. Gerard had his hard face on: the face which meant that he was adamant, not to be shaken. She had only rarely seen it, but she recognised it immediately for what it was.

'Very well,' she said. 'I shall have to consider what I must do next. You do understand that, I hope.'

'And *I* hope that you're not contemplating doing anything rash. Don't engage in anything which you might regret later.'

Trish did not deign to answer that. She merely said, 'I know that you are my guardian, but there are times when

I have to consider my own interests and this is one of them.'

She ran lightly downstairs, laughing to herself a little when she heard Gerard bellow for his unfortunate secretary. She was planning her next moves all the way down to the entrance hall.

I'm sure, she told herself, that Allen will have gone to Mr Nance and that's where I shall make for. I'm also sure that Allen will tell me the truth when I get there. I'll get that wretched butler who dislikes Allen to call me a cab.

This proved unnecessary, however, for when Trish reached the bottom of the stairs the butler was involved with a male visitor who was asking in ringing tones to see Miss Courtney immediately.

'I'm afraid that she's closeted with Sir Gerard at the moment…'

'No, I'm not,' said Trish pleasantly. 'It's Harry, isn't it?' She would have known his voice anywhere. He advanced on her, immaculately dressed and carrying a stick which she had never seen before: Harry collected them.

'I say, Trish, it's most important. I've got one thing to tell you, and another thing to show you.'

'Do you mean the stick, Harry?'

'The stick? No, not that, but it's rather splendid, isn't it? It has a rhino's head carved in ivory for a handle. Quite unique, I'm told.'

Trish nobly refrained from telling Harry that a thing was either unique or not, and 'quite' never came into it. Instead she admired the rhino on top of its black pole and said, 'You'll have to be quick with your news, Harry. I'm about to go out and I came down to ask the butler to call me a cab.'

'Oh, I say, Trish, how jolly fortunate! No need for that, no need at all. I've come to visit you in my new motor, intending to ask you to go for a spin with me. It'll be my pleasure to drive you wherever you want to go.'

And why not? Trish thought. Harry could be useful for once. 'Yes, you can drive me to Mr Nance's shop just off Piccadilly—if that's not too far out of your way.'

'Be my pleasure, Trish, and I can tell you my news on the way there.' His kind face crumpled a bit. 'But why on earth do you want to go Nance's shop?'

'I'll tell you when you've told me your news.'

'Righty-ho, off we go.' And Harry gallantly offered Trish his arm, and escorted her to the waiting motor which stood at the kerb.

'Much better than a horse for getting around town,' Harry told her when he had settled her in it, 'doesn't even champ at the bit. Off we go!'

'Your news, Harry?' Trish asked, once she was sure that Harry was safely on his way.

'Oh, that! You needn't trouble yourself about me being a nuisance any more—I mean pestering you to marry me and all that. I offered for Lucy Chalfont last week—Mother and I were staying there—and when I popped the question she couldn't wait to say yes.'

Quite forgetting the road, he turned his artless face around to face Trish. 'I hope you don't mind, old girl, but you were right; it wouldn't have done. You and I, I mean. Lucy, now, she's more like me, and Mother thoroughly approves of her, too. Her sort of girl, she says. Your turn now.'

'It's Allen Marriott,' Trish said, not beating about the bush. 'He's left Park Lane and I believe that he's staying at Mr Nance's, where he used to lodge. Be a dear and take me there. I can't wait to see him. And, Harry, I'm so pleased for you. Lucy's a great girl.'

'Isn't she just?' Harry agreed. 'Sure you want this Marriott feller?'

'Quite sure,' said Trish firmly.

'Tally-ho, then,' roared Harry, 'we're on our way.' He made the tooting noises of a hunting horn on and off all the way to Piccadilly, the noise the car was making not being enough for him.

Allen was working at the bench and Mr Nance was looking after the shop's customers. Trade had been slow that day, and Mr Nance had made coffee and brought it to the workroom. They were just finishing it when the shop's doorbell rang. Mr Nance sighed and left to see to the customer.

Allen put his cup down and picked up his loupe. At that moment the noise of conversation in the shop stopped. There was a scuffle of feet and a faint cry of 'Allen!' from Mr Nance, which brought him to his feet, intent on discovering what could be going on.

He got no further than the door to the shop, which was violently thrown open as two men hurled themselves through it and advanced on him, obviously with fell intent.

'Come on, Sunny Jim,' howled the larger one, 'your turn now.'

Allen put his right hand behind him to pull off the bench the heavy pendulum of a long-case clock—it was all that he had to defend himself against two thieves who had certainly overcome, if not seriously hurt, poor Mr Nance.

Harry turned his motor into the alley where Mr Nance's shop stood. 'Here we are, Trish.'

He leaped out of the car in order to open the door for her to alight, bowing in imitation of the footman who usually accompanied them in a carriage. He looked around him when she reached the ground. 'Not the best of neighbourhoods, is it, Trish? I'll see you in.'

'No need,' protested Trish. 'I've been here several times before. It's a backwater.'

Harry picked up his stick and offered Trish his arm. 'Won't take no for an answer, Trish. I shan't leave you until I'm sure that all's well.'

Trish thought his sense of chivalry was exaggerated—a judgement which she was to smile about ruefully in a few moments' time. He gallantly opened the shop door for her and followed her in. They could both immediately see that something was very wrong. Everything on the counter and the shelves behind it had been swept to the floor. A moaning Mr Nance lay propped up against the counter's wooden front.

'Allen,' he said feebly. At the same time they could hear the noise of a scuffle going on in the room behind the shop.

'What the devil!' exclaimed Harry. 'Stand back, Trish.' He advanced through the door, his stick firmly clutched in his right hand. Trish, disobeying orders, followed him.

Inside the workshop two men were systematically attacking Allen. One of them, who had his back to them, was holding him, the other was striking him. Trish thought later that it had been providential that it was quite plain who was the victim, for Harry, his blood up, his stick held high bellowed, 'Let that man go,' and advanced on the thug who was striking Allen.

The thug turned round to face Harry, who promptly hit him on the temple with the rhino's head with such force that he fell senseless to the ground. The man holding Allen released him in order to attack Harry, who was shouting 'Tally-ho,' and waving his stick as though it were a Zulu knobkerry.

Allen, dazed and bruised, one eye swollen and black, picked up the pendulum which had earlier been ripped from his grasp by the man lying on the floor and struck his attacker with it.

Reeling under the blow, and faced by two young men advancing on him, both armed, even if with unlikely weapons, the thug raised his hands and shrieked, 'Give over, guvs. I don't want no more.'

Reluctantly Harry lowered his stick. Allen raised the pendulum menacingly and said, 'Lie down on your face on the floor.'

The thug, thoroughly cowed, did as he was told. Allen laid the pendulum on the bench and picked up a length of strong cord. 'Keep an eye on the other chap; he might wake up,' he told Harry, and knelt down beside the thug to pinion him first by the wrists and then the ankles.

Now that the battle was safely over, Trish ran back into the shop to look after Mr Nance. Allen kicked the thug over with his foot.

'Who paid you to do this?' he snarled, thrusting his face into the thug's. 'It was Norris, wasn't it? Were you meant to kill me?'

The thug's face paled. Their patsy—as Norris had described him—was on to them and no mistake. Norris had told them that he would be unable to defend himself and would have no idea who was attacking him or why he was being attacked. And here he was, shouting Norris's name. The game was well and truly up.

'Yes…no…' he blurted out.

'Well, which is it, damn you?' Allen had caught the thug by the throat and on his face was the rictus of savagery. Harry Norman gazed at him in fascination. However had he come to call this man a solemn lump?

'Leave go, guv,' came out in a muffled moan, 'and I'll tell yer.'

Allen loosened his hold. 'Go on.'

'It's yes…' babbled the unfortunate thief, tenderly feeling his bruised throat. 'I'll turn Queen's evidence, that I will. Norris said the job would be easy. Little he knew.'

'And who paid Norris to hire you—and follow me?'

'Don't know. And how did you twig you wuz bein' follered?'

'Never mind that. I'm going to call the police and you may tell them what you do know. Your name, please—and his.'

'Collins, Joe Collins, and his moniker's Bob Jackson,' he uttered in a despairing wail. Who could have guessed that Norris's patsy would turn out to be such a hard man?

Allen rose to his feet and walked over to where Harry was guarding the still unconscious Jackson, but not before giving Collins a savage kick in the ribs.

'That's for what you did to Mr Nance—and it's a lot less than you deserve. Norman,' he said turning to Harry, 'we've a great deal to do. We have to send for a doctor, the police and Sir Gerard Schuyler, in that order. If you keep guard over this pair of beauties I'll go round the corner to Hatchard's, who have a telephone. The manager knows me and will let me use it. While I'm gone best tie up number two in case he comes round—use the cord on the workbench.'

He thought for a moment, and then gave number two a kick to match his partner's. Harry was gazing at him in awe, not only because of Allen's short way with his attackers but for the speed with which he was organising things.

'I say, Marriott,' he shot out admiringly, 'I had you all wrong. I thought you a proper molly, and no mistake. You and Trish will make a splendid pair and—'

Allen stopped him with a raised hand. 'Cut it out,' he said brutally. 'We've no time to waste in chuntering. I need to look after Trish and Mr Nance before I go to Hatchard's.'

This harsh rebuke only served to increase Harry's admiration for Allen: it reminded him of his mother's short way with him.

Trish was holding Mr Nance in her arms. He had insisted on trying to talk to her, even though she had told him gently to keep quiet in order to save his strength.

'Allen,' he kept gasping. 'What are those monsters doing to Allen?'

Once the noise of battle from the workroom had died down, Trish had laid him gently back on the floor before peering round the door to see what on earth was going on. A few minutes passed before she returned to the agitated Mr Nance.

'I shouldn't worry about Allen,' she told him cheerfully. 'It's more a case of what he and Harry are doing to the monsters than the other way round.'

Her reassuring message was borne out a few moments later when Allen came in and knelt down beside her. If she was shocked by his bruised face and black eye she didn't let it show, only pressed his hand and whispered, 'I don't think that he's badly hurt. But he does need a doctor. He was more worried about you than about himself.'

Mr Nance, who had closed his eyes on hearing that Allen was safe, now opened them.

'All's well?' he whispered.

'Very well,' said Allen, 'except for you. I'm going to send for a doctor.'

'For your poor face, too,' said Mr Nance.

'Oh, that's nothing,' said Allen, rising—something he found painful. He thought that one of his ribs might even be broken, but he had no time to worry about that with so much to do. 'You'll be safe while I'm gone. Norman is guarding the two brutes who tried to kill us—we tied them up between us. I'm afraid I damaged the pendulum of Burnside's clock beyond repair, but that's a minor worry.'

He smiled at Trish. 'I haven't time to ask how you managed to arrive at exactly the crucial moment, and with Harry Norman, too. We can talk about that later.'

* * *

'Later' took a long time to arrive. First the doctor came and tut-tutted over Mr Nance. Then a local copper arrived, and after that a Detective Inspector from Scotland Yard, with a Sergeant who stood over Joe and drawled at him, 'Not again, Collins. Who's been paying you to misbehave this time?'

Out it all came: Norris's name, and the assurance that neither he nor Jackson knew for whom Norris was working. 'Someone with a lot of tin, that's for sure. It's all down to Norris, that it is.'

'Norris, eh?' said the DI, staring meaningfully at his partner. 'The bent ex-copper at it again. When we've done with these bright beauties we'll have a word with him.'

Jackson, who was now conscious again, was, like Collins, only too anxious to put the blame to Norris.

'He told us all wrong,' he kept saying, as though that excused them, 'said he was a patsy.' He pointed at Allen. 'Some patsy—and that posh friend of his was as bad. Hit me with his stick, he did. Could have done for me.'

'Aye,' said Collins eagerly, 'and that un' kicked me in the ribs, didn't he?' he pointed at Allen too. 'And me tied up and unable to defend meself. Kicked Bob, too.'

Both policemen looked at Allen's damaged face. The doctor had already told them of his badly bruised torso, and Harry, on being questioned, had revealed that he had come upon the two thieves thrashing him.

'Resisting you, was he?' said the Sergeant. 'I suppose I ought to run him in, too, for defending himself.'

This sally set both policemen laughing.

After that Allen took them on one side and informed them that it was possible that the two men had not been engaged in a simple act of robbery, but were unknowingly part of a larger conspiracy.

'I have sent for Sir Gerard Schuyler, my employer,' he told them, 'and I would prefer to wait until he arrives before

I say anything more. We shouldn't have to wait long for him—and he can corroborate my somewhat improbable story.'

Gerard's name, that of a friend of the Prince of Wales, was powerful enough to gain the Inspector's agreement and Gerard arrived in his motor, to find the police, Allen, Harry Norman and Trish in the kitchen, drinking tea and eating cream buns fetched from Fortnum's round the corner by Harry.

'It's better than a play,' Harry kept saying excitedly. He had already promised the police the use of his new motor should they require it.

'Wait until I tell Mother about this,' was another repeated statement.

Mr Nance was safe in bed, being looked after by a nurse for whom the doctor had sent. The two miscreants were locked up in Mr Nance's outhouse—minus tea and buns.

Gerard, Allen and the police retired to the workroom with Collins and Jackson, from which Gerard emerged a few moments later to suggest that Harry might like to take Trish back to Park Lane. To soften the blow he kissed Trish on the cheek and shook Harry warmly by the hand.

'Your behaviour has been exemplary,' he told them both. 'I understand that the police already have your statements and will act upon them.'

Trish said anxiously, 'You will look after Allen, won't you? He's rather more hurt than he's prepared to admit.'

'And you don't want my motor?' asked Harry sadly.

Gerard shook his head. 'They have the use of mine, and I think that I know where we shall be going next.'

'I should like to speak to Allen alone before I go,' said Trish, in the most determined voice which she could summon up. 'After all, I came here to see him, and so far we've only said about two words to one another.'

'Very well. Harry may wait for you in his motor and I'll

send Allen in here. But don't keep him too long, mind. We've work to do.'

Trish was shocked all over again when she saw Allen's face. The bruises had spread and looked more horrid than ever. His smile for her was unchanged, though.

'You've been a brave girl,' he said, kissing her.

'Who, me? I didn't do anything. You and Harry did it all.'

'Yes, Harry was a real brick, wasn't he? But so were you. You didn't run about screaming and having hysterics, and you looked after poor Mr Nance until the doctor came. He was telling me how kind and loving you were while Harry and I polished off those brutes in the workroom.'

Trish shivered. 'Wasn't it lucky that Harry arrived at Park Lane just as I was about to call a cab, which would have taken much longer to reach you than Harry's motor did? I hate to think what I might have found here if I'd arrived after those monsters had—'

She had difficulty in not breaking down. Delayed shock was setting in.

Allen took her into his arms and kissed her, not passionately, but gently. 'Shush, my darling. Harry did call and everything was OK. Don't think about what might have happened, because it didn't.'

Trish gave him a watery smile. 'I'm being stupid, aren't I? And I promised Gerard that I wouldn't keep you. Don't do anything dangerous, will you?'

'Oh, I think that the danger is almost over. If Gerard and the police permit, I'll tell you all about it when I return to Park Lane.'

'But I thought that you had been dismissed...'

He kissed her again. 'Never mind that now. Explanations later.'

She kissed him back, and he carried the memory of it into the room where Gerard and the police were laying plans to trap both Norris and Jordan Foster, his paymaster.

Chapter Fourteen

Trish and Torry were seated in the drawing room when Gerard and Allen arrived back in Park Lane. They had just taken tea. Torry had earlier told the butler that she was not At Home.

Torry exclaimed when she saw Allen's face. Not only because of his black eye and his bruises but because weariness and tension had taken their toll of him. Around his bruises his face was white.

'What in the world has been happening to you, Allen? Gerard, are you in any way responsible for this?'

Allen shook his head, but Gerard said, 'To be truthful, my dear, in a way, yes.'

'Before either of us offer you any kind of explanation of that I'm sure that you will be pleased to learn that Allen is back with us as my secretary, but only until he has trained Barstow for me. After that, having agreed with Grimthorpe that I am wasting his talents, he is going to be my second-in-command at Schuyler's—I can't have him going to Rothschild's, can I? Wouldn't do at all. Bad for the company and bad for the family.'

He walked over to the sideboard and poured brandy for himself.

'Before we go any further I would like to toast my new aide. Schuyler's has become much more complex of recent years, and I can do with someone at my side who is as bold a buccaneer as I am but is also as clever at using the law to his own advantage.

'To my cousin Mr Allen Marriott. Welcome to the Board.' And he raised his glass high before drinking its contents down.

'Now, my dear, let us adjourn to our private quarters and leave Allen and Trish together. We both promise to tell our women as much of our recent adventures as will make sense to them. Trish has doubtless informed you of what passed at Mr Nance's this afternoon—I shall add to that, as will Allen. Come, my love.'

He threw a sly grin in Trish and Allen's direction before leaving with Torry on his arm.

'I have no doubt, Marriott, that you will also have much to say to Trish which will be to her liking once you have satisfied her quite natural curiosity about our goings on. I wish you all the best.'

'What in the world…?' began Trish, once he had gone.

Allen started to laugh. 'That was Gerard's way of saying that I may propose to you. I shall immediately disobey him by doing that at once, instead of waiting, as he ordered.'

He went down on one knee. 'For the second time, Miss Courtney, will you marry me? Your guardian has already blessed our union.'

Bewildered, Trish said, 'I thought that my guardian had dismissed you in disgrace; now you tell me he is willing for us to marry. Of course I will marry you—I've already said I will—but only if you will tell me what is going on and why someone should wish to kill you and Mr Nance.'

'Oh, they didn't want to kill Mr Nance. They wanted him left alive to tell the tale of how two thieves burst in, robbed the shop, and then killed me when I tried to stop them. Only your and Harry's timely arrival thwarted them.'

'But why should anyone want to do that? And why did Gerard pretend to dismiss you?'

'Oh, it's a long story, which I shall try to shorten. Briefly, Jordan Foster, through Robert Hall, Gerard's late secretary, was robbing Gerard and stealing his secrets. Hall found out, by accident, that I was on to him and was on the verge of uncovering his clever tricks. Foster decided to make it look as though I was the one who was robbing and cheating Gerard, and manufactured faked evidence to prove it. He might have succeeded, only Gerard, for a variety of reasons, had begun to trust me.

'He trusted me even more when I showed him what Hall had done. I was also able to tell him that Mr Nance had found out that I was being followed by a man named Norris whom Foster was employing to keep an eye on me. We both thought that Gerard's appearing to dismiss me might keep him quiet while Gerard investigated him and Hall, which he began to do immediately after I left.

'Are you still with me?'

'I think I am,' said Trish doubtfully. 'It's such a complicated business. Was Mr Foster really as dishonest as that?'

'Even more so, for when he suspected that Gerard was not convinced of my guilt, even though he had apparently dismissed me, he decided to have me killed, because he thought that it might stop Gerard pursuing the matter further. Hence the attack today. In a sense we had made me bait. We didn't foresee that Foster would stoop to murder.'

Trish shuddered. 'What happened after Harry and I left?'

'We called on Norris. Gerard knew his address because, ironically enough, the cream of the sorry joke is that Gerard had engaged Norris to work for him to try to find the swindler! That had made it even easier for Foster to feed false information about me to Gerard. When the police arrived and Norris found out that the game was up, he fell apart. Writing lying reports about me for Gerard was one thing, but a botched attempt at murder was quite another. Of course, if they *had* murdered me he would have been as happy as a sand-boy! Like the two thugs you interrupted today, once caught, he ratted on the man who had employed him and confirmed my—and Gerard's—belief that it was Foster.'

Trish was fascinated. 'Harry was right. This is better than a play. What happened next?'

'Gerard drove us all to Foster's office, where we and the police confronted him. He denied everything until the police produced Norris! They began shouting at one another. It was quite a scene. Then they dragged in Collins and Jackson, whom Norris had hired on Foster's orders, and the fat was truly in the fire. After that the police read the Riot Act and arrested them all. Of course, Norris and the other two were confessing like mad, hoping to turn Queen's evidence.'

He began to laugh.

'Gerard thinks that Foster was in a bad way financially and that led him to undertake such desperate measures. The police impounded all his books and papers, and expert auditors will be going over them. There was a bit of a scuffle before they left and Foster got a bloody nose.'

'Well, he ought to get more than that!' exclaimed Trish indignantly. 'Plotting to murder you is no joke.'

'True, and he might even swing for it.'

Allen laughed again. Trish wondered what was pleasing him so much. He did not tell her what had actually happened there in Foster's swank office after Norris and the others had been formally arrested and taken away.

Foster, realising that he was cornered and about to be arrested himself, had begun to shriek and swear at them.

'Damn you, Schuyler,' he had roared at Gerard. 'You're going to come out of this smelling of roses, while a poor devil like me who has only committed half of your villainies gets caught the first time I do anything wrong.'

He swung on Allen. 'As for you, Marriott, Schuyler's prig of a cousin, I can only wish that Norris's men had done the job they were hired for—and finished off that old fool of a clockmaker as well.'

It was Allen who responded to him, not Gerard. The fury which had been building in him since he had seen Mr Nance lying wounded in Trish's arms finally exploded into action.

'Prig, am I?' he exclaimed, without raising his voice. 'Well, take this from a prig on behalf of Mr Nance, and enjoy it.' And he struck Foster as hard as he could in the face, so that he fell on the floor, blood pouring from his nose.

'Take witness,' he shrieked when he could speak again, 'that this man wantonly struck me. I demand that he be arrested for assault.'

The Sergeant hauled him up from the floor and slipped the handcuffs on him. 'Shouldn't have been trying to resist arrest, should you, sir? We'll all bear witness that the young gent struck you when you was trying to escape. Ain't that the truth?' he asked, appealing to Gerard and the Inspector.

'And I warn you, sir, if you don't stop shouting and swearing at us, *I'll* give you a fourpenny one as well.'

Regretfully, Allen thought, that was one part of the story which he couldn't tell Trish. He remembered what Gerard had said to him when they were walking downstairs to Gerard's motor, while a furious Foster had been hauled away in a Black Maria which was being driven to Hall's home for him to be added to the list of failed conspirators in gaol.

'Yes, you really are like me, Allen, and you have the advantage that you look as mild as milk, while everyone can see what a tough I am. That was a splendid facer you planted on Foster. Who taught you to do that?'

'Oh, I visit a gym occasionally to keep in trim. I can't say that I'm sorry I lost my temper, but it was rather a rash thing to do.'

Back in the present, he kissed Trish again.

And again.

Where all that would have ended, Trish wasn't sure. She was enjoying herself too much to care. There was a knock on the door. They both sprang apart and a footman entered.

'Sir Gerard asked me to tell you that dinner has been put back half an hour. Oh, and I was to be sure to inform Mr Marriott that the butler has been dismissed without notice and without references. He is to leave the premises by lunch-time tomorrow. That is all.'

And he bowed himself out again...

'What was all that about?' asked a bewildered Trish.

'You mean about dinner being late?' Allen said naughtily.

'No, silly, about the butler...'

Light dawned, and she struck her forehead theatrically. 'Oh, of course—he was helping Mr Hall, wasn't he? That was what I overheard. Gerard must have dismissed him for being a spy in the camp.'

'True. We're not sure whether he helped Hall in his frauds, but he did spy on me and Gerard. The police will pick him up here first thing in the morning and take him in for questioning. Incidentally, it was you telling me that you had overheard him and Hall talking, and Hall offering him money, which confirmed my belief that something criminal was going on. In a way you were indirectly responsible for everything which followed.'

'But why didn't you tell Gerard about your suspicions then?'

Allen sighed. 'At that point Gerard, for reasons which I

won't go into, didn't trust me, and to cast suspicion on Hall, whom he did trust, when I hadn't any real evidence to offer him would have done no good at all. Gerard is very hard-headed and wouldn't accept or act on what he would think of as whim-whams. Later, things changed.'

If he were going to be Gerard's right-hand man then loyalty demanded that he could not tell anyone—even Trish—of the cruel bargain which Gerard had struck with him after his father's death. Particularly when he now had to recognise that in Gerard's place he might well have done exactly the same!

Trish shivered. 'It's all over, though, isn't it?'

'Not quite. There's Foster's trial to come—but, yes, basically it's over, and you and I can get married with everyone's blessing.'

'Instead of no one's,' said Trish irrepressibly. 'I was quite looking forward to a secret wedding. Now I suppose we shall be compelled to have all the trimmings—and what a time that will take.'

'Impatient, are you?' said Allen, taking her in his arms again.

'Well, I was beginning to enjoy myself immensely just now when the messenger of doom came in with his news. Do you think, as actors say, that we could reprise the last bit before the door opened—or have you forgotten your lines?'

'I can't remember that I actually used any lines when I was busy pleasing you a few moments ago. There was no room for words, was there?'

'Not really,' agreed Trish happily. 'I suppose that we shall have to restrain ourselves sufficiently for me to appear in white at the wedding without actually wearing a lie.'

'It might be arranged, Miss Courtney—but with extreme difficulty if you look at me like that.'

'Then I'll shut my eyes.'

'Even worse,' groaned Allen, remembering that dinner, duty and every other damned thing in the world lay in wait for them before they were safely in bed together and might do as they pleased.

Nevertheless they had a joyful few minutes before all the 'd's which Allen had dreaded brought them back to the busy, demanding world again.

'Do you think,' panted Trish, when she was reorganising her clothing so that she became respectable again, 'that it will be any easier in the twentieth century for engaged couples to enjoy themselves properly before the wedding ceremony?'

'I think that you mean *im*properly there, my darling,' replied Allen, rebuttoning his shirt. 'But, yes, I believe it will. Even if we don't form a Society to press for it, someone else is sure to. Free thinking is all the rage these days.'

'But in the meantime we burn, as the old poets said,' Trish sighed. 'I could never understand what that meant, but now I know.'

'Not long now, though,' whispered Allen, kissing her chastely on the cheek now. 'Not long.'

'Marriage—or the twentieth century?'

'Both,' said Allen, and he kissed her again.

Epilogue

New Year's Eve, Sunday, December 31st 1899

Trish Marriott had stars in her eyes, Tom Moidore noted indulgently when he entered the drawing room where Gerard's guests were waiting for dinner to be announced. That unassuming gentleman Allen Marriott must be a dab hand at pleasing his wife if her expression was anything to go by. Was there no end to the list of his talents?

Gerard had been lyrical about his new right-hand man when Tom had lunched with him at his club two days earlier. 'I never thought I'd find anyone who thought and acted as exactly as I would—I can safely leave things to him which I've always had to look after myself.'

He had had the opportunity to thank Allen for his hard work and co-operation by asking his mother, Alicia, and her new husband, Frederick Hurst, to come over from the States to attend Allen and Trish's wedding, on December 6th, and then spend the New Year at Park Lane. They had been only too happy to agree. Alicia approved of Trish and Allen approved of Frederick Hurst, who was a steady gentleman, the opposite of his late father.

'Happy?' Tom asked quietly, after making his way to

where Trish sat, not far from Alicia, who was talking eagerly to Torry—another new friend.

'Supremely,' Trish said with a little sigh, and then, with a touch of her old mischief, 'I shouldn't be enthusiastic about being married, should I? It's not done. I suppose I ought to drawl "so-so," but I can't.'

Tom's laugh was genuine.

'Be your charming self, my dear. I can't offer you better advice than that.'

'For that you shall be a guest at my first dinner party, when we have a home of our own in which to give one. At the moment Gerard is allowing us the use of a suite of rooms while we house-hunt. He's been unbelievably kind, not only to us but to Mr Nance. He had him brought here to be looked after when he had a relapse shortly after he had been attacked, and he also arranged for a manager to run the shop in his absence. He is Mr Justus Parker, an old friend of Allen's, whom I met at Greenwich.

'Mr Nance was naturally disappointed when Allen accepted Gerard's offer and didn't take over the shop from him, but Allen persuaded Gerard to buy it instead, so that Mr Nance could go back there when he was fit again. Allen will use the workshop to relax in occasionally.

'Mr Nance is here tonight—another kindness from Gerard. Torry says that the older he gets, the more sentimental he grows. I think it's her influence.'

'Undoubtedly,' said Tom. 'On the other hand she wasn't sentimental when Jordan Foster shot himself just before he was due in court.'

'No, indeed. She simply said, "Well, that's saved the expense of a trial which could have had only one ending, hasn't it?". On the other hand she did approve of Gerard paying poor abandoned Mrs Foster's passage back to America.'

'True,' remarked Tom grimly. 'Once the police investi-

gations began they uncovered more and more of his villainies.'

'Who's talking about villainies?' said Allen, smiling. He
had been speaking to Harry Norman, who was present with
his new wife, née Lucy Chalfont. His mother was not with
them: strong-minded Lucy had banished her to the Scottish
fastnesses, saying in her pretty voice, 'I'm sure that now
Harry is safely married and he has me to look after him
you'll be only too happy to devote your time to caring for
your poor husband.'

'We were commenting on Jordan Foster's villainies,'
said Tom, 'but not any more. Not tonight. Tonight is a night
for celebrations, even if the Transvaal war has muted them
a little.'

'True,' said Allen, and for a moment the three of them
were silent. Many of the families they knew had fathers,
sons, brothers, husbands and other relatives in the army in
South Africa, where the war was not going well. One result
had been that public festivities were very limited. Instead
private dinner parties were being held, and at midnight Gerard's guests would be on the terrace of his Park Lane home
to hear the church bells ring in the new century.

If Tom thought that Trish was not the only one of the
newly-wed Marriotts who was enjoying being married, he
kept it to himself. Both that, and the security of his new
relationship with Gerard, had softened Allen's previously
austere expression a little.

'You're not to look sad tonight,' Torry told her guests.
'I know that the war news is bad, and it's a pity the new
century has to begin in strife, but I think that we can be
allowed to greet it with some enthusiasm so long as we
don't overdo things.'

A sentiment with which all her hearers agreed.

'Happy?' Allen whispered in his wife's ear, echoing Tom
Moidore's earlier question.

She turned her shining eyes on him. 'You know I am.'

'So noted,' he said, giving her his small smile which had the power to turn her heart over.

Her wedding night had been a revelation to Trish in more ways than one. She had hoped that Allen would be gentle with her—indeed, she had never doubted that he would be. She had thought that her own innocence might be a drawback which would prevent them from achieving true fulfilment on their first night together.

No such thing! What she had not bargained for was that once the first surprise of marital lovemaking was over, eased for her by the kindness of Allen's loving and patient initiation, they would discover a vein of abandoned passion which she would not, could not have believed beforehand that they would experience—and she would share.

It was as though they had awakened the tiger in each other as sensation followed sensation. Even now, in the drawing room, surrounded by other people, far from the marriage bed, merely to think of it set Trish's heart bumping. To calm herself she tried to think of other things.

Unfortunately she looked at Allen and was lost again! Who would have thought that this quiet, self-controlled man could take them both to such a peak of ecstasy. The daylight man and the night-time man were two separate beings.

Or were they? After all, when it was needed Allen showed not only courage but a fierceness of purpose which was beginning to surprise not only her but, from what she had heard him say, Gerard as well.

They sat opposite to each other at the dinner table. Torry had put Mr Nance on Trish's left, to ensure that he would have a friendly face to talk to, and Frederick Hurst on her right.

'I had never thought to find myself here,' Mr Nance

whispered to Trish. 'It is a far cry from my kitchen at the back of the shop, is it not?'

'Some of my happiest days were spent there with you and Allen,' Trish told him truthfully. 'We don't really need damask cloths, fine china and priceless glass to enjoy ourselves, do we?'

She looked around the splendid table. 'Not that I don't enjoy all this magnificence; I do. But I wouldn't want to live like this every night. I'm looking forward to being in my own little home with Allen and entertaining you as you have frequently entertained me.'

This cheered up Mr Nance no end. He had been a little daunted by the grand company, even though Tom Moidore had talked kindly to him before dinner.

He said little but listened attentively to the conversation of those around him. He had already realised what a hard man Gerard Schuyler was, that he was also clever and shrewd, and that he loved his beautiful wife dearly. He liked the Hursts as well. They were tactful enough—unlike the Fosters—not to talk about the twentieth century being an American one.

Gerard was laughing about an old number of *Blackwood's Magazine* which someone had given him to read. In mock Gibbonian prose it prophesied the decline and fall of the British Empire, which it attributed to a variety of reasons including the rise of the bicycle, which was a symbol of the nation's degradation since it meant that people were preferring a mechanical toy to a living creature—the horse.

'Oh, there are always those who prophesy doom when things change,' said Tom Moidore robustly. 'I have seen an over-great love of sport by the working man given as another sign of decline. Since *The Times* sees fit to include the Football League Table in its august pages we can scarcely suppose that it is only the working man who is interested in the game. On the other hand I am inclined to agree with those who consider that the recent sharp rise in crime is due to lenient magistrates and judges.'

This started a series of lively discussions around the table to which Frederick Hurst made some shrewd contributions. Gerard, having started several hares on their way, quietly drank down his wine and remarked *sotto voce* to Lord Rainsborough that there had been at least two good pieces of news this week.

'Oh, and what were they?' asked m'lord eagerly.

'Why, that the Bank Rate remains at six per cent and that stocks in Anglo-American Telegraph have risen,' replied Gerard, in what Allen had come to recognise as his teasing voice.

'Oh, business,' said m'lord a trifle dismissively, much to Allen's amusement. If Trish had been nearer to him he would have winked at her.

Discussion then turned to a variety of society scandals which were exercising Mayfair and Belgravia and which concerned people of whom Mr Nance had vaguely heard, but in the pleasant haze which good wine and food produced he allowed the sound of voices to wash over his head, speaking only when Trish asked him if he were enjoying himself, to tell her that he was.

After dinner the ladies and gentlemen did not separate, as was usual. Instead they moved to a drawing room on the second floor which opened on to a terrace which overlooked the London scene. The ladies had brought their fur wraps with them and the gentlemen their scarves, for the night was cold.

Coffee was served and the chatter rose to a roar. Allen sat by Trish and held her hand. Mr Nance lay back in his chair and dozed. Harry and Lucy Norman held hands in another corner of the room.

A lively argument about the Transvaal War broke out

among those who supported it and those who thought it to be a great mistake. Public opinion generally was greatly divided over it. Before the discussion could grow too heated footmen entered carrying trays of champagne, and as though this were a signal Gerard rose and called for order.

'Ten minutes to go,' he said. 'I suggest that when we adjourn to the terrace we take our glasses with us and toast the new century as it arrives.'

No sooner said than done. The room slowly emptied and, wrapped in their furs and overcoats, the company spent the last minutes of the nineteenth century holding their glasses and continuing their interrupted discussions.

At first Allen and Trish held hands, but later were separated in the crush as more and more guests arrived outside. Looking for her, Allen noticed that Gerard had disappeared from the chattering crowd on the balcony.

He also saw that Trish and Torry were talking animatedly to Tom Moidore and his mother and stepfather. Moved by a sudden impulse—a rare thing with him—he walked through the terrace doors and back into the drawing room. Someone had lowered the lighting and Gerard was sitting alone in the semi-dark, his glass of champagne before him.

He looked up at Allen and gave him a wry smile. 'I decided to wait here until just before the fateful moment. I have given enough homage to the coming century this past year. What's your excuse for deserting the party—or haven't you got one?'

Allen sat down opposite to his cousin. 'Now that we are alone and unlikely to be interrupted I have something to say to you—and now is as good a time and place as any to say it.'

He didn't wait for Gerard to answer but continued, his voice as even and steady as it always was.

'Nine years ago I came to you bankrupt and penniless,

a pampered young man raised in luxury, the son of a wastrel father and, what I can now admit, a spendthrift mother. I asked you for help for my mother and me, which you gave, but the price of it was a hard bargain for me to swallow. You also asked me a question which I could not then properly answer. What would *I* do if I were in your position? My answer was that I didn't know. I couldn't imagine myself in your position.

'Now I am not exactly in your position, but I am, as it were, next door to it, and I know what my answer would be if a similar untried boy from a family with a bad record came to me asking for help. It would be the same as yours was then to me.

'The bargain was a cruel one, but it made me the person that I am. What I would have been without it, I do not know. What I do know is that I worked and slaved day and night to be revenged on you. In my early, childish days with Schuyler's I had silly dreams of ruining you—God knows how. As I changed I came to understand that my best revenge would be to prove you wrong in underestimating me by achieving success by my own efforts. Cope chose me to be your secretary because I was his best man. I was better than he—or you—knew.

'And when I could have taken my revenge on you by colluding with those who were intent on ruining you, I used what I had become to help to save Schuyler's, not ruin it. In fairness to you, I thought that I ought to tell you this.'

He fell silent. Gerard did not immediately speak. Instead he picked up his glass of champagne, raised it high and said, 'Thank you, Marriott. Let us toast the future.'

Allen clinked his glass against Gerard's, and they emptied them together.

Gerard refilled their glasses and walked Allen out of the room. The crowd on the balcony, intent on their own affairs, had noticed neither their departure nor their return. Gerard moved over to where Torry stood.

'I missed you,' she told him quietly, taking his arm and steering him a little away from his guests. 'Now that we have a quiet moment I have something to tell you about the coming year, and I think that this is a suitable occasion on which to do it.'

Gerard turned to her, his face questioning. 'Something important?'

'Yes. I learned on Friday that we are expecting another addition to the family—who will arrive in the new century. I have the feeling that it may be a boy.'

'Nicholas it will be, if it is, and Kitty if not,' Gerard said with all his usual energy.

'Almost,' Torry answered him, smiling. 'If it's a boy I would like his second name to be Allen. We owe Allen Marriott a great deal—and, after all, we scarcely deserve what he did for us.'

'True, and by the way in which he is shaping in his new post we shall owe him more. Nicholas Allen it shall be. I shall be quite the patriarch before we are finished!' Disregarding those around them, he kissed her on the cheek, saying, 'Clever girl!'

Trish's greeting to Allen when he joined her was equally loving. 'Here you are at last, my darling. Where did you go and what were you doing?'

'I was clearing up some old business with Gerard,' he told her, 'and now it's time to attend to the new.'

Even as he spoke Gerard raised his glass high. It wanted but five minutes to midnight.

'Come,' he announced, 'let us be ready to welcome in the New Year.'

His guests stood silent and attentive. Tom Moidore had told them earlier that all the boats on the Thames would hoot as the New Year arrived. 'Unfortunately, we are too far away to hear them.'

What they did hear as Big Ben chimed the magic midnight hour was all the church bells in London beginning to ring in 1900.

Allen took Trish into his arms and began to kiss her. Other husbands and wives followed suit. English reserve in public was briefly shattered.

'Happy New Year, my darling,' he whispered into her hair, 'and let us hope that it will be a happy new century and a happy new life together.'

* * * * *

MILLS & BOON®

Makes any time special

Enjoy a romantic novel from Mills & Boon®

Presents...™   *Enchanted™*   TEMPTATION.

Historical Romance™   ✚ MEDICAL ROMANCE·

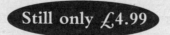

FREE
2 BOOKS
AND A SURPRISE GIFT!

We would like to take this opportunity to thank you for reading this Mills & Boon® book by offering you the chance to take TWO more specially selected titles from the Historical Romance™ series absolutely FREE! We're also making this offer to introduce you to the benefits of the Reader Service™—

- ★ FREE home delivery
- ★ FREE monthly Newsletter
- ★ FREE gifts and competitions
- ★ Exclusive Reader Service discounts
- ★ Books available before they're in the shops

Accepting these FREE books and gift places you under no obligation to buy; you may cancel at any time, even after receiving your free shipment. Simply complete your details below and return the entire page to the address below. *You don't even need a stamp!*

YES! Please send me 2 free Historical Romance books and a surprise gift. I understand that unless you hear from me, I will receive 4 superb new titles every month for just £2.99 each, postage and packing free. I am under no obligation to purchase any books and may cancel my subscription at any time. The free books and gift will be mine to keep in any case.

H9EC

Ms/Mrs/Miss/Mr ....Initials ....
BLOCK CAPITALS PLEASE

Surname ....

Address ....

....

....Postcode ....

Send this whole page to:
UK: FREEPOST CN81, Croydon, CR9 3WZ
EIRE: PO Box 4546, Kilcock, County Kildare (stamp required)

Offer valid in UK and Eire only and not available to current Reader Service subscribers to this series. We reserve the right to refuse an application and applicants must be aged 18 years or over. Only one application per household. Terms and prices subject to change without notice. Offer expires 30th June 2000. As a result of this application, you may receive further offers from Harlequin Mills & Boon Limited and other carefully selected companies. If you would prefer not to share in this opportunity please write to The Data Manager at the address above.

Mills & Boon is a registered trademark owned by Harlequin Mills & Boon Limited.
Historical Romance is being used as a trademark.

MILLS & BOON®

MISTLETOE *Magic*

Three favourite Enchanted™ authors
bring you romance at Christmas.

Three stories in one volume:

A Christmas Romance
BETTY NEELS

Outback Christmas
MARGARET WAY

Sarah's First Christmas
REBECCA WINTERS

Published 19th November 1999